For Stephen,

My Best —

2014

HORRORSCOPE

A Novel By

Brian Evans, Helen Marie Bousquet, and Mark A. Biltz

Edited by Enrique M. Grullon

Published and distributed worldwide by H Infinity Books, Inc.

www.h8books.com

info@h8books.com

Printed in the United States of America

1st Edition, January 2014

Hardcover ISBN: 978-1-6192-7789-2

Cover and Design by: Rebecca Rodriguez-Smith

Edited by Enrique M. Grullon.

Additional editing by Lee Ann from FirstEditing.com.

Proofread by Marley Magner.

Library of Congress Control Number: 2013922127

HORRORSCOPE

A Novel By

Brian Evans – Helen Marie Bousquet – Mark Andrew Biltz

www.h8books.com

ACKNOWLEDGEMENTS

Thank you, Jesus, for giving me the last year that you did with my mother, and for giving her to me at all. I didn't deserve such a wonderful mother, but I thank God that I had her. She will always be "the mama."

I want to thank the following for their help in supporting my efforts throughout the years, and for sticking by me when many did not. The entertainment business is an industry where things are always hard to accomplish when you're on the downside of advantage, but sticking to it is what results in things such as the book you are now holding in your hands; or thanks to technology, reading it on your iPad or elsewhere.

First I want to thank my mother, Helen Marie Bousquet, for all you have given me, which was your all, so that I could write this book and do all of the things you enabled me to do that were good. You gave me everything you had, and no one will ever be to me what you were, for the rest of my life, and I hope you're there to greet me in the next one. You will always be my sweetie pie, mom.

I want to thank Edward A. Howes, who also supported me when the going was tough, and whose dreams for my future were very much appreciated.

Mr. and Mrs. William Shatner, I appreciate your help over the years, and thank you for giving me credibility in a business that rarely sees the likes of people like you both. Your smiles change lives, and you likely don't even know it.

Elliott Lott and Steve Levine of ICM Partners, thank you for helping me to land many of the most profound experiences I've ever had. You put a smile on my mother's face with your efforts, and while I may not have been the easiest person to deal with at times, you gave a woman you didn't even really know many, many smiles, and for that I am truly grateful.

I would also like to say thank you to: Arthur Olson, William Evans (my dad, who was there for me when I needed him), Betty Wilson (my grandmother, who inspired me to sing the style of music that I do), Matthew Waters, Joanne Rosier, Irene Gigliotti, June March, Denis Boder, Brenda and Jim Lacostic, Rebecca Lacostic (and her son Michael), Henry Lacostic (my brilliant cousin), Nick Riccio (for giving my mother her dream home), David Mendenhall, Jon Voight, Valerie Harper, Johnny Carson, Frank Sinatra, Lincoln Colpitts (who brought Naugatuck to my attention), Joan Rivers, Jay Leno, Dionne Warwick, Mayor James Fiorentini, Dan O'Leary and Carrot Top (for all of your support), Rich Little, Felix Rappaport, William Wilson, Jr., and Richard Bousquet. Thank you to my niece and nephew Amanda and Kyle Evans, and to my brother, Billy Evans. I also wish to thank Lori Comeau, Senator Bruce Tarr, and Senator William Brownsberger, Cheryl Driscoll, Deepak Chopra, David Ortiz, Noah Parets, Keenan Gumahad-Hinez, Tom Hanks, Danny Paolino, Alphy Hoffman, Mark Ragonese, David Pratt, Carolyn Berry, Paul Baker, Ines Hellendall, Marley Magner, Anthony Federico, Dolores Jacoby, Dawn Matney, Billy Jacoby, Sandy Finnigan, Bobby Jacoby, Ernie Boch, Jr., Snooky & Jodie, Neil Sedaka, Kathleen Genova, Kathleen Hays, Tom Dreesen, Keith Coogan, Mr. & Mrs. Tom Arnold (for your honesty and patience), and Narada Michael Walden.

Thank you also to Mark "Andrew" Biltz, The Self Realization Fellowship in Los Angeles, Enrique M. Grullon, Tony and Rebecca Incorvia, Adam Taheri, Chris Weber, Sonny Southworth, Jeremy Miller, Murphy Beatrice Seifert, Shep Gordon, King Martin, Christian Marcantonio, Byron Thames, Hal Sparks, and especially to Howard Grunes (a thousand times, thank you, Howie), the best friends I could ever ask for, and undoubtedly do not deserve.

Finally, thank you to Nancy Gentile and Kathy Vaccaro, my mom's cousins. You are both very special to me, for obvious reasons; and to Teresa Gentile.

Please visit www.sleepapnea.org to learn about this very serious health condition. Most people afflicted with it do not even know they have it, and MusicDrivesUs.com, an organization founded by Ernie Boch, Jr. that seeks to help the youth of our world through music.

And thanks again to you, Mom. I love you, and I miss you. *You did this.*

- Brian Evans, December 17, 2013

Mark Andrew Biltz would like to thank his father and his mother, Mark and Vicki Biltz. He would also like to thank Chief Golden Light Eagle, Chris Biltz, Kevin Clark, and Dawn Matney.

Enrique M. Grullon would like to thank his mother, Tammy Grullon-Sands. Enrique would also like to thank Brian Evans, Mark Andrew Biltz, Helen Marie Bousquet, Alejandro Grullon, Miranda Mitchell, Arthur Lecolst, June Lecolst, Mimelfis Altagracia-Caceres, Jose Francisco Grullon, Jose Manuel Grullon (my father), Cindy Orozco, Stephanie Orozco, Jeffrey

Comeau, Parker Rogers, Lawrence Askew, Xavier Simms, The Schlosser Family, Jay F. Sands, Patricia Moran, Diane and Peter Kokaras, Donald Pierce, Bill and Anastasia Pied, Sherri Goulet, Miranda Trussell, Dalma Aponte, Billy Mitchell, and all the residents at Atria Merrimack Place in Newburyport, Massachusetts. Also thanks to the artists and entrepreneurs who have inspired me, including Jay-Z, The Weeknd, Sean "Diddy" Combs, J. Cole, and Drake.

For Helen, my mother.

I love you, mom.
Love, Brian

TABLE OF CONTENTS

Acknowledgements	vi
Chapter One	1
Chapter Two	6
Chapter Three	13
Chapter Four	18
Chapter Five	26
Chapter Six	31
Chapter Seven	42
Chapter Eight	50
Chapter Nine	57
Chapter Ten	62
Chapter Eleven	69
Chapter Twelve	75
Chapter Thirteen	83
Chapter Fourteen	90
Chapter Fifteen	97
Chapter Sixteen	105
Chapter Seventeen	110
Chapter Eighteen	118
Chapter Nineteen	126
Chapter Twenty	133
Chapter Twenty-one	139
Chapter Twenty-two	145
Chapter Twenty-three	154
Chapter Twenty-four	161
Chapter Twenty-five	168
Chapter Twenty-six	175
Chapter Twenty-seven	179

Chapter Twenty-eight 190
Chapter Twenty-nine 198
Chapter Thirty 208
Chapter Thirty-one 217
Chapter Thirty-two 225
Chapter Thirty-three 233
Chapter Thirty-four 241
Chapter Thirty-five 250
Chapter Thirty-six 259
Chapter Thirty-seven 265
Chapter Thirty-eight 272
Chapter Thirty-nine 280
Chapter Forty 288
Chapter Forty-one 295
Chapter Forty-two 302
Chapter Forty-three 309
Infinity – Helen's Notes Retrieved by Detective Merton Howard. 316
ARIES 322
TAURUS 325
GEMINI 326
CANCER 327
LEO 328
VIRGO 328
LIBRA 330
SCORPIO 330
PISCES 331
AQUARIUS 332
CAPRICORN 333
SAGITTARIUS 334
OPHIUCHUS 334
About The Authors 338
About the Editor 340

CHAPTER ONE

"I wish I would just fucking die," said Wendy Henaghan, as she sat across the table from Helen Wilson, who for $25 would give you a half-hour reading from her home in Naugatuck, Connecticut.

The 62-year-old psychic was known around town as the cute lady who liked to read "those tarot cards." Few took her seriously as her hand-written sign, in red ink, displayed in front of her small cottage "PSYCHIC READINGS $25." The kids in the area would often joke among each other with smart-ass remarks such as "This house...is clear," referring to Zelda Rubenstein, the actress who portrayed the medium in the movie *Poltergeist*. Helen looked nothing like her, but her height and frame were similar, enough for the kids to justify the humorous remark about the psychic lady who told your future who lived in the old cottage down the road.

But it was a living, and Helen had her clients. With the exception of her gardener, a man named Elliott Lott that she would give free readings to, her clients were women, mostly housewives wondering whether or not their husbands were cheating on them. That particular subject was never easy for Helen to get into, and oftentimes, she'd avoid the answers her clients sought if she thought it might cause that cheating husband doom. Helen liked to keep it light, regardless of the fact that sometimes her feelings got a little dark; sometimes too dark for a client paying $25 for a fun reading to handle.

“Every time I think about him, I feel like there may have been something I could have done!” Wendy cried.

Helen had seen this movie before. On many occasions there were numerous individuals who would pay to tell her their woes, and all believed she had every answer. Unfortunately for them, she just didn’t. Things “came” to Helen. They arrived through a cosmic messenger that even she could not understand or comprehend in terms of its origin.

“I can only tell you what I feel,” said Helen. “On occasion there are specific details that I see, but what I feel is, this just wasn’t your fault.”

Wendy had not divulged enough information for Helen to know whether there was even something for her customer to be faulted for. The look on Wendy’s face made it clear to Helen...her $25 psychic was onto more than she had divulged.

“Ski. Do you ski?” asked Helen.

Again, the look on Wendy’s face fell to a deeper shade of pale.

“Yes. We were both on a skiing trip that he didn’t want to go on. I feel as if I made him go, and the day was beautiful when it began. Then, while we were halfway down the slope, everything just went white. I couldn’t see anything, and Roger just disappeared in front of my eyes. I managed to stop myself, though I don’t know how. When I stood up and opened my eyes, the clouded air before me was suddenly clear again. That’s when I saw Roger, and I knew the moment I saw him, that he wasn’t here anymore.”

Helen looked at Wendy as she told her story, and suddenly felt an urge to turn her head to the left.

“What?” Helen asked. She wasn’t looking at Wendy.

Wendy seemed puzzled. There was no one there. Wendy looked in the direction it appeared Helen was looking towards, watching as Helen appeared to begin a conversation with absolutely no one.

"I will," she said.

Helen looked back towards Wendy, and then the psychic that everyone in the neighborhood called insane, looked down at the table.

"You need to start going out more," Helen said. "You need to be able to have a life again. This wasn't your fault, but know this...you'll meet him again."

Wendy looked puzzled. She believed in psychics on a very minor level. This was just one of those things she'd do for fun, which became something not so fun after losing Roger. Suddenly the late-night tarot card readings held a stronger meaning, and she looked at Helen for something more.

"How do you know this?" Wendy replied.

Helen looked straight into Wendy's eyes with a knowledge. A clear confirmation that held no doubt.

There was a pause as Helen closed her eyes, her head again dropping towards the floor. Slowly, she lifted her head back up to Wendy.

"Because he just told me so," replied Helen.

Helen Marie Wilson was born in Ipswich, Massachusetts in 1950. She loved to dance, and was the girl every boy longed for as she would walk down the small-town roads in search of herself. In the 1980s, her long-term boyfriend, Edward Howes, and she lived together in California. They had met at a local hotspot in Bradford, Massachusetts called The Yacht Club, and it became a relationship that would last for over a decade.

It was in between her days of Ipswich and Bradford, Massachusetts that seem a bit foggy. The loss of her father by suicide as a child was overwhelming, and something she had never quite been able to move on from. He was unable to deal with the killings he'd had to carry out while in World War II, a time when there were no programs or hospitals to really deal with the after-effects of such a catastrophe. Her father decided that since he couldn't be who he was before the war, then who he had become after it was not something he could further put his family through. Helen had blanked out those unspeakable acts as she tried to get over the tragedy.

It was also, however, a period of intervention by something bigger than herself. While she'd blocked out a certain period of her life, it would come back to her in bits and pieces; enough to know that she didn't want to remember. The period was like someone in the closet, who knew something that nobody else did, but couldn't tell anybody about it. People would look at her differently, when in fact, they should have been in awe of her ability to not care about what other people thought. It was after Edward died of a brain aneurysm while taking a bus to work that Helen changed. She couldn't realize or understand why she hadn't been able to predict it. Why had no one told her that was about to happen? Why would she only see other people's futures, while being unable to see her own?

Wendy Henaghan stood up from the table following the reading, shaken and stirred. Her eyes didn't have the same sadness as they did when she'd come into Helen's house to plunk down that $25. She'd have mortgaged her house for Helen to obtain the information she'd just received. Wendy looked at Helen at the door as she was about to leave, Wendy sticking her hand in her purse.

“I don’t accept tips. It’s $25,” said Helen. “You paid already.”

Wendy looked at her, confused. She could have been reaching into her purse to grab just about anything. A pen, maybe a notebook to make a new appointment. Gum.

“Why don’t you go home now? Inhale what I’ve just told you, and listen to what he has said,” Helen said.

“Okay,” said Wendy. “I, well…well, thank you, Helen. I really appreciate what you did for me today.”

“It wasn’t me. I’m just the messenger,” Helen replied.

Helen watched from her porch, a sprawling lawn in front of the house, a cottage that seemed like it was in the middle of nowhere, or in New Orleans somewhere. Her house was very different than the rest; small, cozy, surrounded past her lawn by residential homes. Like a corporation whose building had a house next door to it, her house just seemed not like the others, but not out of place, either.

Wendy got to her car, a 1979 Pontiac Sunbird, and looked up at Helen. She waved, then got into her car and drove off. Helen turned to her door to walk back in when she got a feeling and stopped. She slowly turned around and panned across her front yard. Someone was there. It wasn’t a neighbor, and it wasn’t a kid playing around; it was someone else. She wasn’t entirely certain as to whether or not it was a feeling or a fact, but she felt someone was watching her. However, in the world that she lived in, she always felt like someone was, which made it hard to distinguish whether or not her current feeling of being watched was real, or merely a feeling that awaited her next client who would soon be plunking down another $25 for a reading with her.

CHAPTER TWO

"When I tell you to fucking pay, you fucking pay. I don't want to hear any more of your bullshit," a voice could be heard from the sidewalk as a couple decided to walk the other way. They just happened to be passing Craig's Safari Bar in New York City, a small bar about three blocks from the old Twin Tower buildings.

"All right, all right...relax man, I've got you," another voice replied.

The bar was previously a coffee shop, until Peter Vaughn inherited it from his father, who had passed away just a year before. Inside, Luigi Nicolo laid down the against-the-law on Vaughn, threatening the man as he intended to do about fifteen more times that day in various stores, cafés and bars that answered to the Nicolo crime family. The family wasn't new to New York City, but they were the typical mafia organization. They killed people. They stole. They received shipments by barge that contained large amounts of drugs. Those just beginning to become useful were handed the task of extorting money out of local businesses until they were able to climb the ranks of "the family." What wasn't typical was the violence; beyond gory, and always meant to convey a very strong message: Do not fuck with us.

As a result, none of the other "families" in New York or New Jersey would associate with them. Because of the blood that connected them all that flowed out of Sicily, it was best just for the remaining families to look the other way, rather than to end up looking like a scarecrow in a cornfield, which the Nicolo family had done before…just to send a message. Minus a head.

What gave the Nicolo family carte blanche was their brutality. Given the nature of the mafia in general, you were something special if all of the other families came to the conclusion that it was just best to stay out of your way.

After Luigi had squeezed out the $2,600 that Peter Vaughn had to offer, Luigi looked down at his cell phone to see a text message from Omar Rosario, trusted assistant to AC Nicolo (Antonio Christopher Nicolo). Omar and AC went to school together in Sicily, and when the family had moved to the USA in 1966, AC made certain that Omar came along. AC worked his way up the ranks of the New York City mob, and by 36 years old was known as the head of the Cosa Nostra in the city that never sleeps. Anyone who challenged him did nothing but sleep, but it was the sort of sleep where they'd never wake up.

"AC is in the living room."

Translation: Get your ass to the house right now, as something serious is about to go down.

Luigi breathed a sigh of relief, knowing that if he was about to be killed, the invitation would have been a much friendlier one. The kind of invitation where you thought "the boys" would simply be sitting around the bar and downing shots of whatever fit their fancy. Most of the family feared AC as much as the rival families, who long ago had realized that any attempt to interfere with AC's dealings made a bullet in the head appear like a massage. There simply was no easy way to die in this crew, and they weren't like the Chicago bosses who would direct their Las Vegas counterparts to merely bury you in the desert somewhere. If AC had his way, the bodies of his victims would be pinned up on the billboards that lit up Times Square. He just didn't give a shit, and lived his life as if it were over long ago. There was just no instilling fear in a man like that.

The twelve-minute drive to the East Side in New York, 82nd and Park Avenue, seemed like a long drive to Luigi. He never heard directly from Omar unless something serious was about to occur. Usually Luigi, low man in the chain of command, would get a call from AC's son, Thomas, if for nothing more than to give him something to do. AC's intent was to keep Thomas away from the violence; but after Thomas was caught killing animals and bringing them to show off to his middle school, AC realized that some things just run in the family. AC gave Thomas the light work of playing air traffic controller, sending the family out to do the deeds, and letting them know when it was clear for take-off and arrival. Still, Luigi didn't feel fear as much as he did anxiousness over having to have any sort of direct discussion with AC.

"Fuck, fuck, fuck, fuck, fuck," Luigi said, as he pulled up to the tall building that his uncle owned. A young man of about 20 years old approached the car from its passenger side, and kneeled down to the window as Luigi used his automatic window control to bring it down.

"I am to park your car myself today," the young man said. "Omar said I should tell you that."

Now Luigi was concerned. Typically he would just pull up to the valet, who would give him the garage code number of the day, and he'd self-park. The code was changed daily to keep out the occasional pain-in-the-ass investigator or FBI man who was seeking another notch on his belt.

"Really?" replied Luigi.

“That’s what he said; he just wants you up there. I don’t know more than that,” the young man said.

Luigi got out of the car and handed the keys to the valet.

“Be careful driving it; I just got it waxed,” Luigi said.

The red 2012 Mercedes-Benz SLS AMG was Luigi’s pride and joy, putting him in the hole to AC to the tune of about $200,000. It was a hole Luigi had best earn quickly, unless he wanted to be put in a hole himself.

“I will, Mr. Nicolo,” the young man said. Luigi watched the 20-year-old Xbox fiend drive away in his pride and joy.

“Fuck,” said Luigi once again.

The doors to the tower that AC lived in and owned were framed in gold, and had bullet-proof glass. The glass was so thick that you couldn’t see clearly into the lobby until you opened the door. Men were stationed in that lobby 24 hours a day

Nicolo was greeted by the three security guards (using the term lightly, given they were all convicted felons).

“How are you, Nicolo? Welcome, welcome! Go right up, he’s waiting for you,” said Manuel Pietro, who looked like Steven Seagal in a very bad mood at all times. Just getting a “How are you” from the man was a surprise to Nicolo.

“I’m good, Manuel, I’m good. Everything good?” asked Nicolo.

“Everything is fucking peachy,” Manuel replied.

The other two men stationed in the lobby were Michael Bonanno and Massimiliano Milano, two individuals who have been many a passerby’s worst nightmare when strolling through an alley at night, should such people happen to walk by when they were both doing a deed initiated by AC.

Manuel, Michael, and Massimiliano were Station A on AC's security team. They were the first group of men you'd see before all hell broke loose, should you be attempting to walk through those doors without an invitation. It was their job to make sure that whoever came through those bullet-proof glass doors belonged there. If they didn't, they didn't leave the building unless they were either cops, or that by vote they were granted an exit. Most of the time they were two out of three for letting someone go; but on one occasion, all three decided to take a man by the name of Tom Diego out of the building via a meat grinder. It had become clear that Diego had intentions of putting a little Brown Recluse Spider in the old man's flat. Although Tom didn't know what was contained in the package thought to have been a gift from the Giulio family, a family that once thought it could outwit the Nicolo family for a takeover, it was a failed attempt, and cost Tom his life. The Giulio family, all of them, have not been heard from to this very day.

Daily visits from the FBI became almost routine, as well as the occasional New York City Police Detective. The Nicolo family were always ten steps ahead of any plans by authorities to bring them down. A few members of New York's finest were on the payroll, and those who didn't agree to do so, either transferred on their own, or were transferred by the Nicolo family to a grave. When that happened, there were usually four or five body bags accompanying each officer whose decision not to play ball led to early retirement.

Luigi stood in the elevator with Manuel as it brought them up to the penthouse suite. Thirty-six floors high, it left thirty-five floors beneath it to make any attempt on AC's life. AC had grown accustomed to the attempts, and the penthouse had proven to be a safe haven to all, with security that would have made even the most sophisticated special agencies envious.

The elevator doors opened slowly as Manuel and Luigi stepped out. Luigi stood about 5'11", and was small compared to the height and size of the monster-like security guard.

"He said to just have a seat, and he'll be out in a minute," said Manuel.

The guard stepped back into the elevator and headed back down to the lobby. Luigi looked around at the spectacular living area of AC Nicolo. No matter how many times he'd seen it before, it was a sight. The large white sofa, the gold lamps, the maroon walls, the mahogany wood that surround the living space; it looked like something out of a movie. The horse statues and awards from organizations that catered to the ego of AC were spread across the left side of the room when facing it from the elevator. It looked like a museum of wealth and power, and AC was the curator. This museum, however, was built on murder, extortion, threats, beatings, and drugs. Looks were deceiving, as the room, as well-decorated as it was, held no indication that the man behind it all, AC Nicolo, was the master of a criminal enterprise feared by even members of his own family.

Luigi was no different. He was terrified to get any sort of phone call from AC, especially from Omar. Given Manuel headed back to the lobby, Luigi felt a little more comfortable. It was just him and the living room, and he took his seat and waited.

As he sat on the sofa, AC's brother walked into the room. Mauro Nicolo looked like an accountant, but he'd slit your throat for milk if he thought you were trying to pour it in your bowl of cereal before he poured it in his first. He had one of those insincere smiles that led you to wonder whether the man actually genuinely laughed at anything in his life.

“How are you, Luigi?” inquired Mauro.

“I’m good, I’m good. Where’s AC?” Luigi replied.

“What, you got somewhere to be?” Mauro laughed. “Let me get you something to drink. What’ll it be?”

“Anything, you choose, I’m easy.”

Mauro grabbed a bottle of Grey Goose and slowly poured it over ice, while giving his guest a stare and not dripping a drop. He handed it to Luigi.

“So, AC has something for you. A trip. He wants you to do something for him, something a little different,” Mauro said with an inviting feeling, as though he were doing Luigi a favor, like maybe a trip to somewhere he’d enjoy.

“Anything; where?” said Luigi.

“I’ll let him tell you all about it. Have a seat. You like soccer? I taped the game from earlier,” said Mauro.

CHAPTER THREE

Jens Maes was a 48-year-old businessman living in Belgium, whose trade was to hawk gems to various associates in China, many of whom moved from Belgium to partner up with various "organizations" in Asia. Recently returning home from a trip to Kaoshiung, Taiwan and Hong Kong, his next trip to the United States was to New York City.

Living large, Jens had so much success that he went from living with his parents in a basement for most of his twenties to actually castle-hunting in Belgium before he hit thirty. Eventually settling in Oudergem, he started a family he rarely saw, redesigned the interior of a castle he was barely in, and lived the life of a single man while his wife was at home spending his money. His two children, Max and Priscilla, ages 11 and 13, both had spent most of their life being raised by a nanny.

Jens was never at a school play. Instead he was trotting around the world to fund his lavish lifestyle…at first. But now he was way past the need for money. He likely didn't even know how much he had. He was long past the days of the initial spending spree one does when first coming into money after having none. Now he was looking to wrap up a few more final deals that would make retirement final. He had come to a point where the traveling seemed boring, the one-night stands repetitive, and was actually showing signs of guilt about being an absentee father. He had come to the conclusion that sleeping around was boring, and he was ready for a stable life. His wife Laura never cheated on him once, and justified her husband's excursions on his job. It was simply the life she wanted, and his pending retirement was an opportunity for them both to begin a new life.

That was the plan, anyway.

New York was to be a simple trip. He would fly in, drop off gems valued at about $6 million euros, and then return home to prepare for a few final trips to Asia before calling his career a day. The profits of the gems would then be split between himself and a partner in Hong Kong, the same man he intended to do his final deals with after his forthcoming trip to New York was all over.

Without any fanfare from his family, Jens picked up his suitcase, gave his hugs and kisses, and off he went. Perhaps it was their ages, but his kids barely seemed to bat an eyelash when Dad went on another journey. It was part of the job, provided well for everyone, and they wanted for nothing. Collectively, the entire family seemed excited about their father's retirement. It was almost going to feel weird to have him in the house all the time. They all wondered what exactly he intended to do when he was done with all the trips, and all the gems.

Jens had talked about perhaps writing a book about his travels. While he didn't have a publisher in mind, he knew he had the financial resources to get any publisher to support such a book. He'd realized early on that the world was all about money; who had it, and who didn't. He wasn't going to be living in a basement again.

As the town car driver he hired brought him to Brussels Airport, all he could think about was what there might be to do in order to kill a few days. He'd been hiring private planes to go all around the world, but began missing the company of commercial flights for some reason. He once couldn't stand the screaming of children in the coach section, but now longed for any voice at all that wasn't his own, or the boring attendants that the private jet companies would assign him. This time, he decided to go commercial; but wasn't willing to go overboard. He was still flying first class.

The only downside was there was no immediate return flight in first class, so he had two options. Either he could rent a jet one-way from New York back to Brussels, or stay in New York for a few days. Why not? It was August; it was nice weather in New York. Maybe he'd catch a few shows. With these options at hand, he booked a round-trip flight on Brussels Airlines.

Grabbing a *USA Today* in the airport after a pretty boring ride, Jens was determined to do something normal on this trip. Flipping through the sports section of the paper while waiting for his flight to board, he caught an article on Alex Rodriguez. A famous New York Yankees player, Rodriguez had signed an astronomical contract worth somewhere in the neighborhood of $250 million. This seemed like something that might be fun, so he went online and ordered one ticket to see a Yankees game. Although available, he wasn't going to buy a box seat, or anything that felt "VIP," as that would defeat the purpose of what he wanted to do. He just wanted to see a ball game along with everybody else. He had everything he could ever want, and wanted to bring his life back to a time when simple things were important.

The long flight landed at about 8:00 p.m. at JFK, and Jens headed to the Waldorf Astoria. There were certain things he'd never give up, and flying first class and staying at a nice hotel were two of those things. He was all done with the escorts and the late-night flings. Any woman he might meet would be more interested in getting her rent paid than spending quality time with a gem dealer, even though he never told anyone outside of his family that he was one. He had the nice clothes on, but he didn't brag. He was more interested in preparing his life for his family. The single life was over. He was 48, and it was just time to grow up. His family had been tolerant for all of these years, but he didn't want his kids growing up being raised by nannies and their mother, and having no clue as to who Dad was.

As the taxi drove up to the Astoria in New York City, where he'd spent many nights doing more than planning on a trip to the baseball park, he received an email while confirming plans with his gem buyer. The email merely confirmed the buy, and it would be one of the easier transactions. The hardest part of doing the international transactions outside of New York was the hassle customs would sometimes give him. However, he always had the correct paperwork to coincide with the gems, regardless of who might have died to obtain them. That wasn't his business. How gems were obtained were the business of someone else, someone he'd never want to know. He was in the business of selling diamonds, rubies, and other rare stones. How they ended up in his hand to sell, well, the less he knew, the better.

The New York trip was small in comparison to what he would typically sell. Six million sounded like a lot, but there were transactions in Asia that exceeded one hundred million, and there was far less fanfare in the Asian airports than he ever had in New York while trying to get out of JFK. On this Wednesday night, his plan was simple. Check in, order room service, and fall asleep to a movie on Spectravision that offered pay-per-view movies. He never actually watched a single one of the movies he'd buy; he usually just had them on in the background to keep him company.

When he got into his room, his phone beeped. It was an email from the New York Yankees ticket customer service department, confirming his seat at Yankee Stadium. It was the newer stadium, and he always regretted not having attended a single game at the old Yankee Stadium, despite his numerous trips to New York. He'd drop off the gems on Thursday afternoon at around 5:00 p.m. at his dealer's office, then catch a Broadway show, though he didn't know which one he would go to. His intention was to wing it, and just stroll down Broadway and find something with an available ticket after confirming that a $6-million-euro wire had been confirmed as sent. Following that, Jens was going to make Thursday and Friday night fun nights for himself, and would leave on Saturday night.

He was feeling quite good. He was almost done in the gem-selling game, a game that had put a strain on his personal life. It was time to do something else.

The days of acting self-absorbed while having a wife and two kids at home were coming to an end.

CHAPTER FOUR

Wendy Henaghan wasn't very good at keeping secrets.

It wasn't as if Helen told her never to discuss what goes on in a reading; but her phone began to ring off the hook. In just the week after Wendy started posting her description of the session with the local psychic onto her Facebook and Twitter feeds, Helen was uncomfortable with something she had never experienced before.

Lines.

Her front yard suddenly had a barrage of people lining up for readings. General readings, medium readings, tarot card readings, and whatever happened to occur in the reading. Some of them didn't seem to have a name, but Helen delivered whatever message she felt was important, and was always smart to avoid conveying any message that could injure someone else. So far, there weren't any horror stories for Helen to tell, no need to alert authorities. On occasion a customer appeared too disturbed for her to continue the reading.

When Matthew Berkowitz showed up, she got a sense almost immediately as he walked through the door that she should tread lightly. There was something off about this guy. In his mid-twenties, Matthew was a handsome man who stood about six feet tall, and had brown hair and bright-blue eyes. The looks, however, didn't match the mind.

He sat down across the table from Helen, a round table in her living room that she only sat at for readings. She'd bought the old table while in California with Edward Howes. After attending the Self-Realization Fellowship in Los Angeles, she had met a woman there named Irene Gigliotti who would often have yard sales. She always called Helen first to check out the sale before she brought it out on her front lawn, and this table just grabbed Helen. Its engravings on dark wood were of the various zodiac signs. Helen felt an immediate connection to the table, not knowing much about its origins beyond Irene's intentions to get rid of it for $100 if there was a taker. Helen bought it for $75, and Irene decided it was worth the loss just to not have to lug that thing out of the basement, needing to climb sixteen stairs to do so. Helen paid cash for it, and Edward took it out of the house. Edward hit his head on a light above the stairs while attempting to drag the table up the stairs, and required four stitches. Helen always believed that his death that would occur months later might have been initiated by that head blow. He didn't just cut his scalp; he really banged his head good. It almost took him down the flight of stairs.

Uneasy about the fact that people were now lining up to see her, never altering her reading price of $25, she put a "Line starts here" sign at the base of her stairs in front of her porch so that onlookers or those waiting in line wouldn't stare through the window. Quite frankly, she didn't enjoy the attention.

Helen just looked at Matthew Berkowitz and didn't say anything.

"So, is there something I should do?" Matthew said.

Helen just looked at him. There was compassion in her like no other you'd ever meet. So even though this guy had a screw loose, she let him in.

He paid his $25. He would get his reading, whether he liked what she had to say or not.

"Matthew..." she said.

"Whoa, how did you do that?" he replied.

"I didn't do anything," she replied.

"I never told you my name," Matthew said, surprised.

Even Helen didn't know she'd done that until Matthew responded to it. She'd have let it go right by her and continued on to the reading had it not been for him bringing up his name, which she had no way of knowing.

Helen thought for a moment, and looked back to Matthew.

"Okay, well...that happened. Let me just tell you what I'm getting."

Helen exhaled, not knowing she had been holding her breath.

"You need to leave her alone," Helen said quietly. "It's not who you are meant to be with."

Enraged, Matthew shot up from the table.

"What the fuck do you know about it, bitch?!" he said, with the look of hell in his eyes.

It wasn't the same man who had walked in and gently sat down, placing the $25 on the table. Helen, while trying to be calm about what she was receiving, this energy that said "Something is seriously wrong with this guy," just let him in. She's the one who let him have the reading, and it was at this moment that she realized she might need to consider having someone in her home while doing them. It wasn't safe for her to be giving readings to people like this. Looks were indeed deceiving, and despite Helen's feeling before the reading that the guy was a little crazy, she accepted the fact that it was she who had let it proceed.

"Listen, Matthew. You need to calm down. What you're feeling, we have all felt. The loss is unbearable, and regardless of what you're thinking of doing right now…"

Matthew slammed his fist down on the table.

"What exactly do you think I intend to do, huh? What do you think?" he demanded.

"I don't really know, Matthew. It isn't good though, and if you came here looking for the specifics, which I know you've done, that will have me helping you to do it, then you knocked on the wrong door. You need to chill out, and look for someone else. Look in the damn mirror; you are a great-looking guy. There's no reason you need to obsess on this one person who you've known all along doesn't love you," Helen said sternly.

"But she does love me!" Matthew screamed.

"No, she doesn't, and you've always known it. The only reason she even got involved with you is because you scared her!" Helen yelled back. "You need to get a grip!"

Matthew just stood there, staring Helen down.

"I don't know what this is," Matthew said. "I don't know what you're doing, or how you're doing it, but whatever the fuck it is, it's fucking bullshit."

Helen stood up.

"Matthew, it's time for you to go. This reading is over," she said.

Matthew stared her down as Helen handed him his $25 back. He stared at her for what seemed like ten minutes, but in fact it was only seconds. A knock at the door by the next customer in line broke it up. A film over Matthew's eyes seemed to disappear, one of rage, to one of the normal guy who walked in, realizing someone was witnessing his next move.

"You keep the money. I got my reading. I'm sorry I snapped at you," Matthew said.

Helen walked around the table, leading the walk to her own front door.

"I think what you need to do is go home, relax, watch a little TV, and think about what you're doing. Be careful with what you're doing. Don't do anything you can't take back," Helen said.

A calm Matthew, almost eerily calm, turned to Helen before walking out the door.

"I don't know what this is," Matthew said.

"It's what you paid for, Matthew. Now go home, right now," Helen said.

He walked away without any further words, and in came Tammy Waters.

"Hi, Tammy…how are you?"

Helen just repeated her last ability unknowingly, and the jubilant, fun look on Tammy's face turned to "This isn't just a woman who gives readings" look in an instant. Helen looked out the door, watching Matthew walk down the street in a huff. She closed the door.

Tammy's reading lasted about half an hour. It was a lot calmer than the previous session with Matthew, and the tarot reading was what was called a "Seven Card Spread." It was typically a spread for direct questions. The first card related to the past, the second card related to what was happening now, the third card told you the future, the fourth card detailed what to do, the fifth card described external influences, the sixth described hopes and fears, and the seventh card described the final outcome. It was a reading she would have been scared to give Matthew. For Tammy it was a simple reading, one that Helen welcomed after the last, and related to her children. When Tammy stood up to leave her reading session, Helen was a little envious of her.

"A perfect life. Good for you," Helen said.

Despite her customers' general consensus that every psychic would likely tell you what you wanted to hear, Helen wasn't one of them. Tammy didn't realize how lucky she was.

It had been a long day, and Helen was no doubt going to be here for a while. She walked out of her front door onto the porch with a sign she'd made, and walked down her stairs. She had a little limp, from a problem she couldn't pinpoint. She also wasn't interested in learning about it. She walked past the line of people who looked at her with a curiosity and interest she was unfamiliar with. She didn't look at any of them as she ended the line of about sixteen people. She stood behind the last person and nailed it into the ground.

"The line ends here. Please come back tomorrow."

Sixteen people, and it was only noon. She'd be giving readings until about 8:00 p.m. on this night. She turned around, walked back up the stairs to her porch, and turned around to the crowd.

"I appreciate you all coming, I'll be getting to you all, but please tell anyone else you might see come here to come back tomorrow. You are all the end of my day. I'll be right out to bring the next in line in, as I need a few moments to prepare," she said.

In truth, Helen was tired. She hadn't expected to see so many people show up. She was lucky if she saw sixteen people in a year, relying mostly on the social security benefits she'd just begun to receive after working a series of odd jobs just to keep the lights on. To have sixteen people show up before noon was surreal to her, and let her know that she was going to have to organize herself a little better than this in the days to come.

While spraying a little Pledge wood shiner on her reading table, she stopped when hearing a series of what appeared to be sirens screaming by her house. She walked over to the news radio station she always had on and turned up the volume. It had been in "on" mode during all of the readings, but not loud enough for anybody else to hear while giving those readings.

"....thew Benvenuti, 26, was shot twice at the scene and was killed by officers of the Naugatuck Police Department. The man apparently was distraught over a woman's refusal to continue a relationship. While the woman, whose name is being withheld, was not hurt, the man, whose name again is Matthew Benvenuti, did manage to shoot a man who was apparently the landlord coming to the woman's defense. He is in critical condition at Waterbury Hospital in Naugatuck. A dog was also shot by Benvenuti, but is expected to survive."

Helen turned the sound down.

"He didn't listen. My God, he didn't listen," Helen said out loud to herself.

Helen walked to the front door and opened it.

The line all looked up to her as a man began walking up the stairs, believing he was next in line.

"Wait," said Helen.

She looked out at them, and directly at the man who was next up for a reading.

"I need you to come back, please. I cannot read anymore tonight. Please come back tomorrow. My hours of operation are from 10 a.m. to 6:00 p.m. every day, with lunch at 12:30 for half an hour. The sign I posted will always be the end of the line."

Helen had just taken her first step at organizing.

CHAPTER FIVE

"I want you to do something for me," said AC.

This always meant you're *going* to do something for him. There was no need to be overly okay with the request. There was no need to say, "Anything, boss, just name it."

AC already knew he could name it. If his words were directed at you, you already knew that you would do it. In a white robe, as he had just come out of the shower, the man who was now in his late 60s walked into his living room with the presence of a king, one that would burn your city to the ground.

Luigi stood up frantically. Mauro remained seated. AC looked at Mauro with soulless eyes.

"Mauro," AC said with stillness.

Mauro shook his head yes, stood up, and left the room. AC strolled to the glistening window of his penthouse suite and looked at the city below.

"You know, that's the one thing I miss about not having a house. I can't see anything. No matter what angle I position my body, I just can't see anything below me. It's nothing but these buildings. I miss a house. I picked my life, though. I picked it, chose it all myself. Every floor that has brought me to the 36th was a chapter in my life you wouldn't wanna know about; but I'm here," said AC.

Luigi sat there, listening, surprised that AC was talking so much. He never talked this much. A fear came over Luigi as to where AC was going with all this, and what it had to do with him. If this were one of his friends, he'd likely say, "You brought me all the way over here, let some dumb-shit kid drive my Mercedes, to tell me you miss your home?"

But no. Luigi liked driving that car no matter who parked it. He sat there and did what he should do. Shut up and listen.

"Do you know why I don't talk to people?"

It didn't require Luigi to provide a reply, and AC just continued.

"Because there's not much to fucking like about them. They lie, they do it to your face, and then they smile and pretend it never happened. I remember my ex-wife once cheated on me and lied about it, thinking I actually believed when she left that morning that she was headed to some shopping mall. What she didn't know was, I *own* the mall. Not only wasn't she at the mall shopping for some fucking candle or something else she said she was gonna get, but she was fucking some wannabe guru she met at a yoga class," AC said.

Luigi then replied, something he regretted the moment it came out of his mouth, but it was out of it now, and he'd have to hope AC was all right with being spoken to at all.

"I didn't know you were married," Luigi said.

A pause came over the room as AC just stood completely still. Only his neck moved, while still trying to see a tree from some angle as he twisted his head around the window, pretending he actually cared about what Luigi's thoughts were.

"It wasn't a conventional marriage, and it was also not a conventional divorce," AC said, as though he were telling you a story about something he'd read in a *Reader's Digest*. It was just a bland reply that held no emotion, as he basically had just said she likely never left the hotel she'd met her new lover in.

AC smiled as he walked to his bar and grabbed a bottle of Hennessy.

"Do you see this bottle? It's called Beauté du Siècle, and there's only 100 of them in the world," AC said with a grin. "This bottle cost me a quarter of a million dollars."

As AC opened the bottle, Luigi's mouth about dropped. He poured the expensive Cognac into two glasses. The bottle had never been opened before, and had sat in a small silver chest on the bar before AC decided to open it up. Luigi knew even an intended end of his life wouldn't be worth opening a bottle like this, so he suddenly felt at ease.

AC walked over to Luigi and handed him the glass. He then sat down at the L end of the wrap-around couch and sat back.

"I have an interest in sports. I also have an interest in gold, rubies, diamonds, and rare gems. And...there's a friend I have that met this guy at a buy, gems, nothing illegal, who lives in Belgium. Anyway, it's an area I'm interested in," said AC.

"Belgium?" said Luigi.

This brought about a pause to the conversation.

"No. Not Belgium. Gems. I'm interested in gold. What the fuck would I be interested in Bel...just listen," said AC, a little irritated.

"Sorry," replied Luigi.

Luigi gave AC the floor, realizing he'd just interrupted a man who would put his head in a vice with the same ease you'd go to the store to buy a Kit Kat candy bar. Or perhaps bury you up to your head on an ant farm as your eyes were eaten out.

"I got wind of a...a baseball game this guy is gonna go to. He's going alone. He's about at the end of his little gem run. Guy's made a fortune doing it, selling diamonds, shit like that. He has a lot of pull with some pretty influential people in Asia; and that, if we're talking about my interests geologically, is right behind my interest in gold. I want you to go to that game. You'll be seated a row behind him, Mauro will give you a little map of what it's gonna look like, and I want you to introduce yourself to him, chat, find out more about him, who he is. I want an intro to that world," said AC.

These are more words than Luigi had ever heard come out of AC's mouth in his lifetime working for his family. AC was not the talkative type. Maura was usually the mouthpiece for the organization.

"Well, can I ask you something?" said Luigi.

"Now you can, yes," said AC, quietly reminding Luigi that he'd been interrupted.

"Why me? Why couldn't I park my own car? I mean, I don't know much about gems or any of this stuff. I pick up your money," said Luigi, as he reflected on Peter Vaughn earlier in the day.

"What you pick up in those places; that isn't my money. I don't even see that money. None of those few thousand dollars are money to me. What you pick up is your pay. It's what pays for your little fuck-mobile, you and the others. That isn't my money; but I'll guide you prima donnas until one of you is ready," said AC, while at the same time wondering if Luigi was his "guy" for this, given the Belgium remark versus his interest in gems.

AC continued.

"I'm gonna give you this. I wanna see what you get for me. And I had a valet pick your car up because it's gonna stay here for a couple of days in the garage till you get back. I want you doing all this shit for me very low key, nothing flashy. You like to do things flashy. That's okay; I was you once. Then you get to be my age, and you become a little more strategic about this and that. So, I'm being a little more strategic. And why you?" said AC. He stood up and walked back towards the window.

"I don't know. I just feel like it's you that can do this in the way I want it done. I don't want to scare the guy out of the gate. Hopefully he never gives me a reason to scare him."

"Okay," said Luigi.

"Now, Mauro will take you to your room on the 33rd, and you're going to the ballpark tomorrow. It's a 1:00 p.m. game, and you get to see the Yankees knock the red out of the Red Sox for us," laughed AC.

Luigi stood up as Mauro walked back into the room without being summoned. The brothers had each other's moves down to perfection. Mauro knew when to leave, and felt when to come back. He was always spot-on.

CHAPTER SIX

"Fuckin' dog!" said Helen, as the Miniature Schnauzer walked beneath her feet. Helen had just walked the dog, who had a habit of running beneath her feet. She was always torn about whether or not she even wanted the thing, but it beat being in that house alone. On one occasion she returned home, believing she didn't need to tie the dog up when she left, only to return to see her carpet thrashed as the dog decided to chew on a piece of string that hung from it. It ended up pulling the entire carpet right down the middle, almost separating a section of it from the rest of the carpet.

This wasn't the first time the dog had almost tripped her in her own home, and Helen let the dog run off in the house as she sat down on her recliner chair, but not reclining it. She rested her hand on her head, and turned on an episode of *Little House on The Prairie* for the hundredth time.

Michael Landon was crying about something again.

The phone rang, not giving Helen much time to situate herself after her dog walk that almost resulted in her falling on her behind. It was her neighbor, Sandy Finnigan.

"Helen?" Sandy asked.

“Hi, Sandy, what’s going on?” Helen replied, glad that it was someone she actually knew, rather than a person trying to make a psychic reading appointment.

“Brett’s father didn’t pick him up again, and I bought him two tickets to the Yankee’s game on Friday. If I miss another day at work I’m not gonna have a job, and I was just wondering if you liked baseball,” said Sandy.

Helen didn’t. She did, however, love Brett. Brett is Sandy’s 11-year-old son. When Sandy divorced her husband of seven years, the girlfriend he was cheating on Sandy with would become his next wife. Once her husband was married to his new wife, the son they had while they were together barely got the time of day. Oftentimes her ex-husband would never show up on Sundays, even though they had agreed when they separated that would be the day the ex would see their kid. Many times Helen would watch Brett on the porch on a Sunday as the kid sat there, crying, because his piece-of-shit father just wouldn’t show. It broke her heart, but there was nothing she could do. Even with all her abilities, she couldn’t make a bad guy a good father.

“Well, what time is it tomorrow?” Helen asked.

“It’s a one o’clock game at Yankee Stadium, the new one they just built. They’re playing the Red Sox,” said Sandy.

“I’ll bring him,” Helen said. “No problem.”

Sandy cried on the phone.

“I’m sorry, Helen. I hate to push this shit on you, but his father is such an asshole. I don’t understand how he couldn’t want to pay more attention to his own flesh and blood,” Sandy confessed.

“He’s only concerned with his *own* flesh and blood, the blood that heads in the wrong direction,” said Helen.

Sandy accepted the remark, not sure whether or not Helen was telling her this as a friend, or knowing something that she didn’t. With Helen, you never knew.

After speaking with Sandy about plans for Saturday night that might bring them both to Atlantic City to play the quarter slots, Helen hung up the phone. Helen never played anything higher than the quarter slots, afraid she’d attract attention she didn’t want. After all, she always knew the right slot machine to play, and never walked out of a casino, ever, without winning that particular slot machine’s jackpot. On one occasion she had “felt” the need to play a $1 slot, one of those that are in the back of the casino that no one ever plays. After the attention she brought onto herself in winning $44,874.22, and the sirens that accompanied the win as the machine went berserk, she had decided she needed to be careful about stepping into a casino. Some of the employees were even barking about her ability to win the jackpots on the nickel machines, which she’d play by herself once in a while, because she always won. So long as she kept to the nickel machines, however, management didn’t seem to bother with her.

She was just lucky.

Getting ready for her day, and realizing she’d have to get up a little earlier the next day to beat traffic to Yankee Stadium on a Friday, she intended to keep her schedule light. She’d put up a new gate in front of her house, with a sign that stated that readings had to be by appointment only. Her $25 fee never changed. After all, she was always afraid that a reading could one day be wrong, and she never wanted to charge more than she thought she needed. If things got too tough financially, there was always

Atlantic City. Helen was frugal though, never spending more than she had, and always paying her bills on time.

Her first appointment was a man named Kris Newquist. He had heard about Helen through Wendy Henaghan's Facebook posting, and decided he could kill two birds with one stone by both visiting Wendy and checking out this new psychic, who might be able to answer a few burning questions that he had.

Kris was 24, and his father had recently passed away from a heart attack. About 5'10", he had light-brown hair and was a light-hearted young man. There was something very innocent about him, and Helen liked him instantly.

"Hi, Kris," she said as he walked in. "Why don't you have a seat?"

Kris obliged, and took his seat at the table that even Helen did not know the history of. As Helen sat down, a prick to her finger occurred as she put her hand on the corner of the table. That had never happened before. What caused this?

Looking down at her finger, she saw a drop of blood coming from her finger, a small black spot at the base of the puncture.

A splinter had entered Helen's finger.

"Son of a bitch!" she yelled, startling Kris.

"Are you all right?" he asked.

"My finger…a splinter…that's all. Sorry for freaking you out, I'll be right back."

Helen walked to her bathroom and turned on the faucet, rinsing the blood off her finger. Finding a pair of tweezers, she carefully opened up the wound a little more in order to pull out what now lay beneath her skin.

"Fuck," she said out loud, but not loud enough for Kris to hear her in the living room.

Pulling out the piece of wood that cut into her finger, she looked at it. There didn't appear to be anything sharp, either side of it, to have punctured her. In fact, the tiny piece of wood looked like a butter knife on each side. Not thinking anything of it, she opened a trash can next to her toilet using a foot lever, and into the trash it went.

Helen walked back out to the living room to find Kris sitting there, texting someone on his iPhone. Kris looked up at her.

"Are you okay?" he asked, as he put the phone down.

Helen laughed. "I'm fine. I just got a splinter, that's all."

"I think you left a, there's a tiny spot of..."

Kris tried to finish the sentence in a way that didn't get to the word "blood," but Helen looked down and saw what he was getting at. A tiny spot of Helen's blood was in the place of the eye on the Leo engraving. It was the exact size of the eye on the lion, and didn't appear anywhere else on its body. Helen wiped it off with a Kleenex that was on an end table behind the table.

"Thanks for telling me that. I probably wouldn't have even noticed. Gross," she said.

"So, tell me about yourself, Kris. What's your sign?" she asked.

Kris was a little harder to read because he seemed pure. He looked like he had just gotten out of the shower, even though he hadn't. He had a clean appearance that looked like he actually cared about taking care of himself. There was a pleasant way about him.

"Well, I'm a Scorpio, and I've had a difficult time with the loss of my dad. My mother and I have been trying to make ends meet, and before he died, my dad had said he left me something in a box that he'd tell me about one day. That day never came, but after he left us, the bills certainly continued to pile up," Kris said.

"I see. Well, come over to my side of the table. Bring the chair," Helen asked.

Kris stood up and walked over to Helen. He put the chair down at the corner of the table and sat down. Helen took his hand.

"Don't say anything," she said.

Kris nodded his head in agreement as Helen closed her eyes.

Helen continued to close her eyes, and smiled as she held Kris' hand. His hands were too soft to be a laborer.

"You're in school to be an attorney," she said. "Environmental law."

"Yes, I've been going to USC. My mom works there as a secretary. I've also been working a job at the school on the days I'm not in school. They got me working in the dental section, working for some dentist who's in charge of their smoking cessation program," Kris said matter-of-factly.

"I'm feeling like money," she said.

"What?" Kris asked.

“Shhhh,” Helen said.

Helen was able to feel the inanimate. She could become what you were looking for, and see where “she” was. In this instance, she was seeing that she was in a locker, locked up. There was a combination lock in front of her. She looked at it as if she were literally standing in this locker.

“You’re right, Kris. He did leave something for you and your mother,” she said. “It’s still there.”

It had been eight months since he’d lost his father, a mechanical engineer for Ford Motor Company. His father headed up the department that submitted various products that Ford would add to the vehicles to Washington for approval. For instance, if Ford developed a new windshield wiper component, it was Kris’ father who would ship, or deliver, the product for government approval prior to any components being manufactured on a mass level. With Ford, it was always a mass level.

“It’s not a bank, though,” she said. “You were very close to your father.”

“I feel like I still am.”

Helen looked up at Kris, seeing his father standing behind him.

“You have no idea,” she replied with a smile.

“Kris, there’s a locker at Burbank Airport. The month and day of your birthday are the first two numbers in its combination. The month is also the third number of that combination. I can’t see what locker it is because I’m looking at it from the inside...”

“You’re what?” Kris exclaimed, with surprise in his voice.

“Shhh,” she said.

“Sorry. Please, go on,” he said.

A pause silenced the room. She opened her eyes.

“I’m afraid you’re going to have a long day, but the good news is, it’s a big locker. You’re going to be at Burbank Airport for a while, but I have a feeling, in fact, I know, that it’s a day that will end well for you and your mom,” Helen said.

“Burbank Airport?” Kris asked.

“Burbank Airport.”

Helen continued on with her reading, but there wasn’t much to say about Kris. His life was about to get better when he would discover within the locker a bag containing $970,000 in cash, a Mickey Mantle rookie card in a plastic case that said “PSA 10 - Gem Mint” on its top right-hand corner, and a deed to land in Boulder, Colorado for eighty acres of land he never knew his father owned.

“See you later, Mickey,” she said, as Kris walked out of the door.

“Mickey? I’m Kris,” he replied.

“I know. Have a good time now, Kris. Be well. You’re going to be all right.”

Kris walked out as Helen’s next appointment, Mary Taheri, walked up the stairs for her reading.

Mary was about 5’4”, 130 pounds, brown hair and blue eyes. She looked like she was angry, but it wasn’t anger she could direct at Helen.

“Are you the psychic?” Mary asked firmly, as if Helen owed her money.

"Yeeees, come have a seat."

Mary sat down in a huff, as though Helen was already wasting her time. She seemed stressed out and sat down with a *plunk* onto the seat. Helen looked at her and smiled, trying to lighten the air that suddenly was surrounding them both like a heavy weight.

"What's on your mind?" Helen asked.

"It's my husband," Mary said, getting straight to the point. "I want to know if that motherfucker is cheating on me, and if he is, who she is, and where that fucking bitch lives."

Helen didn't like this language, but also knew there were some people Mary's age, in this case 33 years old, who had the mentality of a teenager.

"Well, first you need to relax, or you're going to be very hard for me to read. You seem very upset, so I want you to sit there and relax. I can't help you if you're too wound up," Helen said.

"Ok, ok, I can do that," said Mary.

Helen closed her eyes, but wasn't thinking. She opened herself up on this one, letting direction come from her Source, whatever it was. Her face went from pleasant to "oh, shit" in about thirty seconds.

"Mary, I know why you're here, and I know what you want to know. I also know what you intend to do, and it's going to backfire. And one other thing...he's not your husband," Helen said.

Mary got up, livid. Clearly, Helen had hit her where it hurt.

"Well, he's practically my husband. We've been together for two years now!" she screamed.

"Mary, you haven't been with him in more than three months, and he has been with April for some time now. He was seeing her before he ever met you, and the two of you only got together while he was broken up," Helen said.

"So what am I? You're telling me I was the break-up girl? I was the in-between bitch while he made that whore jealous? Is that who I am?" Mary yelled, as if Helen had done something to her.

"Listen, Mary. I'm just the messenger. You came here for a reading, and that's what I'm giving you. You didn't even need a reading on this one, because there's nothing that I'm telling you that you don't already know," Helen said.

"How did you know her name was April? Did that asshole GPS my phone again?" Mary said. "Has he talked to you?"

"I don't know how I knew her name was April. I don't know how I know most of what comes out of my mouth. What I do know is that you need to move on from this. Let it go. He's not coming back," Helen said, sounding more like a parent than a psychic.

Mary sat down, staring at Helen while toying with her car keys on the table.

"I know what this is. I know how you know all this," said Mary.

"Mary, he isn't that good a guy to begin with. Even if you ended up with him, he's a possessive guy, and you'd never be able to do the things you like with this guy. He's a jerk, and yeah, if you sit around waiting you'll probably hear from again. Everything, and I mean *everything* that comes out of his mouth is a lie. He says he loves you, but you know in your heart that you can't trust him. There's a reason he put a GPS on your phone.

There's a reason he doesn't want you looking at his text messages when he's with you. You just fall for it and let it go, because you love him more than he loves you. Get rid of this sack of shit. There's nothing there for you to get back!" Helen replied.

"What do you fucking know, you stupid bitch! This is all just a bullshit set-up. He talked to you!" Mary yelled. "I'm not stupid!"

Stupid is exactly what Mary was. Just one of those girls you see at the mall who forgot she's not a girl anymore, or who is in denial about it. The type who hangs out with twenty-year-olds and tries to look like one of the girls.

Mary walked out of Helen's house angrily, never looking back, appearing to have a new direction, a new purpose.

"What is the problem here?" Helen yelled at her. "What am I saying that's making you act like that?"

Mary got into her car and sped off. Helen shut the door and leaned up against the doorjamb.

"I don't know how much more of this shit I can take," Helen said to herself.

She walked over to grab a glass of Bailey's, and walked over to her couch. She sat there, grabbed the remote as if to turn the TV on, and put it back down without doing so.

"Yankee Stadium," she said. "8-3 Yankees. How boring."

CHAPTER SEVEN

1939 - Costa Brava, Spain.

The barge pulled into the Costa Brava port on Saturday, March 3, 1939, en route to the United States after a stop in Nice, France. The shipment contained a dismantled castle that a rich businessman named Arto Sharif decided would look good on about 2,000 acres of land he'd purchased in Los Angeles. Raised by a single mother, his father had died in a bar fight when Arto was a child. He had become self-made, indulging in the finer things in life. He purchased a home in Reseda, California for his mother, Irene, and made the United States his home. Prior to his arrival in America, his home was never a single residence, but a series of moves with his mother by his side.

The barge also had a space on its top level for unrelated shipments. It was a space that could be purchased for shipments of personal items from various families to another, including artifacts from museums.

It was lot 34A00F that caught a bored Sharif's eye as he strolled the barge, accompanying his would-be home as it braved the ocean to its final destination. Sharif curiously lifted the blue carpet covering it to see the various statues, some which appeared to be Italian artifacts. They were sitting on a table. The table was engraved with various carvings of the signs of the zodiac, and was tagged as an individual shipment. It probably wouldn't have been much comfort to whoever was expecting it to be delivered to the

United States to know that a four-hundred-pound artifact was sitting on top of it the entire trip to New England, where the barge would eventually arrive.

It was the same table that would one day end up in the home of Helen Wilson some seventy-plus years later. But where it came from had helped to imbue it with a history and personality of its own. Helena Petrovna Gan, later known as Madame Blavatsky by those who received readings from her in 1884, had originally purchased the table while in travels. Her travels were motivated by escaping her husband, who was much older than she was. Born in Russia, she spent much time in Egypt and Rome, never able to keep her feet planted in one place as word got out about her abilities, which in that day was seen as evil rather than as the gift that it was.

It was in 1886 that she had met Daniel Dunglas Home. He was from Scotland, and was a renowned medium known throughout Europe as having a personal line to the afterlife. When Helena had decided she'd had just about enough of moving around all the time due to what some called "witchery," she had given the table to Home as a gift, along with other personal items that she believed would help him on his path as a psychic. One of those things was a glass vase that her mother had given to her. Two years later, Helena herself had met the hereafter. This, however, did not conclude the conversation with Home, who would speak to her, and occasionally see her, when Home would find himself in trance-like states. This would usually occur at night.

But Home wanted to know more about the origins of the table than Helena did. To her, it was a table with engraved signs of the zodiac that aided in her cause, gave comfort and credibility to those she'd read to, and just fit the part. To Home, there was something else going on with this table. It appeared to be put together in a way that wasn't customary to the day. There were no signs of screws in it, or nails, or anything that would have kept it together in the typical way. It just was. There didn't appear to be any real wear and tear, and although it certainly didn't look brand-new, it didn't look as old as he knew it was. He really couldn't understand exactly how it was put together. The engravings on it seemed spectacular. The precision seemed exact. There were no dings around the signs, no scratches, and each sign seemed to have what appeared to be a silver frame to it, entirely surrounding each sign of the zodiac. The way the metal surrounded the signs was equally intriguing to Home, as it was perfect; too perfect for the time.

Looking beneath the table, Home stared for hours for some sign of its origin. He was unable to determine where it could have been made. But at the end of one of the legs he made a startling discovery that Helena had apparently never become aware of in the two years or so that she had owned it herself.

What appeared to be an old piece of tape was covered the bottom of one of the legs of the table. When Home had placed the table in his study, he had recognized that it would constantly look unbalanced. It was always leaning when it shouldn't be. So one Saturday morning, Home turned the heavy table over to inspect it further. He had assumed he might have to add tape to the remaining three legs of the table in order to balance it out, when in fact all he really had to do was remove the tape that covered the bottom of that one leg. Carefully, he peeled the tape back to discover an engraving on the bottom of the leg. He couldn't make it out, as pieces of the tape seemed to get embedded into the engraving. Trying to find something small enough to clean out the pieces of left-over tape, or whatever adhesive material it was, he found a small pencil, sharpened it, and slowly began picking off the remains of the tape that seemed to have been swallowed by the bottom of this old table leg.

After about an hour of picking at it, he was startled to realize exactly what it began to reveal itself to say. It would have had to take weeks to engrave this name so perfectly. It was perfect. What tool had been used to create this writing in such a way that was so clear, once the pieces of fiber-like material had been removed? This was not a day where fine print existed. During this time, agreements were very to the point, so there was never a need for an asterisk.

"Michel de Nostredame - 1562," it read.

Home shot up in disbelief at what he had before him. The table was not from the 1700s, as he'd expected; but during a time when he and John Dee, a psychic to Queen Elizabeth II, had ruled the planet in terms of their credibility and predictions. This table was much older than he had thought, and the engravings more spectacular than he'd originally assumed. It was clear to him that the energy that attracted him to the piece had far more history than he had believed. It was at this table that Michel de Nostredame would write his thoughts. Michel de Nostredame, known to the world as Nostradamus.

After Home's death in 1886, an unknowing family member had sold the lot of his property to Mason Billingsley, a man who scoured Europe in search of property left behind by those whose walking, talking bodies were history in themselves. While Billingsley never cared enough to research the actual pieces, he enjoyed the visual aspect of the items he'd buy. He would travel the world to sell what appeared to be artifacts to the rich, who thought they had it all. In the case of what he had purchased from the

Home estate, he simply did not know what he had. Or the table didn't want him to. This table had a knack for ending up where it wanted to be.

Its travels from 1886 to 1939, where Sharif was now looking at it on a barge headed for the United States, remain a mystery. Over fifty years had passed since Billingsley hawked it to someone. Many of his auctions were to the nameless who showed up, paid their money, and left. This table simply had a tag on it as it readied for an ocean journey that stated "USA." There was no name on it. It had no street address, or family name. It almost looked as though someone was just trying to get it out of Europe. The day had come to simply get it out of there.

Sharif pondered to himself why someone didn't just take a hammer to the thing if they wanted to be rid of it. He approached the barge captain, Neil Jedrey, with a question that was said in a manner of no importance. He didn't want to give away his interest. Jedrey was a small man of about five foot three, and looked as if he had just jumped off of the Captain Crunch cereal box.

"That space down there, what's it for? Where is it all headed?" Sharif said.

"I've no clue, mate. They pay, I take it," Jedrey said with a grunt.

"Is it all one shipment to one person?" Sharif replied.

"No, but when we arrive there's usually a group of ten or fifteen people who stand in line and board when we arrive. They grab what's theirs, and off they go. It's not the main cargo, but I have the space, and it's a quick way to make a few extra bottles of whiskey," Jedrey said.

"What if no one picks it up?" Sharif said, now engaging Jedrey's own curiosity as to the question.

"Then it goes overboard," the captain said. "I don't store; I deliver."

Days felt like months on the barge as it traveled to the United States. The rough waters made the journey feel like agony, and it was hardly a cruise ship. By the time the boat had arrived in Ogunquit, Maine, most of the crew had been injured in one way or another. Sharif himself had banged his head in his own room while sitting at his desk. He never did figure out what had hit him, but it would most certainly leave a scar. When one is on the waters as they were, during this time, anything could happen, and usually did.

After pulling up to the port, a line of people, six men and eight women, waited on the dock to pick up personal shipments that were in this odd section of the barge. Lamps, a statue that it took four grown men about an hour to figure out how to carry off the ship, and finally, the table that held Sharif's curiosity.

No one.

No one had arrived for this unique table, one he had never seen the likes of before.

"Bottle of whiskey, and I'll owe ya for the next haul," Sharif said to the captain.

"For that?" Captain Jedrey balked. "It's yours."

Lifting the table off the barge was easier said than done, so Sharif had the men who hauled the statue off the barge help him with it for a few beers at the local tavern. Sharif didn't lift a finger, despising physical labor.

Loading the table into a pre-arranged truck that awaited his arrival, off he went to his home in Los Angeles' Mulholland Drive area of the big city. This table was all that was on his mind, almost forgetting that he had just spent weeks on a barge that delivered a castle to California for him. It would take months to put together his new digs, and while he had yet to sell the home that he had been living in while he put his new castle project together, it was the table he had been obsessed with. He wanted to know everything about it. This was one of those one-of-a-kind pieces that he'd be able to show off to his friends, the friends who would walk around his castle, take free drinks, and who actually cared less about him than the gum on their shoes. This was a man who had money, and in Los Angeles, that's all it took to garner friendships. It was the land of Hollywood and wealth, so this table would provide conversation that merely knowing him wouldn't. It was a land of what you have, and a land that cared nothing of those who had nothing.

Arriving at his home, he called to the three men who awaited his arrival to help him unload the vessel with four wheels, the only vehicle he could manage.

"The table," he said. "Be careful with it. Put it in my library."

The men, burly and strong, lifted the table and did as they were told. After the truck had been unloaded, Sharif grabbed a bottle of whiskey and poured himself a glass.

He sat at the table, pulling up the chair that was usually behind his desk. Resting his elbow on the table, his hand held his head up as he looked down at the engravings. His drink in the other, he just stared at the Taurus sign.

"Where did you come from?" he said to himself in a whisper.

"Where?"

He shot up as if a bolt of lightning had just exploded in his living room. In this case, however, the explosion was in his chest. His face became dark-red as he realized that he was about to know all of the answers about everything he had ever had a question about. He looked down at the table, his whiskey falling to the ground, and slowly rested his head on the table.

The answers to all of his questions were about to be revealed as he began his journey to the afterlife.

Somewhere in Los Angeles, there was another Mason Billingsley on the prowl, and a castle that would never be erected.

The table itself would decide who its owner would be, and a playboy who brought his own castle to the United States was not where it belonged.

CHAPTER EIGHT

"The Boston Red Sox fucking suck!" a group of Yankee fans chanted, as Luigi stood in line for a beer. Luigi wanted to punch everyone in that group in the face. He wasn't a Red Sox fan, but he wasn't really a Yankee's fan, either. Luigi was a Mets fan, and to him, everything was about respect. This group of drunks who stood next to him had none.

The line seemed as if it went on forever. A never-ending line that would end with him having to pull out a twenty for a beer, and hoping there was change. The $1.5 billion ballpark opened in 2009, and was huge, nothing like its predecessor that closed in 2008 after 85 years of baseball. In 1923, the original Yankee stadium only cost $2.4 million to construct. How times had changed; not just at Yankee Stadium, but throughout the world. The house that Ruth built was now a park, and here he stood at the new stadium. Waiting seemed to be what he did for a living.

Luigi hadn't slept well the night before, readying for the task of setting up a meeting with a gem distributor and his boss during a baseball game at Yankee Stadium, wondering how he'd ever pull this off. He knew that he had to, or it was his ass when he reported back to AC. He'd spent the night before nervous about the game, falling asleep to the movie *The Shawshank Redemption*. For some odd reason, the movie relaxed him, and seemed to bring his own ego down a peg every time he watched it.

Grabbing his beer, he walked back out to the huge ballpark and found his seat. Already sitting in front of him, just one seat to his left, was Jens Maes, the gem dealer that AC had hoped would be his key into the Chinese market. The Chinese had quite the amount of disdain for what Americans simply called "The Mafia." How on earth was he going to manipulate this situation at a Yankee's versus Red Sox game filled with thousands of people? AC saw to it that most of the seats in the row Jens sat in had been purchased, seated with "family" members whose job was to keep their mouths shut while allowing Luigi the opportunity to accomplish what he was meant to. Members of AC's clan eyed Luigi as they slowly walked into the row in front of him, and he felt the pressure to deliver even more. He nodded at each familiar face. Jens just stared obliviously at the ballpark, completely unaware of the set-up that was occurring just to get him in front of AC for an hour.

The two seats in front of Luigi were empty, but then, out of the corner of his eye, Luigi watched as everyone stood up to his right in the row in front of him. These two particular seats had been purchased, and it was Helen Wilson and Brett Finnigan.

Luigi felt a little uneasy, looking at the rest of his family who sat to the right of them. One family member just gave Luigi an "I don't know" shrug. Luigi just shook his head.

"Shit," he thought.

Brett was all about the Red Sox, clearly. Blasting out of his CD headphones he heard blaring lyrics "Gonna spend the day over at Fenway," a song that had become popular among Red Sox fans in Boston. Its music video featured William Shatner as the home plate umpire, and Luigi recalled seeing the video on *The Today Show*, and laughing at the thing.

Good thing this kid had headphones on; but the boy was going to be deaf by age twelve with the volume he had the portable CD player on. Helen gave him a little nudge along with a hand gesture that resulted in Brett turning the thing down.

"We're at Yankee Stadium," she said softly.

"So?" replied Brett.

Both turned their heads back to the ballpark.

Jens just looked to his right and gave Helen a smile, nodding his head.

"First time to Yankee Stadium?" Jens asked her.

"First time to this one," Helen said, referring to the new ballpark. "I liked the old one much better."

Brett couldn't hear the dig at the new park with his headphones on, now listening to Neil Diamond's "Sweet Caroline." Helen looked at Brett.

"I love Neil Diamond," she said to Brett.

Brett pulled the headphones off.

"Who is Neil Diamond?" Brett replied.

"He's the guy singing that song, that's "Sweet Caroline." That's Neil Diamond," she said.

Brett put the headphones back on, as Helen was reminded about how old she was.

"Wow," she said, looking at Jens, who was chuckling at the conversation he'd just overheard.

After a performance of the National Anthem by Neil Sedaka, who is famous for such classics as "Happy Birthday Sweet Sixteen" and "Laughter In The Rain" and dozens of other singles, the game began.

Planted to Jens' left were several other family members of Luigi's large "family," and Luigi was beginning to see the broader picture of all of this. Luigi gave Tony Incorvia a look, one that said: "Get up, follow me."

Standing up in a row of regular fans, none too thrilled with having to stand up as soon as the game started, Luigi squeezed himself past a dozen legs and followed Tony up to the top of the stairs near various concession stands.

"All right, man, what's the deal here? I wasn't expecting the entire fucking family to be here. I'm freaking out enough just trying to figure out how to get near this guy. And what's with the woman and the little bastard in front of me?" Luigi said.

"Listen, we got this worked out. Mark Pistone is with me. I'm gonna start talking about you like I know you're some big shot, and loud enough for Jens to overhear. I'm gonna pretend like he's not even there, just being loud enough for him to hear me build you up. You just gotta trust me on this, the shit works every time. Otherwise you're gonna look stupid trying to just get the guy's attention. All this shit has been worked out," Tony replied.

"AC could have told me about this before, so I had a little heads-up, you know what I'm sayin'?" replied Luigi, sounding like he just walked out of a scene of *Goodfellas.*

"Tell AC that; I'm sure he'll be cool with you telling him what he coulda done. We're here; just watch the game and let me do what I do," replied Tony.

This seemed like a zoo to Luigi, who felt completely out of control of the situation. He had thought about how he was going to approach Jens all night. He had a plan. It was going to work. Now all of a sudden he had Tony Incorvia here telling him he was going to play out an acting role in front of him to get Jens' attention. He couldn't understand why AC didn't just have Tony ask the guy for a meeting with AC; but AC set the entire thing up so that it would be Jens' idea to reach out to Luigi, and not the other way around. In a way, it was brilliant; but Luigi would have liked to have been in on the plan, rather than seeing his entire family watching his every move instead. All Luigi could think about was how many "reports" AC was going to receive from the row of family members, now given the task of making sure Luigi just does what he was told. He always enjoyed playing "big shot," and now he was getting his opportunity to be one.

They both walked back down to their seats as casually as any other fan, pissing off the Yankee fans who yet again had to stand up to let Luigi back into his seats. Those is Tony's row all had the same blood flowing through their veins, knowing the plan for the day. Standing up was no big deal for them, even though most of them would rather be at the horse races.

Luigi just had to watch the game. He looked to the row in front of him, seeing the back of Helen's head as she nudged Brett to take off the headphones.

"Did you come to see the game? Or to listen to that thing?" Helen said. "We didn't come all the way here so that you could listen to your headphones, so take them off, or we're going back home."

Brett took them off with a huff, but then, realizing how sweet Helen was, gave her a smile.

"You're right. I'm sorry, Helen."

"It's all right," she replied. "Just watch the game. We came all the way here, sweetie."

Brett looked like he had a convenience store at his feet, as Helen treated him to all the goodies. An orange Sunkist, nachos, and a pretzel were at his feet. Brett was certainly not going without during this game.

Laughter came from Jens' left, with a sudden halt as Tony looked towards Luigi, then back at Mark Pistone.

"Holy shit!" Tony said. Jens quickly looked to his left game-neighbor, but without saying anything. Jens looked back towards the game, pretending not to listen, but intrigued.

"That's Luigi Nicolo. That guy is fucking loaded," Tony said, loud enough for Jens to overhear, but not so loud as to sound obvious.

"Get the fuck outta here, for real?" replied Mark.

"I'm telling you, that's him. That guys worth a couple hundred mil. What's he doing down here?" Tony asked. Tony looked up at Luigi.

"Hey, man, aren't you Luigi Nicolo?"

Jens looked at Tony as he asked, but wasn't about to turn around to see who Tony was talking to. Instead, he just heard the voice behind him reply.

"Yes, and I'm just here to watch the game, buddy. Just like everybody else," Luigi replied in Oscar-worthy lies. For a moment, Luigi knew what it felt like to be AC. He liked the feeling, and seemed to enjoy this role. Of course, he couldn't fully envelop himself in the role while realizing there was a kid in charge of his Mercedes over at AC's building. Luigi was a man who kicked ass to bilk money out of small businesses. Today, he was royalty. It would have seemed stupid if it wasn't working like a charm, and Jens was clearly intrigued, trying to move around in his seat and give himself an excuse to turn around just to get a glimpse of what he loved: Money, and the prospect of getting just a little more before he was all done in the gem business.

"Do that thing you do," Brett yelled to Helen.

"Shhhhhhh," said Helen.

This caught everyone's attention. Luigi broke out of character, and Jens actually looked at Helen with a quick smile, then turned back towards the game. Tony sat there, biting his lip with a "fucking fuck" look on his face. So close. The zone had been interrupted, simply because Sandy Finnigan bought those two damn seats through Ticketmaster before he could buy the entire row that Jens had bought one seat in, a seat that was easy to find with a name as unobscure as his. That and $50 to a ticket booth clerk about three days earlier. Jens told the ticket agent about his excitement over attending the game, and that little story had one of the most horrific mafia family members in modern history surrounding him, and Jens didn't even know it.

For now, however, all eyes and ears were on what exactly this little woman in the middle of them all could "do."

Luigi just sat back in his seat. He shook his head, then folded his arms.

Even though it was Yankee Stadium, it seemed like the most quiet place on the planet.

"This better be fucking good," he thought to himself.

CHAPTER NINE

Mary Taheri wasn't how Detective Merton Howard anticipated his day would begin. The Naugatuck lawman was 60, and closing in on retirement. He was a very black and white fellow, standing about 6 feet and 190 pounds. He'd seen it all, heard it all, watched it all, and even had to pull the trigger twice in his thirty-year career. On one occasion it was during a bank robbery attempt; the other was during a custody dispute that went to hell in the courthouse lobby between a man and his ex-wife.

After being given joint custody, Eileen Welch pulled a gun on her husband, prior to the use of x-ray machines that would have otherwise caught a piece being walked into the court. Eileen was upset about the judge in the case granting her husband joint custody, namely due to the fact that he was cheating on her with another woman prior to filing for divorce. It had little to do with him being a good father, which he was. He just wasn't as good of a husband. The consequence for Eileen was experiencing what it felt like to be shot in the leg. Her leg healed, but her anger for her ex-husband never did. Several months after she was released from a two-year stint in jail, she attempted, armed and ready, to kidnap her then-six-year-old son and was again shot by another officer. This time, she did not get up, and her son no longer had a biological mother. It was one of those stories that made Merton even more ready for retirement.

When Mary Taheri walked into his office, which was inundated with reading materials and old newspaper clippings that seemed to follow his latest, and hopefully last, homicide investigation, Merton appeared irritated that this woman had been sent to his office. He didn't typically handle these sort of complaints. Mary, however, was adamant that she speak with somebody, and the police officer at the station's front office refused to even consider writing the police report.

"So, I understand you wanted to speak with me. What was the problem out front?" Merton asked, already in the loop that a woman who appeared to be shaken, not stirred, had attempted to file a pretty bizarre police report.

Mary Taheri appeared just as angry as she did when she snapped in Helen Wilson's living room. This time, however, it was caused by the insinuation that she was crazy, by the officer's refusal to even take a report. She was at least relieved that she was being given face time by someone, as the officers at the front desk huddled and laughed at her as she was buzzed into the station's detective unit.

"Listen. I am not crazy. I am not on medication. I am not some lunatic coming off the street. There is someone I need you to check out," Mary said adamantly.

Merton sat down in his chair, a donut in one hand, and a coffee that appeared to spill a little in the other.

"Have you ever heard of constitutional rights, Miss Taheri?" Merton said.

"Of course I have," she replied. "What do you think, I'm an idiot?"

"Well, here in America, I can't simply check people out on a whim. There needs to be probable cause before I can start walking into someone's house and invading their space and privacy. Tell me what it is this woman apparently did. It's a woman, right?" Merton said.

"I don't know what the hell she is. But a lot of times people come walking into a police station with a story to tell. The story is ignored, and then something bad happens. There's this woman, Helen Wilson, and she claims to be some sort of psychic..."

Merton decided interruption was necessary.

"Wait. A psychic?"

Mary knew where this was headed.

"Listen, I know how this sounds. This woman is connected to something that is wrong, I can feel it. People line up in front of her house every day for these readings she's giving, and she gets paid to do it," Mary replied.

"How much is she charging people?" Merton asked.

"Twenty-five dollars," Mary said, a bit embarrassed by the answer.

A pause took over the room.

"OK, so, here's the deal, Mary. People charge more than that at carnivals for readings and, shit...just to win a stuffed Cat In The Hat doll. She doesn't sound like she's breaking any laws, and we're a bit strapped as it is, budget-wise, to be combing through some woman's life who is charging people a whopping twenty-five bucks to have their damn horoscope read to them," Merton said. "I don't know what you want me to do, but the reality is, there's nothing here for me to investigate. She hasn't committed a crime, and until she does, there's nothing that I can do," Merton said in a more affirmative manner. "I'm dealing with murderers, and you want me to break away from grieving family members because some twenty-five-dollar psychic hit a little too close to home? Don't you know that's what these people do?"

Mary stood up, not getting any of the answers that she wanted to.

"I'm sorry I came. Obviously I look crazier than this woman I'm here to tell you about; but remember, I came here. Remember this day, and look at the clock on your wall. I came here, and I told you about this woman. There's something very wrong here, and there's no way this lady could know the things she did. It's a scam. It's a fraud of some sort, and that's a crime you need to look into. She's working with someone. I don't know who, but she knows shit she couldn't possibly know. I mean, don't people accepting money for services need some sort of business license? Something?" Mary said angrily.

Merton walked over to her, ready to see this bizarre storyteller out of his office.

"Listen, Miss Taheri. Write her name and address down, give it to the officer at the front desk, and I'll hang onto it. If something comes up, I have her information, and I have yours. I just cannot tell you that I can go prying through this lady's life without her committing a crime. These psychics are on every block these days, and if we went after all of them for fraud, then there'd be a lot of murderers getting away with what they've done. I have to say, however, that this will go down in my journal of the more interesting complaints I've received. I, however, have a missing kid case that requires my attention more than hocus pocus."

Mary turned to him, readying to leave his office.

"I'm telling you. There is something to this that you need to check out," she said.

"Well, then I'll have all of her information in the event I need to, thanks to you," he said.

Mary smiled at him, feeling the condescension.

"I'll leave the information with your officer, Detective Howard."

"Thank you," he said.

Merton closed the door and walked back to his desk. Sitting down, he looked up at his clock.

"2:33 p.m.," he said. "It's 2:33 p.m."

Merton didn't like the way this woman talked. Even more, he didn't like the way he was feeling, as he now had this time stuck in his head.

In front of him, he picked up a copy of the *Hartford Courant*. He flipped through it, a bit intrigued, to the comic pages. At the bottom right-hand corner of the page, he saw the section marked "Daily Horoscope."

"Aquarius."

He read his sign, which read: "You are about to conclude a journey, and the last thing you want to do is inquire into the impossible. You feel you must though, and you won't know why. There will be a reason you do, and you will then understand that the word *impossible* actually also spells "I'm Possible," and sense will be made of it."

Merton put the newspaper down.

"Fuck."

He looked back up to the clock. It said 2:35 p.m.

"Fuck."

Merton Howard was going to take a drive.

CHAPTER TEN

Brett Finnigan held his horses. Luigi, who sat behind him, would rather be betting on them. Jens pretended to watch Alex Rodriguez step up to the plate, while his right ear seemed zoned in on the conversation, which for some reason had him oddly listening in on a conversation between a woman and the boy next to him.

“Popcorn, Reece’s Pieces!” yelled a young man as he walked up the stairs of the stadium, throwing bags of the candy across rows and then collecting the money as he got closer to the customer. The kid seemed like he’d been doing this for lifetimes, regardless of the fact that he looked about 18.

The family row, minus Helen and Brett, didn’t break a sweat. Brett practically had a convenience store at his feet, and the family that awaited Luigi’s task of hitting up the gem dealer for an appointment with AC couldn’t have cared less about candy.

“Well?” Brett said to Helen, as he drank his orange-flavored Sunkist. “Do it!”

“Wait, wait, I’m working on it,” said Helen.

Luigi eyed his family, who sat quietly, but also listening in on this chat out of nothing more than bizarre curiosity. Helen looked around, and Jens, Luigi and his family all did a terrific job at not paying attention, or coming off as if they weren’t paying attention to the conversation they were actually glued to. Lying was what the mafia was good at, and Jens was from Belgium. He was just there for the experience.

He was about to get one.

"A double," Helen replied. "That man is going to hit a double."

Rodriguez stood still as a pitch flew by him, making the count 1-2. One ball, two strikes.

"I don't think that's happening, Helen," said Brett, with an antagonizing smirk.

Clay Buchholz threw his next pitch. This one, for some reason, seemed to indicate something was off. A change had occurred in the ballpark. It was a feeling. The pitcher for the Red Sox seemed a little confused, as if something had changed his mood. The ball flew over the head of Rodriguez. The crowd gasped as the count went to 2-2, two balls and two strikes.

"A double, eh?" laughed Brett.

"Wait and see, Brett. Wait and see," said Helen.

The pitcher walked around the mound as John Farrell, the pitching coach, ran up to the mound, his hand covering his mouth. Covering your mouth became routine in baseball after it had been discovered teams had actually hired lip readers to watch the TV monitors in their respective club houses in order to convey pitches to the batters. Coaches would issue signs based on those lip readers to the various base coaches, who would then sign to the batter as to what pitch was coming. After a brief conversation, Farrell returned to the dugout. Buchholz set aim at home plate, preparing to throw his next pitch.

After winding up, the pitch was thrown in what felt like slow motion. Helen knew what was about to occur. And it did.

Rodriguez smashed the ball into center field and over the head of the outfielders who scrambled to catch the ball. Rounding second base, Rodriguez counted his blessings and remained at second base.

A double.

Luigi looked at his family members with a look of surprise, his eyebrows raising as he tried to explain to himself what he just saw this woman do. Dumb luck, he decided. Jens barely knew anything about baseball, but could see that Alex Rodriguez appeared to be standing on the second base.

Yes. It was a double.

An announcer blasted out the name of the next Yankee player as the crowd continued to thunderously react to Rodriguez's double. They all found out it was a double after Helen did, but none of them heard her proclaim a double was on its way. If so, they might have been reacting directly to her. Instead, it was only a Belgian gem dealer and a group of mafia members who were in on the experience. Dumb luck.

Vernon Wells stood up at the plate.

"Ouch," said Helen. "This is gonna hurt."

The pitch to home plate struck Wells in the ass as he turned to avoid the pitch coming right at him. The umpire directed him to first base, with Rodriguez remaining at second base.

"Watch that man on second base. He's a crook," Helen said.

As the pitcher began his wind-up, Rodriguez took off to third base, stealing the base. It was now first and third in the third inning. The Yankees were on top, 6-1, with nobody out.

The look on Luigi's face, and indeed his entire family, and even the Belgian to her left, said it all. All of them had the very same look on their face, and it was a look that said:

WHAT THE FUCK??

Ichiro Suzuki stood up to the plate, but now all eyes were on Helen. Helen was lucky enough to always have eyes on her, and the older she got, the more people paid attention. Hers was a beauty that maintained itself both inside and out. Unfortunately for Helen, the eyes currently paying attention to her were from a family whose living was made by crime, and the worst kinds of crimes. Murder. Robbery. Extortion. Intimidation. Beatings.

And they all had their eyes focused on a woman in her 60s, who was sitting next to an 11-year-old boy.

"All out," she said.

"All out? Everybody?" said Brett.

The runners' leads off the bag looked to be about five feet each.

Before Brett could finish his sentence, Ichiro Suzuki barely touched the ball with his bat and it looped into the pitcher's glove for out one. The pitcher then fired the ball off to Dustin Pedroia, who was covering second, to take out Rodriguez. Pedroia then tagged Wells as he ran a little too close to second base.

A beautiful triple play had just occurred.

“Oh, the pizza guy’s not going to be happy, either,” Helen said to Brett.

“Why?” Brett said, as he looked at a young guy selling mini-pizzas to fans.

“They sell everything. But not his in about 5, 4, 3, 2…”

The young man tripped, dropping all of the pizzas on the stairs.

“Sorry, guys! I’ll be right back with more!” the young man said to the fans, some with not-so-happy looks on their face.

Luigi was shocked. Jens was shocked. The family stared up at Luigi as if to say:

WHAT ARE YOU GOING TO DO ABOUT THIS?

Jens had seen enough, and realized he just had to start a conversation with this woman. It would have to be a conversation that wouldn’t give away the fact that he’d just overheard a conversation that wasn’t meant for him. The Nicolo family suddenly found themselves eager to know more about this woman than the gem dealer, and their tactics would likely be a tad bit less sensitive than Jens would be.

“Excuse me, miss...do you know what time it is?” said Jens.

Helen pointed to what appeared to be the 100-foot Jumbotron in center field. The time appeared to be about twelve feet high. It was 2:29 in the afternoon.

“Oh, oh. Stupid me,” laughed Jens.

Helen smiled and looked back towards Brett. She looked back to Jens with a look of curiosity, but she didn’t really understand what she was curious about. Her attention was aimed at him enough to realize that he’d overheard her every prediction, or the criminal behind her, and those to her left.

“I need to go to the bathroom,” said Brett. “But that was awesome, Helen.”

Helen laughed, and family members to Brett’s right all stood up, indicating to Helen that everybody around her had heard Brett’s request to use the restroom. Still, though, she thought nothing of it.

“Do you mind watching his grocery store?” laughed Helen, as she pointed to Brett’s array of snacks that he’d devour during the game.

“Absolutely, I’d be delighted,” Jens said, as he looked into the eyes of a miracle.

As Helen stood up, her ticket fell to the ground in front of her seat. Jens remembered that when he picked up his own ticket for the game at the will-call of Yankee stadium, his name was printed on it, along with the credit card and its last four digits used to purchase it. He decided not to tell her that she’d dropped it, knowing that so long as she remained in the stadium, she wouldn’t need it to get back to her seat. If she did have any issue by not having her ticket, she had eager fans around her who would gladly vouch for her. And Jens had the ticket she dropped to confirm that she was indeed seated there. It was a ticket, however, that Helen may have wished to secure a little better as Jens picked it up.

Helen Wilson. Visa. 8831.

Luigi witnessed Jens’ review of the ticket, and could tell that he wasn’t the only one to witness what he’d just seen. He now realized that the man he was sent to secure a meeting with AC was also very aware of what appeared to be an astonishing act by a woman neither of them knew at all.

Jens placed the ticket back on her seat, upside down, so that it was not obvious that the ticket had been looked at.

But it had been.

Very closely.

Helen returned to her seat with Brett, and watched the game without further play calls by her.

Her ticket had been removed from the seat, the ticket Jens had placed on it face down.

CHAPTER ELEVEN

Jens sat in his car in the Yankees parking lot, unable to explain what he had just witnessed. What he did know was, he was intending to spend at least a couple of extra days in New York City. His intention was to look up Helen Wilson, and do a little digging on the lady. Using his cellular, he brought up Google on his phone's internet browser, and looked up her name.

Unfortunately, there were about 100,000 search results for the name, none of whom was the lady who had just shocked him at Yankee Stadium.

HELEN WILSON FORTUNE TELLER.

Nothing.

HELEN WILSON YANKEES

Nothing.

HELEN WILSON PREDICTIONS.

Nothing.

PSYCHIC HELEN WILSON.

Bingo.

Helen Wilson was a psychic who lived in Naugatuck, Connecticut. She would give readings for $25 at her home, though no address was listed.

The Google search result brought him to psychics known in Connecticut, but there was no actual Web site for her or her services. A photo accompanying a publicly run "psychic research" website displayed her photo. And it was her. He had just watched this woman shock him at a game that was meant to be a last hurrah in New York before the long flight back to Belgium. Instead, he was now sitting in his car, wondering what the hell it was that he had just seen. Scrolling down the listing, there was a "Next Live Event Section" for "This Web site," which clearly indicated that the web page was not run by her, but by someone that just gave information out about psychics online. The "Next Live Event" by Helen Wilson would be held at Naugatuck High School's gymnasium, for free, to anyone who wanted to ask her any questions about psychics, mediums, the horoscope signs in general, and the tarot cards. It would be at 1:00 p.m. the very next day.

Behind Jens' rental car, Luigi Nicolo also sat in his own vehicle, watching the back of Jens' vehicle, but clutching the ticket he'd swiped after Jens had put it down. In the midst of the game and Brett's needs, Helen simply didn't notice she'd ever dropped it or misplaced it. Luigi just watched Jens, taking down the license plate of the rental car that would be pretty easy to track, enabling Luigi himself the ability to find out where the man was staying once he had a friend pull the car rental documentation. The Nicolos had friends everywhere. If he were really lucky, AC may have owned the car rental agency himself, given he did own several; but he doubted it, given how many agencies in New York there were. He'd cross his fingers. He decided it was time to go tell AC that not only had he not obtained a meeting with Jens for him, but that he'd witnessed a woman who called plays during a Yankees game.

AC was going to fucking kill him with this story; but his only potential salvation was that other family members witnessed the same thing that he had as they sat in the same row as Helen, several of them able to clearly overhear what he just had. He was hoping that their corroborating stories would at least save his ass. If he'd ever gone back to them with this story without other Nicolo members as witnesses, he'd likely have been killed just for the sake of it. It would send the message to the rest of the family that when AC gave an order, it would be kept. For now, Helen Wilson was a secret yet to be told to AC. Those who lived in Connecticut knew her as the sweet lady that gave fun readings; but the longer she conducted the readings, the clearer and more precise those readings became. This was hitting nerves with some clients, as Detective Merton Howard had recently learned when he himself had received the oddest complaint he'd ever received when Mary Taheri walked into his office.

For now, Luigi just had to think on his drive back to AC's from Yankee Stadium about exactly what he would say, how he'd say it, and how this would all be perceived by a man who could erase him from the planet and not lose a second's sleep about it. He was even more concerned about how Mauro, AC's brother and assumed silent underboss, was going to react. AC listened to Mauro most of the time, but not all of the time. This had caused some pretty heated debates between the brothers, but AC did consider Mauro as trustworthy above all others. Mauro could raise his voice when speaking with AC, and was the only person on the planet granted that right. Mauro realized he had that right when he screamed at AC over a bank heist gone wrong several years ago, and lived to apologize about it the next day.

Pulling up to AC's building, the weight of the conversation that would begin in about eight minutes weighed heavily upon him. He had no idea how he would possibly begin this conversation, and justify to AC that the news he brought was worth his inability to secure a meeting with a gem dealer he was sent to obtain.

"I'm gonna fucking die today," he whispered to himself, as the same young valet driver holding his Mercedes hostage opened his door to let him out.

Luigi didn't say a word to the valet. He just shot out of the car he had been supplied with for the game, looked at himself in the glass windows of the building he was about to enter, and wondered to himself if this would be the final time he would look in the mirror during his lifetime. In this case, that mirror would be on the ground floor of the apartment of the very man who might kill him. The brutality associated with this family did not remove the possibility that murder could be the option AC might take against disobeying, and not achieving, a direct order. You listened to AC, or you died.

Security had obviously alerted AC as to Luigi's arrival, and Manuel was again on security detail as he opened the door to the ground floor of the building and walked Luigi to the elevator. Accompanying him, Manuel didn't say a word. Luigi held back on unnecessary verbiage as well, instead focusing on how exactly he intended to begin this conversation.

As the elevator doors opened, AC and Mauro sat on the couch, awaiting Luigi's report.

So Luigi assumed.

"Come in," AC said, with a smile on his face.

This was not the reception that Luigi expected. He had spent the entire drive from Yankee Stadium both trying to figure out what he had just witnessed Helen Wilson do, and how she did it, as well as what he would say to save his ass when AC was up close and personal.

"I know what happened at the game," AC said. "I want you to do something."

Luigi breathed a sigh of relief, glad to hear that another family member had already filled him in on the events of the Yankees game. Luigi would live another day.

"What you did today was good," said AC. "But what you're gonna do tomorrow…let's just say it's gonna tell me whether or not you get your Mercedes back with you sitting in it, or under it."

There was a pause, and then both Mauro and AC burst into laughter.

"I'm just fucking with you, Luigi; don't get all sensitive on me," AC said, putting his arm around Luigi, a gesture he had never made in his lifetime before.

"How did you find out? Do you know who she is?" asked Luigi.

Mauro stood up.

"Luigi, we knew who she was the second we had her seat number. The ticket idea though; I heard you snatched it up. It woulda been a good idea, had we not already had a few people at the park in place. I like the way you thought."

Jens Maes actually came up with the idea, but for the moment, he'd be someone AC got to a little later. He'd learned that Jens had extended his stay at the hotel, and it had to be something pretty special to make a man change his flight to Belgium for a $25 psychic.

AC didn't live in Belgium. He lived in New York. He owned much of it.

And he had an extra $25.

CHAPTER TWELVE

"You have a different way of sight from the other side," said Helen. "Once you cross over, you don't have the earthly components you are used to having. It takes some time adjusting to it, so you can't take it personally if you're not dreaming about your loved one right away. When you pass away, it's like a rebirth. The good memories come with you, and the lessons you've learned were usually from something negative happening. Those lessons were learned. It's why your time is chosen. In the next life, they are not allowed to come with you. There is no need to learn what you already have, and therefore God does not permit you with the ability to bring that baggage with you. It would defeat the purpose," said Helen to a group of about three hundred people who had come to see her at the gym of the Naugatuck High School.

It was the first time Helen had ever done something like this, but the lines were beginning to become way too long, and even neighbors who considered Helen a part of their lives were becoming agitated by the traffic going to her house.

"I'll now take some questions," Helen said to the crowd. Sandy Finnigan decided to help out by walking through the crowd with a microphone so that everyone could hear the questions clearly as Helen stood at the front of the crowd, but not on the stage. She never wanted to make the crowd feel as though she were above them. She never wanted them to think she was better than they were. For some reason, Helen Wilson had this gift to speak with those who had moved on, to predict the future, and rather than reading a tarot card, she let the card talk to her. The figures on those pages spoke to her. From Helen's view, it was never just a card with a picture on it, but moving figures that spoke to her. The cards spoke through her without words, and she translated that cosmic language through her earthly vessel, which was herself. There is a bliss on the other side that Helen and a few like her knew about. She was given the keys to experience just a tiny bit of what happened when one dies, but enough to know that those on earth know nothing.

A man stood up. He looked to be about 30 years old, and sat next to someone who appeared to be his sister, given their resemblance.

"What about Jesus? Do you believe in Jesus, in God?"

"I do believe in Jesus, yes. I do believe in God. I believe there are different figures for different cultures, but that it all leads to the same One God," she said.

A male voice rang out that no one could see.

"What a crock!" the voice could be heard saying.

Helen didn't even bother to ask who had said it, and the standing man who posed the question had a look of "what an asshole that guy is" on his face.

"Listen, let's discuss Jesus in this way. I'm not here to teach religion; it's not what I do. I don't know why I can do the things I do, or why I've been chosen to do them. It wasn't how I thought my life would turn out, but it did. That part is not up to me. All I'll say about Jesus is, he must have done something pretty incredible to capture the world during a time when there was no Internet, no David Copperfield props, and whose death made the world restart its clock. Whatever Jesus did, it shook the Etch A Sketch of the planet. The world, collectively, agreed that time itself, the calendar itself, despite the world being here long before His appearance on earth, began at this man's death. Now, I don't care how many streets are named after someone, or how many public libraries are named after former presidents. When Jesus Christ died, the world agreed that time had actually begun. So, from that perspective, I'd say that not only did Jesus exist, but that he shocked the world with abilities the world recognized, and recognizes to this very day," said Helen. "In fact, every year before him came with a BC…Before Christ. So time didn't just begin when he left, but his name was retroactively added to years of the past. I would call that making an impact."

There was a silence in the room. People were actually listening to her. It was a point they had not heard before. It was something to think about. What did Jesus do that made the world begin time upon His passing? What does one have to do to begin the clock of time itself all because of what they did? How did those activities spread so fast throughout the world when there was no Internet, no newspapers, no Wells Fargo wagons? What happened?

A woman named Elizabeth Stanley stood up with a question of her own. In her mid-forties, she was a beautiful woman, an athletic woman.

"You obviously believe in a hereafter," she said to Helen.

"There had to be a herebefore as well, in some way. I don't know those answers. My abilities typically are aimed at one person."

"God's way of letting us know that He does listen to each person?" Elizabeth replied.

"I believe that, yes. Sometimes it's needed," Helen said. Helen continued. "There's a lot of pain and suffering in the world. We feel sorry for our losses. That's our own ego talking. We miss them when they leave, because our own egos think everything is all about us, not realizing that when this life ends, a beauty begins that we'd be jealous over. We're only sad for ourselves, because if we knew what they were experiencing in the hereafter, we'd be relieved."

Elizabeth began to sit down, but clearly had another thought she wanted to ask. Helen sensed it.

"You have something else on your mind?" Helen asked.

"Well, yes. What about the people who cause the atrocities of the world. Does everyone deserve the same bliss you talk about?" asked Elizabeth.

"Well, that's above my pay grade," said Helen, and some of the audience members started laughing. "But I will say what I feel, which is all I ever have to go by when I'm asked questions like that. I'm not God. I believe wholeheartedly that those who commit such acts are not in the same realm as those who have love in their heart. Beyond that, we're getting into a philosophical discussion that I don't believe I'm qualified to answer. In fact, I don't think that anybody is. Scientists who claim absolute knowledge have the same life span as we do, and not to minimize their work, but if they knew all the answers, you all wouldn't have so many questions. The weather man can't even get it right a lot of the time, and he has all that fancy equipment that's supposed to warn of impending doom. How many devastating hurricanes were supposed to hit your town that ended up being a shower? One's biggest mistake is to try to understand what God thinks."

A hand raised from the last row, though his face could barely be seen behind a larger man sitting in front of him.

"You, in the back...stand up, please, to ask your question, so that all of these folks can see you," Helen asked.

Sandy Finnigan walked over to the man, who rose from his chair.

It was Luigi Nicolo.

"I got a question. Seems like you know a lot. Why you only charging $25? Why talk to everybody like this for free? Didn't you ever hear the ol' don't-do-nothing-you're-good-at-for-free thing?" he asked. Once again, some of the audience seemed to laugh. Luigi looked around to see who it was. He wasn't trying to be funny.

"Well..."

Helen paused. She felt something from this man. Her answer would sound a bit firm, more so than the other questions. She could "feel him" this far from where he stood, which only concerned her more due to the fact that the vibe she was getting, halfway across the room, wasn't a good one. She seemed to snap out of the feeling just to answer the question. If not for him, for those in attendance.

"I don't think this is the sort of gift, if you want to call it a gift, I know it comes from good, that you profit from. I keep the lights on. I pay the mortgage. I've lived in the same house for twenty-eight years, and won't leave until it's my turn. I think when it becomes about me, the gift would leave, and it appears to have helped a lot of people. I don't want to risk that. I don't want to risk others not knowing what they need to because I want a nicer car, which I do," Helen said, the crowd laughing. "But in all honesty,

I just don't think it would end well to be given a gift like that and using it for bad."

Luigi stood, trying to figure this woman out. He started to sit back down. Even though Helen could no longer see his face as he sat behind the behemoth in front of him, Helen felt compelled to say one more thing.

"I don't think using this gift badly ends in bliss. I don't think it ends very well at all. For anybody."

Sandy looked at the crowd, and spoke into the microphone that she'd been walking around the audience with.

"Helen and I want to thank you all for coming out today. We hope that she's been able to help you understand her a little better, and what she does. There are pamphlets on the table at each exit for those who may be interested in a private reading, but please know that we are now running about six months out for appointments."

People stood up and began exiting the gymnasium. Helen followed them out. She had a strong personality that didn't believe she had to leave out the back exit. She was one of those people leaving, she believed, and not a celebrity. She never felt this disconnect with those she spoke to, or read for, and knew that maintaining that is what kept her who she was. She would never let ego in the front door, or any window. The awe she would instill in others seemed to roll right off of her.

As Helen walked out, she was approached by Jens Maes, from Belgium.

"Ms. Wilson, may I have a quick word with you?" he asked. Sandy attempted to come to Helen's aid.

"Helen is very tired and needs to..." Sandy began.

Helen interrupted.

"It's okay, Sandy. Yes, what can I do for you?" Helen asked.

"I am from Belgium. I am only here for a few more days, and I wondered if I might be able to set up a private reading before I leave. I simply will not be here in six months."

"Helen does phone reading on occasion," said Sandy.

"No," said Helen to Sandy. "It's all right."

A pause ensued.

"You can set him up with an appointment," she said, looking at Sandy. "It's fine."

"Thank you, Ms. Wilson. I really appreciate this," he said.

"Think nothing of it, and call me Helen," she said.

Jens walked out as Sandy handed him a pamphlet, which Sandy had sketched out herself. On its face was the phone number to call for appointments, though Jens wasn't going to have to wait six months to do so.

As Helen exited, Luigi leaned on his car from across the street, just looking at Helen. Helen looked up and saw him, her feeling getting even stronger that this was not good. She was relieved the gymnasium discussion was over even more now, as the souls that sat between her and Luigi when he'd asked his question had made her direct connection to this man's life all the more clearer.

And all the more frightening.

"Let's go home, Sandy. Right now," she said to Sandy.

As Helen got into the car, Sandy walked around it to get into the driver's side of the car. As she leaned into it, she, too, noticed Luigi.

And Sandy didn't need Helen's powers to realize there was something very wrong with that man.

CHAPTER THIRTEEN

Detective Merton Howard sat in his car in front of Helen Wilson's house. He rested his forehead on the steering wheel and thought about his life, his career as an officer, and how those many years of service suddenly had him sitting in front of a psychic's house. He felt ridiculous, trying to think of how he might explain this to his superiors, should they ever ask how he'd spent this particular afternoon.

There were numerous homicides that remained open cases, and part of him was wondering how to even engage Helen Wilson into a conversation. Mary Taheri seemed very upset, and he just didn't want to "remember that time" on his clock as the end of his career approached. He'd felt as if he'd remembered enough times already.

"So this is what insane feels like," he said to himself.

He opened the door to his black 2000 Mustang convertible, and his eyes flashed at the odometer that read 171,000 miles.

Where had the time gone? Where had he gone to rack up so many miles on that vehicle in a little over a decade? He didn't feel as if he'd gone that far in it, and yet here he was, at 171,000 miles. And now he was at Helen Wilson's house. It took 171,000 miles to drive to a home that was only about an hour's drive from his own home.

Brett Finnigan rode his bicycle past Merton as he got out of the car. Merton watched Brett as he pulled up to the mailbox at the front of his own house, checking the mail for his mother. Brett looked back at Merton, and thinking nothing of it, rode his bike up his driveway so that he could begin his online battles on "Call of Duty," a video game he'd play for hours on end with adversaries all over the world. That was the world we lived in today, going from Pacman to being able to play games online with people in Italy, thanks to the Internet.

Merton crossed the street and looked at Helen's property. A small home, almost appearing as a cabin due to the fact that it sat back about thirty yards from the street, set back in the trees. It had a rather large front yard that was completely groomed. A stone wall with a gate surrounded the property. She'd see him coming as he walked up the long walkway to the steps he'd have to then climb at the base of her front porch.

There was no sense trying to be slick about this, so he just walked up the pathway and prepared to feel stupid to whoever might answer the door.

Standing at the base of Helen's steps, Merton contemplated turning right back around and just going back to the office. There's nothing to indicate anyone in the house noticed him walking up to the house. And perhaps if they did, they might just assume he was another person wanting a reading who'd changed his mind. If they were looking closely, however, the badge that hung from his belt would give him away, maybe even from the sidewalk if the sun above caught it right.

The door opened, and Helen peeked her head through the door to the outside world, and Detective Merton Howard.

"May I help you?" asked Helen.

"Yes, I was wondering if we might have a word," he said.

Helen opened the door, allowing Merton Howard to walk into her living room.

"Is there a problem?" she asked.

"Well, from what I hear, you'd know already," he said.

Helen laughed.

"Well, it doesn't really work that way, but I'm getting the feeling that you're not exactly here for a reading."

"No, I'm actually not here for a reading. I'm a Scorpio, though!" he snickered, as he offered himself a seat on her couch. Folding his legs, he looked around her living room, the table the "readings" might be held at, an assumption he made by its etchings.

"Quite a table you got there. Where'd you get that thing?" Merton asked.

"The origins of it are a mystery to me, but never one I really felt compelled to look into. That would be your job, anyway, I gather," she said.

"Only if you killed somebody with it," he replied.

What was meant to be a joke placed an eerily silent pause between them both as they looked at one another.

"I assure you I can hardly lift one of the chairs that slides up to it," she replied.

She began taking this little visit a little more seriously.

"What can I do for you," she asked.

Merton looked around the room, sitting on the couch as if it were his own living room. He seemed very comfortable in a home that wasn't his. He'd spent many years in other people's living rooms. Usually it wasn't good news when he did.

But this little visit to Helen's was more curiosity. He didn't think she had done anything wrong before the walk up to her front door. Still, Mary Taheri seemed pretty adamant about there being something wrong. Merton just didn't get it, though. This was a sweet little woman who seemed just fine. She read her little readings, earned $25 to do so, and that was it. If people wanted to throw a few bucks at a carnival act, he didn't see the harm. Sure, he could argue that she might need some sort of business permit, but he had more pressing cases than calling up the local business divisions unit for the State of Connecticut, or making some phone call to the attorney general's office. This woman wasn't hurting anybody, in his estimation, and if she were, he'd be all over it.

"Well, let me tell you why I'm here," he said. "I had this woman come in, and..."

"The boy," she interrupted.

Merton had a confused look on his face.

"You're here about the boy," she said.

"No, I'm...what about the boy?" he said.

Suddenly Merton Howard took this meeting a bit more seriously himself, and as his own confusion and curiosity had turned to very well-hidden adrenaline, a flutter in his stomach occurred. It was his job not to get excited about anything.

He'd been investigating the disappearance of an eleven-year-old boy named Christian Marcantonio. Christian had been playing baseball with friends at a local junkyard-turned-makeshift-baseball park. They would use real bats, but chose tennis balls instead of baseballs so as to not smash any of the glass on the vehicles, or the building itself that stood in front of it. The owners of the junkyard didn't have a problem with the kids playing out there, but they still sold the junk in their junkyard, and broken windows or damaged parts on worn-out vehicles weren't worth very much. So if the kids had to utilize tennis balls instead of the real thing, that was fine by the neighborhood kids who would pretend they were playing to a sold-out crowd at Yankee Stadium.

It was there that Christian Marcantonio had been kidnapped by someone who had claimed to need to bring him home on behalf of Christian's parents. The other kids stated that a man in his 50s approached him, but they overheard only bits and pieces of the conversation. The only thing that frustrated his friends at the time was that one side of the team had lost its second baseman. It wasn't until the next day that his friends realized that it was no family friend who had picked Christian up that day.

"There's a plant. It manufactures plastic. It's not plastic used to make bowls, or picnic utensils, or toys, it's..." said Helen. "I need a moment."

Helen got up and walked over to her table, sliding her fingers across the Aquarius sign.

"It's for pastries. This is a plant that makes pastries, like for cupcakes. Oh, my God. There's more than him," she said.

Merton became clearly anxious.

"Wait, wait, what? Where? What are you talking about? How do you know this?" he said.

"There's a city called North Andover, Massachusetts. This man works there," she replied, her eyes now shut.

"Are the kids at the plant?" said Merton.

"No, they're all at his house, a basement. The smell of plastic comes from his home as well. The neighbors...he gives the neighbors free reels of plastic wrap. They like the guy, they don't hear anything or see anything," she said.

"Well, how many are there? How many kids are we talking about?" Merton said, now believing in something he never had thought he would. It had been months since Christian disappeared.

"Three. There's a girl as well, but she's...the infinity sign...no, that's eight, she's eight years old," Helen said, as she opened her eyes.

"Detective Howard," she said directly into Merton's eyes. He felt like his soul had been pierced by this sweet little woman.

"Yes," he replied quickly.

"Now. You need to go there now. He hasn't hurt them yet, but he's going to. One of them is going to escape the captor, but that isn't going to be good for the remaining two. He'll want to be rid of them. You came here for a reason, as most people do, and like many of them...not for the reason you thought," she said. "Whatever it is you wanted to talk to me about can wait."

Merton forgot what that reason was himself.

"I will...I'm going to look into this, Miss Wilson. Personally, and, maybe...thank you for this potential information," he said. "It's not quite why I came by today, but... well, thank you."

It was a reading he didn't intend on having. He's a cop. He didn't believe in this sort of thing. But he had reached his wit's end in trying to track down Christian, and now he was being told there were actually three kids abducted by this man.

He pulled a cell phone from his pocket and began dialing numbers as he walked out the door of Helen's home.

Helen just sat at her table, staring at the engravings.

"Good. Good," she said, breathing what appeared to be a sigh of relief.

Helen was appearing on radars, and some of them were the wrong ones.

CHAPTER FOURTEEN

AC was not the asshole that he normally was. Something was very different about him.

When Luigi walked into his penthouse suite, he was treated like an old high school buddy. He was being treated like a friend, and a close one at that.

He sat on Luigi's sofa with his leg crossed, relaxed in a way where it would appear that he and AC were talking about old times. That, however, was not the case here. AC was intrigued, and confused. These were two things AC successfully made a living off of being neither. If there was someone out there who had something over him, he wanted in, or he wanted it all. It was one way or another, and there was no compromising with him. Not compromising is what made him who he was.

"Spill, Luigi," he said. "I want to know everything there is to learn. Is it a one-man job? Is she working with some technical assistance? Is the whole thing a scam? Because if it's a scam, I'll kill the bitch on principal, and then you and the others will have to explain how she scammed all of you during a fucking baseball game. So for real now, I want to know, tell me what you know about this woman. And I don't want any bullshit or exaggerations," AC said, sitting across from Luigi with a drink in his hand.

Luigi opened up a leather attaché, the kind you might see an attorney walk around with.

"Going legit on me, Luigi?" AC said with a chuckle. As he spoke, his brother Mauro walked in and sat next to AC. Typically Mauro, he said nothing, but did give Luigi an acknowledging gesture that said: "You exist, Luigi." It was about the best he'd get from Mauro.

"Well, here's what I know," said Luigi.

Luigi turned to the second page of his yellow legal pad. Mauro looked at AC with a frown, then looked back to Luigi.

"I, uhm, I believe in what I see. I went to church, I've been baptized, and I believe in the Father, Son, and Holy Ghost. I would have to say, honestly, that I'm not sure if they believe in me all that much. Given what I do, and how I've spent my life, I try not to think of God that much, because then my concern usually turns to what He thinks about me, and I'm sure it's not that great. About any of us, actually," Luigi said.

"Fair enough, go on," said AC. Mauro frowned again.

"There has always been one person I fear in this world," Luigi said.

"Our enemies, no doubt," said AC.

"No, AC. You. I have always feared you. You could have me disappear into dust and no one would even know I existed. Let's be real; most of the people who work around you know that if they want to live, they do what you say. So I can't see God, but I most definitely can see you, and you could end my life just as He could. But you can do it with a gun, or a knife, and I can see it coming; or not see it coming, if you choose. You're a god. You're not *the* God, but on earth, you're kind of a god," Luigi said.

Mauro cut in. "What are you telling us; you fear an old lady who lives in a cabin?" Mauro said.

"I think this little old lady is not old. She moves around, she keeps busy. I saw one of her neighbors who had to be like 80 years old jogging down the street she lives on, so some woman in her 60s isn't actually old. That being said, she became the person I fear, even more than you, the moment I went and checked her out, the way you told me to," said Luigi.

Mauro cut in again. "So, let me get this straight. You see a woman call a few baseball plays, and you fear her more than anyone on the planet?"

Luigi didn't have the patience with Mauro that he normally had.

"Mauro, you send me to these things and ask me to report to you two. It's what I do. I have never come back with anything but information you've been able to rely on. A lot of guys are walking the street in our crew because of the things I told you, because if they hadn't listened, they'd be doing life. And I'm telling you, that this psychic, or medium, they call it, or this astrology thing she does; I'm telling you. I've never seen anything like it, and I think it's something we all need to stay away from. Just follow the gem guy, let me get you guys connected into Asia like you wanted, and just leave this woman alone. I don't see anything but very bad news coming from getting involved in this," Luigi said firmly.

"We tell you what we're going to do. We tell you what we're going to get involved in and what we're not. You don't have opinions; you have instructions, and you follow them. That's what you do. And I don't appreciate input I didn't ask for. We want a report, not a therapy session; you got that?" said Mauro. "I think this entire thing is a load of bullshit. But if we're gonna walk away from it, and we just might, it's gonna be *our* call, not your call," said Mauro.

AC looked at MC.

MC looked back at AC, then back to Luigi.

"It's gonna be AC's decision, is what I'm saying."

"Thank you, Mauro. I'm glad you're taking the advice you just gave Luigi here," said AC, who looked back to Luigi while Mauro just stared at his brother, then looked down at his lap.

"Luigi, I want you to set up a reading. I want to have an appointment with her, and let her read me," AC said.

"AC, with all due respect, I think opening yourself up to a woman like this is a very bad idea. And she's booking six months out, anyway," Luigi said.

"If I don't like what she says, she disappears. I'm not worried about her, not at all," AC replied.

"It's not just her anymore. That gem dealer is planning on a reading, too. That dude just flipped the fuck out over this woman. Canceled his flight back to Belgium. He's seriously going down there and she hooked him, big time. He knows who she is," said Luigi.

Mauro stood up, clearly irritated.

"Listen, we have the opportunity to do business in a country with billions of people, making hundreds of millions of dollars, if not more. Are we really gonna spend our time hovering over a $25 psychic? Is this shit for real?" said Mauro.

"Sit down," said AC to his younger brother. "You are beginning to irritate me."

Silence overcame the room. Mauro had never heard AC speak to him that way in front of other people. Now he was angry at Luigi merely because he could tell the story about it if he wanted to.

"You will set up a reading for me. I want to hear what she has to say. In the meantime, Mauro is going to personally attend to the duties of watching our Belgian friend. I want to know where he is, what he's doing, whether he's engaging in any more gem sales, or if he really is just here for a psychic reading with this woman. What is her name?" said AC.

"Helen Marie Wilson," said Luigi. "Her name is Helen Marie Wilson. She lives in Naugatuck, Connecticut, and I'll tell you, she's either psychic, or knows her shit. That crowd was completely glued to her, and she said things I've never heard anyone else say before."

"Like a false prophet," said Mauro.

Not amused, AC didn't even give his younger brother's comment the respect of bitching him out. Instead, he continued talking to Luigi.

"If this woman is who you say she is, what you say she is, then we may have something up our sleeve, something our competitors do not," he said, standing up. AC then walked to his penthouse window, again looking down as if he might on this occasion see a tree.

"I should plant a bigger tree, just so I can see the head of something from up here," he said off-topic.

Luigi said nothing.

"I want this set up soon. Make something up. I'm not gonna wait no six months to meet with her, so convince her. Lie, say something," said AC.

"If she's psychic, won't she know that's bullshit?" asked Mauro, regretting the sentence as soon as it came out of his mouth.

Again, AC ignored his brother.

"And I want to know Jens Maes' every move. Put a bug on him. I want to hear what this psychic is telling him. Everything," AC ordered.

"I think that could be a little easier said than done, but I'll try," Luigi said.

AC walked over to Luigi. The room was silent. Luigi just sat there, not sure if he had just said something wrong or not.

"Listen," said AC. "Still fear me, because all of the things about me that you fear are true. Those are accurate descriptions of my abilities. You don't *try* when I tell you to do something. You *do*, or you run for your life, and then you count the days until I find you. That's what you do. And don't ever make me make such a statement as this again. When I say it, you fucking do it."

"Yes, sir. I'm sorry, sir," said Luigi.

Mauro kept his mouth shut, readying to take up stalker duties on the Belgian gem dealer. Clearly, Mauro saw this entire thing as way off the direction they should be in, and marked the first time he really didn't understand his older brother's order. In fact, his thought was "the old man is losing it," but could, and would, never say a thing about it to AC's face.

"I'll get right on it. I'll figure out a way to tag Maes, who I think has an appointment tomorrow or the next day. I'll get it done, then I'll schedule an appointment for you. I'll tell you though, this woman seems to know a lot, like, everything. You're also not a face the country isn't familiar with," said Luigi.

AC stood. He was thinking.

"Well, see if she might come here for an appointment. I could send a car for her, see how much she wants. Money is no object," said AC.

"She charges $25. She won't accept more than that, and I'm not sure if she does house calls, but I'll try," said Luigi.

"You'll what?" said AC.

Luigi cringed as he realized he repeated the word *try*.

"I will make one or the other happen. Either a reading at her house, or I will bring her here," Luigi said.

Mauro got up. "Excuse me, gentlemen, there is some actual business I need to attend to. I appreciate this interesting conversation. AC, may I?" said Mauro.

"Go ahead, it's fine," said AC.

Luigi got up and headed for the elevator, clicking the down button. There was no up button, given the top floor belonged to AC.

"I'll keep you posted," said Luigi.

"Yes, please do. I want to be in her office, or her in my living room, with 72 hours," said AC.

Luigi stepped into the elevator. "Yes, sir."

It would be the longest elevator ride down to the lobby that Luigi ever experienced.

CHAPTER FIFTEEN

Mauro sat in the office of his apartment on the 33rd floor of his brother's high-rise, stirring a drink he'd mixed with about three different types of alcohol. He didn't really even remember what he'd made, but he just sat there stirring it, and stewing in an anger he hadn't felt before.

He stood to make millions off targeting Jens Maes of Belgium as a way to bring the family into the Chinese market. Rare gems are big business in Asia, and it was always his belief that through a European counterpart his family could make his way into a territory that frowned upon dealings with the mafia in America. It was simply a way to get into those Asian territories through a back window. In his mind, however, AC was fucking that up by listening to a bunch of bullshit about a psychic who gave $25 readings from her home in Naugatuck, Connecticut, when they should be concentrating on reality.

But even when they were kids, AC seemed to take an interest in reading his daily horoscope. Mauro always thought it was a bunch of bullshit, but it really surprised him to see his older brother, "The Godfather" as it were, take his eye off the ball and order Luigi to start playing into the fantasy. Who the fuck was Luigi, anyway? How did Luigi go from being a punk who collected from local mom and pop shops to suddenly being the Director of Fantasy Land? In the mind of Mauro Nicolo, that's exactly what this entire scenario was. A load of shit.

Mauro sent a text to a Polish friend named Evan Yastrzemski, someone he knew back in the day when stealing cars was their first step up the ladder to the empire built on murder his family had now become. Mauro was going to set up a meeting on his own, and knowing Yastrzemski had set up shop in Brooklyn, mainly dealing in the distribution of cocaine, it was going to be harmless. Besides, Mauro had established loyalty and trust enough in the eyes of AC that he could have these types of meetings without the approval of his boss at every turn.

Anyone who knew Mauro pretty much had the same opinion of him. The guy was a prick. There was a stoic silence about him, like a statue with a heartbeat. Once he had his sights on you, or if you pissed him off, you were going to face a quick wrath that settled the argument with you in the ground.

Expecting a cavalry of his Polish friends after his text message, Mauro flipped through channels of his television, a 70-inch high-definition television that took up practically the entire wall in front of him, with a surround sound system one would kill for. Mauro might have, for all anyone knew; but it was indeed state of the art.

"This guy," said Mauro to himself, as he watched comedian Bill Maher on HBO's "Real Time with Bill Maher."

Drink in hand, the TV was on mute as Mauro just sat there, sipping his concocted drink, and just watched what appeared to be Maher's monologue.

Mauro reached for the remote, preparing to unmute the television, when an intercom in his apartment beeped once. The protocol was, when you needed to get Mauro's attention, it was one beep for "This is security in the lobby and you have a visitor." Two beeps meant "She's here," which referred to just over a dozen women who made themselves available to him, and three beeps meant, "You need to run." AC never had to beep. He just walked into Mauro's apartment when he had to.

Never in Mauro's life had he heard three beeps. There was never a need to run, especially when you ran everything. One beep prevented Mauro from hearing Bill Maher as he appeared to finish his monologue and walk over to a guest who was sitting down to have some sort of discussion. Someone was in the lobby, and his security team was simply letting him know that they were on their way up. The Polish were here, and they weren't there to listen to Bobby Vinton's rendition of "Melody of Love" with Mauro while they all drank good cheer. In fact, Mauro didn't even know what he was drinking, despite mixing it himself.

He stood up as he prepared for the group of men, led by Yastrzemski, to come up the elevator. As the elevator reached his floor, the door opened to reveal Yastrzemski and eight other men, who walked into his apartment.

"Mauro," said Evan. "How nice to see you."

"My sentiments exactly. It's great to see you and your compadres again. It's been far too long," said Mauro. "Why don't you gentlemen have a seat and I'll get you all a drink?"

Fortunately, Mauro was going to prepare a nice glass of Hennessey versus the drink he'd poured himself when he was feeling pissed off. Having Evan and his crew here gave him a sense that he was on the road to some resolution over how he'd been feeling about AC's decisions. In his mind, he wasn't doing anything wrong here by this meeting. There would be a way to be able to spin it as "just looking out for you, AC," if there ever was a need to. A meeting was harmless, and if it happened to appear as though it was just having his brother's back, then there was no harm in it. It wasn't as if Mauro was attempting to set up a deal. In actuality, Mauro was seeking to make sure the deals he believed would one day be in place in China would actually occur. He was protecting himself, but by doing so, was also protecting his horoscope-reading brother.

After pouring the men a drink, he walked them into another room in the apartment that looked like something out of the White House war room, a room with a long mahogany table and chairs, and nothing else. There was nothing on the walls, and the only "art" was the window that displayed the New York City lights. This was a room Mauro used to talk, not to look, and not to show off any memorabilia. It was in stark contrast to every other room that made up his apartment.

"Have a seat, gentlemen," Mauro kindly directed the men.

Evan and his buddies all sat down at the table. Mauro sat at the head of the table, which felt a little strange to him given it's typically where AC would sit whenever there was something to discuss. Any meeting that required more than two people occurred in Mauro's apartment. AC just wasn't into having large gatherings in his penthouse. Mauro got that, and realized that as second man down on the family" list, AC got what he wanted as first man. The meetings in Mauro's home were so many as to annoy him. Maybe once a month. This was, however, the first time a group of men showed up at his own apartment without AC, and just to make sure there was no confusion or doubts, he purposely held this meeting at his own apartment so that security in the lobby could see the men come in.

While AC was trusting, that wasn't to be confused with keeping secrets from him. This was a meeting meant to create a buffer against fucking up deals Mauro had been working to accomplish. A meeting is just fine. He was being uncommonly open about it by having them all come through the front door in full view of AC's security team. Ultimately, the security wasn't for Mauro, and he knew it.

"Gentlemen, what I'm about to tell you doesn't leave this room. You all know me, and you all know what it means to be working with me. You know what it means. So out of respect for all of you at this table, I'm going to let anyone who wants to live, if they might not be able to control their ability to keep my confidence, get up and leave right now, with my respect intact," Mauro said, in a way that sounded eerily professional for what just amounted to a death threat. It felt like Michael Douglas as Gordon Gekko from *Wall Street* if he was more than greedy. In this case, he was also a killer.

Silence was in the air as all of the men just stared. These men had seen everything. War, poverty, murder, rape, and had graduated the school of life in a way no American could ever understand.

"Go on, Mauro," said Evan.

"I'm going to get straight to the point, cut out all the fat on this one. The family has been looking to explore operations in Asia. Gems, including diamonds, rubies, things of this nature. While the big man in the penthouse has his eyes on gems, primarily, I see a bigger picture there that I'm sure I can excite AC about," Mauro said.

Mauro was smart to include AC's name in this conversation, and by saying "I see a bigger picture there that I'm sure I can excite AC about." It was really just a way of covering his own ass in the event someone at the table went to his big brother behind his back to insinuate that Mauro was doing something he shouldn't be doing. Planning something. When he said he could excite AC about something, that really translated to the reality that AC knew nothing of the purpose of this meeting, and any "new idea" that came up couldn't be construed as going behind the bosses back. Call it a surprise Mauro had planned, should anyone at the table be trying to screw him over, or get on his brother's good side.

"I want everyone at this table to have my brother's back in this situation that I'm about to describe. Everybody here is going to be engaging in his preservation, and I just want this, call it low key, to be about making certain that his moves are protected."

What a load of bullshit. Everyone at the table knew it was a load of bullshit. Mauro, himself, knew that what he'd just said was a load of bullshit. Suddenly they were all there just to protect AC, and if anyone tried to make anything other than that out of this meeting, he'd just set himself up to be the hero. Brilliant.

"Why don't you elaborate on what exactly we are going to be doing to, uhm...protect AC. Who does AC need protection from? Who would dare to even mess with him?" said Evan.

Mauro stared at the table and looked up. He looked as if he didn't even want to answer the question. He'd spent years doing AC's dirty work, and while well compensated, was always the man who had to deal with the shit end of the stick while AC was getting blowjobs in the penthouse. The only difference here was that Mauro, like Gekko, thought that greed was good. Asia could mean big business for his family.

Mauro stood up and walked over to the window. Unlike his brother, he didn't give a shit about the trees, and never tried to look down to see if he could see one.

"Did you gentlemen know that Ronald Reagan and his wife Nancy were into astrology?" said Mauro.

Again, there was silence in the room. From what field had this question come?

Evan started to speak, but stopped before a word could come out of his mouth. It would take a second attempt at talking to be able to push his response out of his mouth. The words seemed as if they were being created in his stomach.

"No. No, Mauro. I did not know that your president had once done such a thing."

Mauro turned to the men with the glistening and awe-inspiring city behind him.

"My question earlier applies. Is there any person who sits here right now that would like to leave?"

Without saying a word, a man at the table, a compadre of Evan's, stood up, nodding his head to Mauro. Mauro looked at him.

"I appreciate your honesty, and hope we are able to work together one day. You may show yourself out."

Mauro was weird this way. There would be no consequence for an independent contractor, which is essentially what this Polish group was, in just being honest and wanting nothing to do with a certain matter. It didn't mean they were weak to Mauro. It meant what it meant: "I'm not right for this particular job." It meant the same for Evan. He'd use this man again, just as he had in the past. This particular job just wasn't for him. Better to be honest than end up dead.

"Anyone else?"

Silence.

Mauro looked at Evan.

"Do you believe in psychics?"

Evan just stared at Mauro. There was a lot of silence in that room on this evening.

"I don't really think of such things, to be honest. I will say though, when you called me here, that was not a question I ever expected to hear you say to me," said Evan.

"Well, it is not a question that I ever believed I would be asking, but here we are."

CHAPTER SIXTEEN

Merton Howard accompanied Police Chief Arthur Olson of the North Andover Police Department to China Blossom, a small Chinese restaurant located in Andover, Massachusetts. Marked and unmarked police cars and K-9 units converged on its parking lot as they would begin their plans on scoping out the area of Borden Chemical, a plant that manufactured plastic wrap for various pastry companies so that they could be sold nationally. The chances are, if the cupcakes known as Twinkies were sold at the local grocery store's sweets section, they were wrapped in the plastic wrap manufactured at this plant in Massachusetts prior to being distributed nationally.

Several agents of Boston's FBI briefed the officers as they narrowed down a list of four homes in the area where the "scent" of plastic might be smelled if someone were to live there. As much of the land surrounding Borden was grass and trees, there were only four residential houses in the area. Outside of these four homes, there was nothing else but community stores, such as dry cleaners and laundromats and a 7-Eleven store that had just gone up in the area. Generally, the stench of a plastic wrap manufacturer which had been there for many decades didn't appeal to home builders, or families looking to find themselves a home.

Merton Howard and Arthur Olson stood at the front of the steps that led into the front entrance of China Blossom, and were handed coffees by an employee of the restaurant.

Chief Olson stirred his coffee and looked at Merton.

"This is quite the production for an area like this, I have to tell ya," said Olson. "I'd really like to know how it is you came upon information that there could be a couple of kids being held captive in this area. Doesn't really seem the type of place," he said.

"What is the type of place?" Merton said.

Boston FBI Field Agent Ricky Grullon approached the men.

"Gentlemen, what we've been able to assess at this point is that there are four homes in the area of Borden Chemical. One is vacant, and the other three homes are three- and four-bedroom units. One is owned by a Cheryl Driscoll, one is owned by a Brenda Lacostic, and the other is owned by Irene H. Gigliotti, who has two daughters that are at USC Southern Cal," said Grullon. "So far, nothing that screams anything hopeful, but let's go check them out."

"All right, gentlemen!" yelled Ricky. "This is the plan. We're going to knock on a few doors over there, but I want you to keep your eyes peeled for what's going on around the house, the backyards, anything that looks suspicious. It's mostly a wooded area out there, so look for sheds, keep an eye out for possible deadfalls, and just pay attention. We're looking for a couple of kids; you have their photos in the briefs I've provided you. That being said, let's get to it."

"Just who is this source of yours?" said Olson.

Merton looked at him.

Olson grilled a little more.

“I mean, we’re all out here, you’re from, what is it, Naugatuck, Connecticut? Well, I’d just like to know what you know, and how you know it, just between us.”

Merton sipped his coffee.

“I’m afraid I can’t get into that with you at the moment,” Merton said, knowing the circus he’d created would be shut down in a second had he provided an honest answer.

Olson stood as Merton walked away, nodding to him as he did.

Grullon approached Merton with a bit of curiosity himself, following protocol for interstate accusations for which they had to be a part. It was standard for agents to be sent on wild-goose chases, but the FBI tended to be a little more eager to learn about sources than the local police. Nothing really happened in North Andover, Massachusetts that would warrant such a large group of officers, an officer from a different state, and FBI agents. However, as anyone watching CNN would know, anything could happen anywhere, and everyone just erred of the side of caution. When you’re talking about kids and kidnappings, it wasn’t a topic anyone was going to just let go without checking it out. If they didn’t check it out and there was any truth to it, it would only make matters worse. A public relations nightmare was not what any of the agencies that were involved in this search wanted, and whether they admitted it or not, it always played a part of investigations like this.

Merton personally walked up the pathway to the home of Cheryl Driscoll, finding no one home at all.

“She’s in Berlin visiting her grandfather,” a voice yelling from behind her said.

It was Brenda Lacostic, who owned the home next door.

"She's gonna be there for another month, and I keep an eye out for the place. Is there something I can help you with?" she said.

Merton exchanged smiles with his inquisitor.

"Thank you, I'm just poking around. We're investigating the abduction of a few kids who are rumored to be in the area, and I was wondering if you might have seen any kids, or heard any yelling, anything that would help. Crying kids, anything," said Merton.

Brenda looked at him with a surprised look.

"Kidnapping? Here? No, I haven't seen anything unusual at all," said Brenda. "Same faces have been around here for years, and there are only a few houses in this area, anyway."

Merton nodded.

"Well, thank you, ma'am; I do appreciate your help," he said, handing her his business card. "Please do give me a call if you notice anything suspicious," he said.

"I most certainly will," she said.

Merton began to walk away.

"Uhm, Mr. Howard? I mean, Detective Howard?" she said, as she looked at the business card he'd just handed her. "Perhaps you might want to ask Mr. Arnold. I know he's only lived here for a year, but he does seem to come and go a lot, always shopping for something."

Merton Howard stopped in his tracks. He turned around slowly towards Brenda, and walked towards her without making eye contact, looking around the wooded area he stood in.

"Do you happen to know if there's a vacant home in this area?" he said.

"There are no vacant homes in this area, just the one Mr. Henaghan moved into about a year ago. There was an old couple there that just up and moved, left town. They weren't living there long, then the place was just empty. Course that smell doesn't seem to attract a lot of..."

"Ms. Lacostic," he interrupted. "I do appreciate your help, but I need to go tell my boss that I'm not wasting Connecticut tax dollars," he fake-laughed.

Brenda looked at him, oblivious to the interruption as anything that might indicate what his next move was about to be.

"I completely understand," she said. "Wouldn't want to get your boss mad at ya listening to me," she laughed. "I can talk!"

"No, no, it's fine. Thank you for your help," Howard said.

Detective Howard pulled out his cell phone and called FBI agent Ricky Grullon.

"Special Agent Grullon," Howard said.

"Tell me about that vacant home in the area."

CHAPTER SEVENTEEN

Luigi Nicolo walked up the stairs of Helen's house with a mission. Sandy Finnigan didn't like the look of Luigi the moment she saw him. She'd seen him somewhere before, but couldn't put her finger on where. The vehicle he'd driven to Helen's house in was still running, with the back windows half-open.

Since Helen and Sandy had both partnered up, with Sandy taking on scheduling and buffer duties, life became a little more organized for the psychic.

"I want to schedule an appointment for a friend of mine," Luigi said to Sandy.

Sandy looked at Luigi a bit irritated, as he had clearly walked past the "By Appointment Only" sign posted at the front entrance of Helen's house.

"Helen doesn't take knock-on-the-door appointments anymore," said Sandy. "You'll have to call and make an appointment. It's just the way she does it now."

"I can appreciate that," said Luigi. "But you see, I work for a man who doesn't like to take...ya know, *no* for an answer."

Sandy's irritation was becoming something else. Helen and Sandy had heard some pretty wild stories to get past the waiting list. Sandy wasn't even psychic and she knew that something was off about this person.

"Sandy," said Helen from behind her. "Let him in."

There he was. Luigi went from a thief to local businesses on behalf of AC, to Yankee Stadium to follow a gem dealer, to standing in the living room of someone who was said to be a bona fide psychic.

"I remember you," said Helen. "You were at my talk at the high school. I didn't take you for a believer in this sort of thing."

Luigi looked a bit like a fish out of water in her living room. Even as low down the totem pole as he was in the family, rarely did you see him in a living room that seemed real. Someone's real home. Knick-knacks on the shelves, crochet hooks and spreads, candles lit everywhere. Magnets on the refrigerator. It had been a long time since someone like Luigi had seen anything like this place. A man like Luigi was looking to impress everyone, but for the first time in his life, he felt as if he had walked into a living room of a person he couldn't.

"My uncle would like to talk to you," he said. "He's in the car. I realize this is a bit out of line, but he feels it's very important."

Neighbors, too, were beginning to get uncomfortable over the random people who were beginning to stop over at Helen's house. One neighbor, Brenda Lacostic, could often be seen peeking through her window. Brenda would sit on her porch with her mother, Betty, and although Helen couldn't hear what they were talking about, she knew it was about her. After all, she's a psychic; but she didn't need to be one to know that she was beginning to attract a little too much attention in the area.

As the Lincoln Town Car sat outside running, Luigi walked to Helen's porch and stood there. He put one arm up, and the door opened. Sandy stood behind Luigi. She didn't know who was about to get out of the car, but she knew it was someone. The front lawn was big enough for Sandy to get in a few words to Helen if she had to as this visitor exited his vehicle.

"No. Absolutely not, I don't think so," said Sandy to Helen.

Sandy knew without a doubt who the man was who just got out of the car. AC Nicolo, the most notorious mob boss in New York, known throughout America as a man you did not want to piss off.

"Helen, Al Capone has arrived. This isn't happening," Sandy said.

"You watch your fucking mouth," said Luigi.

Clearly flustered, Sandy was in a bit of a panic. A known murderer was walking up the walkway to Helen's living room. Luigi took a few steps back from the language he'd just spewed out at Sandy.

"Listen, I'm sorry. I just need you to calm down, and give my uncle some time with Helen. Alone," Luigi said.

"I am not leaving Helen alone with that man, so you can forget it," said Sandy.

Helen stepped in.

"Sandy, come over here," Helen said.

"This is something I've felt before. I knew this was coming, and I need you to go home and let me handle this. I will call you later. I want you to leave through the kitchen and cross the yard to your house. I promise, I'll be fine. I'll call you tonight," said Helen.

"You'd better, Helen. And if I don't hear from you in an hour, I'm calling the police," Sandy replied.

“Hey, lady, seriously. Calm the heck down and do what she said, before my uncle reaches those steps. I’ll keep your opinion of him between you and me; that I can do for you. But get out,” said Luigi.

Sandy looked at Helen, nodded, and walked to the kitchen, exiting the house.

Here Helen was standing with a mobster. The Godfather was walking up her walkway. Once AC got about halfway up the walkway, he was out of sight of the neighbors. The neighbors, however, knew exactly who that man was. While Brenda snuck a peek, she wasn’t walking onto the patio this time to get a closer look. She didn’t need one. That was AC Nicolo walking up that walkway, as polished as a tuxedo shoe right out of the box.

As he reached the stairs, he stopped and looked up.

“So you’re her,” said America’s most notorious mobster to a psychic who gave $25 readings in Naugatuck, Connecticut.

Helen just looked at him.

“Yes. I’m her. Come in,” said Helen.

AC Nicolo stepped into the home and stopped just past the front door, the front door remaining open while he did.

“Nice place. It’s very much like a home,” he said. “It’s been a long time since I’ve been in one of these.”

“I’m sure it has. Won’t you please sit down?” she said. Helen then looked to Luigi.

“I need you to leave me and you uncle alone, please. When he is done, he will come to the car,” said Helen.

Luigi looked to AC, then back at Helen.

"I'll be on the porch," Luigi said.

AC looked at Luigi.

"No. You'll do what the lady said. Now," said AC.

After a brief pause to calculate the order in his head, Luigi nodded to AC and left the house.

"Please, come over to my table, and I can better assist you," said Helen.

Helen walked over to her table, and AC sat down.

"Nice table," said AC, as he looked at the engravings. "It's very...psychicy," he said, as he made up the word on the spot.

"Thank you. How can I help you?" she said.

"Well, I want you to tell me what it is you do. I want to know how you do it. Is it all a scam? Or is what I'm hearing true about your abilities?" he said.

"My abilities are aimed at helping people, and steering them in the right direction," Helen replied.

AC wasn't wasting time. "Oh, horse shit. I've been around the block. You know who I am. There isn't a scam out there I haven't seen, and most of them I invented. This is a good racket you've got going for yourself though, I gotta hand it to you. I don't get the $25 thing though; seems you could be doing better than that for yourself."

"I'm not sure if I can help you, and many times, Mr. Nicolo, the answers end up being bigger than the questions you're going to ask me. Some of them you may not want to know. I don't know why or how I'm able to do the things that I do, but I assure you, my integrity is intact," she said.

"Why don't you let me be the judge of what I want to know," AC said.

"You're already off to a bad start. You're not the judge. You've lived a life being one, and there are many unhappy souls that surround you. Many of them wait for a chance to talk to you. There are souls around you that want answers, and there are a few that want a little more than that. You've wrecked a lot of lives. You've got no friends, but you already know that. In fact, I believe that I am the first contact you've had with a regular person in quite a while. Years, actually," she said.

"Ma'am, you are hardly a regular person," AC said. "I don't talk to regular people, and I certainly don't show up at their homes."

AC looked down to the etchings of the table.

"This is all, how should I say it. Exquisite. It looks like something out of a museum. Where did this come from?" he said.

AC ran his fingers over the Leo sign. The lion faced to the left from where AC sat.

"A Leo. That's me. I'm a lion," he said.

"It just ended up here. I'm asked that a lot. I don't know its origins, but most people say that it's pretty old," she said.

"I imagine that it is," AC replied. "Keep telling me about me."

Helen just stared at him. She really didn't want to do this.

"Are you doing it? Is that what you're doing right now?" asked AC, wondering why the uncomfortable stare was occurring. Anyone who normally stared that long were looking at the end of a gun as they pleaded for their life. Helen didn't realize the concession she was getting by looking at him in this way. The stare had nothing to do with the reading. She knew everything she needed to about this man before he reached the bottom of her steps. It's why she let him in. It's why she sent Sandy home.

"No, I'm not doing it right now. I'm just wondering why you want it done at all. People come to me to better themselves. People come to me if they need some sort of advice on their direction in life..." said Helen.

"Ah," he interrupted. "Direction. Now that's something that I need."

Helen slowly stood up.

"Can I offer you a drink of some type? I don't have alcohol, but I do have everything else," she said.

Helen walked to the kitchen and grabbed a drink. As she opened the refrigerator door, she turned around and watched as AC continued to look down at the table. She grabbed two cans of San Pellegrino Blood Orange soda, and walked back to the table.

"Ah, Italian soda," said AC. "Good. Not what I'm usually offered for a drink, but it'll do."

He popped the can open and took a sip.

"So, Helen, I had some of my family attend a baseball game. They had a lot to tell me, and I want to know from you how you do what you do," AC said.

The doorbell rang, and through the screen door it was clearly Brett Finnigan.

"Brett Finnigan?" said AC.

Helen looked at AC, shocked by his knowledge of who Sandy's son was at all. AC looked back at Helen.

"I'm just taking a lucky guess, Helen. So tell me, do *I* get $25?"

CHAPTER EIGHTEEN

Jen Maes wasn't sure of what to make of his excursion to Yankee Stadium, but he was glad he'd at least known the name of someone who made his trip a lot different than he had expected. Sure, he had heard about psychics before, but never had he actually sat down next to one, or spoken to someone who claimed to actually be a psychic. This was not what he came to the United States for.

After attending Helen's speaking engagement at the high school, he was looking forward to the reading he had convinced Helen to do with him. Sitting in his hotel room, he'd rechecked his flight back to Belgium, and made an adjustment to his return in order to accommodate the first psychic reading he would ever have.

Everyone reads their horoscopes, he'd thought to himself. Everywhere in the world he'd ever been, from Europe to Asia to the US and everywhere in between, he'd seen the section of the newspaper that gave its daily predictions based on the birthdate of any given individual. This woman, however, was unlike anything he had ever seen. She was simple. She was short. She seemed incredibly warm, and her smile was inviting.

Unbeknownst to him, Mauro had set up a squad that awaited him in the lobby. Their task wasn't their normal job of taking someone out to a corn field, but merely to follow the Belgian gem dealer and to watch his every move. That was the job, and as strange a job as the Polish group of fellows thought it to be, they would do as they were told. Mauro also had a few of his own family members on site to keep tabs on what was going on.

As Jens put on his dash of Lagerfeld cologne and checked himself out in the bathroom mirror of his hotel room, he stopped and looked at himself in the mirror, thinking of the family that awaited his return to Belgium. He wasn't sure why he felt compelled to have a reading by what could have been nothing more than a fluke at a baseball game. Lucky guesses.

Impossible, he thought. Every play? This woman knew every play? Whatever it was, it was enough for him to look at her baseball ticket, see her name, Google the woman, and end up in a high school auditorium in Naugatuck, Connecticut, when he had just expected to arrive in New York to make what he believed would be a final score before retirement. He had so many contacts at this point, that he knew he could simply make money off of the information he had, without ever needing to get on a plane again. Little did he know that he was about to be followed by New York's biggest mafia family, and a gang from Poland retained by Mauro Nicolo to watch his every move. He wanted to have this reading done for novelty's sake, and then go home to his family and children. He missed them.

Jens walked to the elevator door; it opened with just one man standing inside. That man was there for a reason. As soon as Jens walked into the elevator, the man began texting.

"You get reception on that thing in here, eh?" said Jen with a smile, just making friendly conversation with a man he'd share a twelve-floor ride to the lobby with.

The man didn't flinch. Not even a smile in return. Not even a fake one.

Jens just looked down and waited for the elevator to reach its destination, and so it did. Eager to exit the elevator, Jens sensed something wasn't right. He couldn't put his finger on what it was. He definitely had a sense that he wasn't alone, but also thought he might just be feeling a little weird knowing that he'd soon be having a psychic reading.

The lobby was full of what appeared to be businessmen in suits, all on cell phones, moving and shaking to the hustle that is New York City. If they only knew where he was headed, it would likely take many guesses. A pre-arranged town car pulled up and Jens hopped in. As he sat down, he looked back into the hotel lobby. It was suddenly empty. No men in suits, just the doorman.

"Weird," he said to himself.

"Ah, you ain't kidding," said a voice coming from the front of the car. "Welcome to New York."

The voice was taxi driver Christopher Djan, a man in his 60s with a smile on his face at all times; he was there to please.

"Just seems they all vanished," said Jens. "That place looked packed then *poof*, gone."

"New York, my friend, where everyone comes, and they go and they come and they go. It's like one of those rides at a circus," said Christopher.

"A merry-go-round," Jens said with a smirk.

"Yes! Just like a merry go around," he said with an accent that would lead you to believe he was from either Pakistan or Saudi Arabia. Jens didn't feel like asking the question, a bit haunted by what appeared to be the disappearing act of the men he just walked by in the lobby of the hotel he stayed at.

Christopher held the cell phone to his head.

"Yes, I have him now, and we are on our way to Naugatuck. I will not be available for calls for a bit," he said.

Christopher put the phone down and looked to Jens through the rearview mirror.

"Just checking in with the office, letting them know I have you," he said.

"Got it," replied Jens. "Not a problem."

Jens, unfortunately, believed him. The call was actually to Mauro Nicolo, who wanted to know where the Belgian gem dealer was headed. Part of Mauro thought they were about to lose their key to the Chinese gem dealing business to a flight at JFK airport. Fortunately, he was taking an hour and a half trip out of New York to see a psychic. For $25. The town car ran about $350 each way for this trip, but that didn't seem to bother Jens. It was one of those "one-time things," he'd thought.

"If you do not mind, I'm going to have a little rest on the ride," said Jens, making it clear he wasn't in a real talkative mood.

"No problem, my friend. Rest, and I will wake you up when we get there," said his driver.

The drive seemed as though it were at warp speed. It was one of those rare occasions when you try to take a nap and wake up six hours later. Jens literally only believed he'd blinked, and there he was being tapped awake on his shoulder by Christopher.

"Mr. Jens," he said.

Jens woke up, a little startled by it.

"We're here? It didn't even feel like I'd fallen asleep," he said.

"You must have been very tired, my friend," his driver replied.

Jens stepped out of the car and looked up the walkway to the home of Helen Wilson, the psychic. The driver looked at the sign on the front of the white picket gate that enclosed the front entrance of the home, the sign "Psychic" prominently displayed on the front gate with the words "By Appointment Only" sprawled across the bottom of it.

"Everyone reads their horoscopes," said Christopher. "I always read them."

Jens looked at him and smiled, a bit embarrassed by the fact that his hour-and-a-half-long journey, a journey that felt literally like the blink of an eye, was now known to this driver that he'd just met. Rather than try to explain it, he just decided it'd be best to just proceed.

"Thank you, Christopher. I will be about an hour," Jens said.

"No problem, you take all the time you need. I will be here."

Jens walked up the pathway and looked at his watch. 1:59 p.m. He was a minute early. The door opened to a smiling Helen, who always had the same smile on her face whenever you saw her.

"Last stop to Belgium, yes?" Helen said.

"Yes, ma'am, it is," he replied.

Jens walked into the small home, and Helen directed him to the table. Jens sat down, eager to begin what could just be a fun excursion into fantasy.

Helen sat down across from him. Her smile quickly disappeared, but not in a way that would give one the impression that something bad was about to come out of her mouth. Frankly, Jens didn't know what was about to come out.

"I'm all right," she said, with her eyes closed.

Jens just sat there, not knowing who she was talking to, or if he was supposed to say something or not.

"I'm hearing you," she went on.

Helen opened her eyes and looked to Jens.

"Tell me what you would like to know," she said.

Jens just sat there, unable to really think of what he should ask.

"To be honest, Mrs. Wilson, I don't really know. I just felt like I wanted to try this. I have family I'm about to return to after a small business trip I had in New York, and thought I'd check this out. I was impressed by your reading at the high school," he said. "Getting here from New York was a breeze. I fell asleep the entire way here."

"I did what I could," she replied. "So if anything particular..."

Helen stopped. She looked at her table. Her hands glided over its entire top.

"Jens."

Jens was a bit taken aback. First, he didn't know what she meant when she said "I did what I could." Now she was just saying his name. She continued.

"Jens, here is what I know. I know you have a wonderful family in Belgium that loves you, and that you need to, now, leave this place and go directly to the airport. You will not stop. You will tell your driver to take you directly to JFK where you will board the flight home and talk to no one on the way, not even to your driver."

"I don't understand," Jens said. "Is that all you can see about me?"

"No, it's not all I can see, but I see two things. One of those things is the path I just suggested, and the other, you really do not want to know. I'm not trying to scare you, I'm just saying that you need to go home now. You did what you came here to do," Helen said.

Jens wasn't satisfied.

"I came a long way, I just expected..."

She cut him off.

"What you expected was a reading, and I only give true ones. Your work has caught the attention of some undesirables, and you will be best served if you do as I say."

Jens stood up from the table. He reached for his wallet and put $25 on the table. A twenty dollar bill, and a five dollar bill.

"Well, I have to say, this was interesting. I appreciate your suggestion, and to be honest, I'd intended to go to the airport after this," he said.

"Well good, just no stops, and don't talk to your driver about it; not a word. It will be an easy ride to JFK. Just do not talk to anybody."

Jens shook her hand, exchanged smiles, and walked to the car. He looked back once more at the house he'd just walked out of in Naugatuck, Connecticut.

"I gotta be crazy," he said to himself.

Christopher got out of the vehicle and got in, startled to see a man sitting next to him in his town car.

"Hello, Mr. Maes. I was hoping we could share a ride to JFK," said Mauro Nicolo.

CHAPTER NINETEEN

Helen Wilson had always known she had a sixth sense. She knew things were coming, and had always prepared herself accordingly for the journey ahead of her. She was great at predictions, the tarot, reading one's horoscopes; but when it came to herself, she never seemed to be able to tell her own future.

She had feelings, but nothing as specific as those she provided readings for.

"Oh, God, please tell me what to do. What do you want me to do with my life? Have I done enough? Is there something I'm missing? How can I best serve you? Please let all of my work, and all of my actions, be through You," she said, as she looked in her bathroom mirror.

Something was coming. She could feel it, and she knew that she had to prepare herself for the journey ahead. The problem was, she didn't know if the journey was godly, or just a drive over the bridge to New York again to see another baseball game. Feelings weren't strong enough to indicate that an action should be taken, or prevented. This was the problem with the gift Helen had. She could read others, but she just couldn't read herself.

The words "I'm all right" would continuously be said by her to herself, mostly when alone. She didn't know what she meant half the time she'd say it. "I'm all right."

Helen never expected to be a psychic. She never meant to become the person in the neighborhood that people were talking about, and she most certainly didn't think the head of New York's biggest mafia family would show up at her door. She knew what AC's visit meant, and she knew what he meant by referring to Brett Finnigan by his full name. She didn't have to give him $25 as he had jokingly indicated, but she knew she hadn't heard the last of him.

"Who is it?" she called from her bathroom.

Then the knock at the door came, which was impossible for her to know from her bathroom, had she not been gifted with the abilities she possessed.

Luigi Nicolo stood at the front door. Sandy Finnigan was with Brett at a dentist appointment, but she assumed Luigi already knew that, given AC's apparent knowledge of those Helen was close to.

"Come in, I guess," said Helen.

Luigi walked into the house as if he'd been an old friend, with that same comfortable feeling that one might have if they had been to someone's home a thousand times. He was, however, uneasy about only one thing, and that was Helen.

The thought of pressuring a woman who might be something from God was something he wanted no part of. Sure, he knew he'd done wrong in his life, but this was something else. This was something he had no experience in, and he didn't want any. He was threatened himself, on a daily basis, just with the knowledge that if he had not done as he was told, he could be wiped out by his own uncle. Given that, trust and any sort of feeling of being "ok" just wasn't a part of Luigi's being.

“Sit down, Luigi. Let’s do whatever it is you came here to do,” Helen said.

Reluctantly, Luigi sat down. The comfortable feeling he had of walking through Helen’s front door was quickly replaced with a fear of the unknown. This woman knew things about him. This woman knew things about his future. He knew it. He could feel it. He was there to deliver a message so that it was clear, and regardless of how he felt about the situation, he was simply the delivery boy for AC.

“I know why you’re here, and I know what it is your boss wants from me. I also know his intentions if I do not comply. I have to tell you, though, intimidation may not bring the results any of you want. I can’t tell you for sure if I can help him. His ways are of forces that are dark, and as young as you are, and as able as you are to escape this life, I know that you won’t. You’re afraid, but I’m not, for myself.”

Helen looked to the window where she could see a piece of Sandy Finnigan’s house.

“But that boy, his mother, indeed everyone in this neighborhood, they don’t deserve this. It’s my fault for opening these people up to this situation, and now I don’t really have a choice but to comply with your uncle, now do I?” said Helen.

Luigi just looked down.

“No, ma’am, I guess not. I think we’re both knowledgeable of what my uncle and his family are capable of. In fact, I know what I will be forced to be capable of if they aren’t happy,” said Luigi.

"I've never been 100 percent," said Helen. "What your family is asking me to do could backfire in a very big way. It's not what you want to do. You're trying to use the celestial world to help you commit crime, and I have never attempted that before. I'm not sure it's going to give you the results you want," said Helen.

Luigi just stared at her.

"I don't know how to make this clearer to you, Helen. The fact is, if you're wrong, I want you to look out that window," he said.

Helen complied, watching kids running around, and a neighbor walking down the path of his own home to pick up a couple of newspapers.

"All of those people will die. And not in a way that PETA would approve of," said Luigi.

Helen took her turn at staring.

"Ok. Well, I guess I understand," she said.

"I'm going to contact you when we need your, let's say, advice. I want you to think long and hard about each reply you provide me. It's very important that you know what you are telling us is accurate. If anything changes, you are to call me immediately," he said. "My uncle has a real belief in this sort of thing. My other uncle, not so much."

"I understand," said Helen.

"There's something I need to ask you right now, and I don't want to hear your thoughts on the morality of what I'm asking. You need to just give me an answer. Don't lie to me, don't try to talk me out of things; just answer the questions that come down from AC," Luigi said matter-of-factly.

“OK,” she said. “You don’t know what you’re doing; none of you do. But, OK. I will share no further opinion of my own to you or your family; but you’ve been warned.”

Warned. The Nicolo family was being warned by a short woman who gave predictions for $25.

“Fair enough,” said Luigi. “It’s not just your neighbors you need to worry about. It’ll be you, too, Helen. They will come for you as well. I’d come for you if I had to.”

Luigi stood up and pulled a small piece of paper out of his wallet. He gave it to her. She opened the folder paper up:

“What bank would be safe to take?” it said. Helen sensed that the person who wrote this was not AC, but someone he’d instructed, just as he had now obviously instructed Luigi to sit in her home.

“This is not right,” she said. “This is not why I do this.”

Luigi walked past the comfortably close zone to look at Helen’s face.

“Please don’t make me tell you again, Helen. I have instructions for that, too,” he said. “You don’t want to know what those instructions are.”

“I’m just saying, but OK. And you’re wrong, Luigi, I do know. It’s why I’m forced to tell you that the New York State Patriot Bank on Broadway is going to be ripe for your family on Thursday between 2:00 and 4:00 p.m. There will be no way to fail if you follow the plan you’ve already been developing, the one your uncle has been. I will note, however, that it wasn’t much of a plan. Thursday, though, between those times, and you’ll be all right.”

Helen had just allowed what she never thought she would, and she knew that there would be no turning back. If she left the country, she knew she'd still receive word that her friends were all dead because she did. She had no choice but to stay. She had no choice but to deliver.

"In the end, you will all strike out," she said.

"Well, AC hasn't struck out since I've been related to him. He always wins, and all you are to him is an expedited means to increasing revenue," Luigi said.

"Even if you're playing with the Ultimate Power?" she said.

"On this world, AC is that ultimate power, and you, you are just his latest weapon."

Luigi turned to walk out of the house. He began opening the door to leave.

"Luigi, do not allow this to happen," she said.

Luigi looked back at her.

"Helen, there's probably no one in the world who knows more that this is an impossibility. You have to come through, or AC will rain down something you've never seen the likes of."

Helen shook her head.

"I hear you, but I need you to know, he has yet to see rain of the kind he's playing with," she said.

Luigi just looked at her, looked around the inside of her home, looked back at Helen and smiled.

"I've left my card in your mailbox. If anything changes about anything, you tell us. You are to call me immediately. There will be no "I'm sorry" statements if anything goes wrong, Helen. I'm to tell you that, too."

Luigi turned around and walked out of the house.

Helen walked back to the table she'd provided hundreds of readings from and sat down.

"What do I do?" she said, as she looked at the Aquarius sign. "What do I do?"

CHAPTER TWENTY

"Lucky bitch," said Mauro.

Mauro was not happy. The bank that Helen had predicted would be easy to clean out...was easy to clean out.

This made AC have a confidence in what Mauro believed to be utter bullshit something that now had credibility. Mauro had his own beliefs, and his biggest fear was that this was all part of some elaborate scheme to bring his family to the ground. Perhaps she was working with the FBI. Perhaps she was working with the State Police. The concern that Helen "the psychic" Wilson could set them all up for a takedown was real to Mauro, and AC's blind faith in this woman, after all his family had been through to control the empire that they now did, could be demolished by a woman from Naugatuck, Connecticut.

One of her predictions could lead to entrapment, and that's simply the way Mauro was brought up to be. Paranoia was just another word for heightened awareness in his world, and he didn't like the idea of some woman telling the head of the biggest crime family in America what to do, and when. To Mauro, shit rolled downhill, and he didn't want this woman controlling the puppet strings of that empire.

It was time for Mauro to pick up the phone. This were more than a few Polish friends, and he instructed that posse that it was time to bring in the cavalry, and a call to Poland was made. Next, a call to Italy. This was a lot of "covering AC's" back, so much so that it might even be hard for AC to believe that Mauro was going to such a length to "protect" his older brother.

Mauro was protecting himself.

The bank heist earned his family a little over two million dollars. That wasn't chump change, but the more this woman got right, the more danger his family was in. He didn't really know what to think of Helen Wilson. All he knew was that she called some baseball plays correctly, and scored on a bank job. In his mind, these could both have been some lucky guesses.

Evan Yastrzemski walked into Mauro's suite with a blank look, awaiting words from Mauro on what to do next.

"I want more on this woman. I want a fucking baseball team on this woman. I want to know her every move, her every client, who she's talking to, where she eats her ice cream. I don't want this woman knowing she's being watched, but I want her the most-watched woman in the world. So if you need to bring over some of your men from Poland, tell me where to send a jet to pick them up. I'm bringing some people over from Sicily myself, because I will be damned if I'll let this little woman from Naugafuck bring this family down. I don't know what my brother is thinking about, but he's asked me to be the man who protects this family, and he never said I couldn't also protect him from himself. And he needs my protection. It's my job, and I want everyone in on this because as long as he's playing with the psychic, we've got a problem," Mauro said.

Evan just stood there, and Mauro lifted his chin enough to let him know he awaited a reply.

"Done," said Evan. "I'm going to need some things from you."

"What will you need?" asked Mauro.

"I want credit cards in the names of a list I will provide you. The color of these cards need to be black. I need that jet in Poland within forty-eight hours, and I am going to need hotel rooms for all of them, each in a different hotel. I'm also going to need $200,000 in cash, more if we need it. If you want what you're asking for, then ghosts are very expensive," said Evan.

"Done," replied Mauro. "Come back tomorrow with a list, and you'll have what you need by 8:00 p.m. tomorrow night, if you're here by noon."

"I can do that," replied Evan.

Mauro walked to his window, looking at the glistening city and the buildings in front of him.

"We need Asia to survive. We need an in over there to continue our dominance here. We could stop today and never have to work again, but that's not what has made us who we are. We don't stop, and we sure as hell don't quit. And I won't let a fucking psychic bring this family to its knees," Mauro said. "I want her watched, and I want this Belgian fuck brought into the mix. He's our key into this territory. He's earned a reputation, and the Chinese trust him. We'd never get in without him and believe me, we've tried other angles, and they just do not work. They look at us with disgust over there, and the problem is, they don't need us."

Mauro looked at Evan.

"Do you got something to say?" Mauro asked as Evan stood there, one hand nervously brushing over his face.

"I just don't feel entirely comfortable doing these things without the blessing of AC, no disrespect. This is a man many people fear where I come from," Evan said.

"You need to fear me just as much, my friend. I'll be the man at the post sooner or later, and I will hold these things you do for me with respect and admiration. The time will come when I am the one on the top floor, and when that day comes, my memory will be strong."

Mauro looked down at his cell phone as it vibrated. It was a text message, which read:

SHE DID IT AGAIN.

"Fuck," said Mauro. "I feel like I'm living in the fucking *Twilight Zone* right now."

What "SHE" did again was predict that a horse, Melly, would win at Aqueduct Racetrack. This horse was 20-1 against, a sure loser who on this day didn't lose.

"Mauro," said Evan.

"What is it?" said Mauro. "You falling for this shit now, too?"

"No. I mean, I don't know. I don't know anything about this shit. You asked me to do something and here I am, doing it. I just think you should think about this, all of this, behind AC's back," Evan said.

"I am protecting my brother!" Mauro screamed. "This is what I do!"

"And I'm not saying that you shouldn't. It's what a brother does. All I do know is that sometimes we don't know all that we think we know. What if this woman isn't some fluke? What if there is something to this that is real?" Evan said.

"There is nothing fucking real about a woman in Naugafuck, Connecticut reading fortunes for $25," he said.

“But your brother does appear to have her on a pretty tight leash. I don’t see what the problem is, like you do,” said Evan.

“Then you’re as fucking stupid as he is, because this bitch could predict something that’s a full-scale trap that we walk right into, only to have everything we have, everything we own, taken from us. That is not going to happen. That will never fucking happen. I forbid it, and I am protecting my brother by doing so,” Mauro said.

“I’m just saying that I think we need to be careful. I know you, I know how you are, and believe me when I tell you, I know your capabilities. I know there is nowhere on the planet one could hide from your wrath, which you’ve proven to me time and time again throughout our knowing one another. This, however, is just something I’ve never experienced before myself, and I don’t like walking into things I know nothing about. I don’t know why you don’t just have us take her out,” Evan said.

“If I do that, it no longer is excusable as me simply protecting my brother. If I do as you say, that’s an action that could break my trust with my brother. That would change things between us. This must be about protecting my brother, and by that I mean from himself as well as everyone else,” he said. “But he’s in this thing now. He’s buying it. I don’t. If something should happen to this woman, then it will undoubtedly come back on me. As much as I trust you, I know that in the end, your family would support him over my opinion,” said Mauro.

“Well, with respect, I need you to know that we would. All of us would. I’m here because you said you need us to help protect your brother, but make no mistake; we would kill you as quickly as we did anyone AC ordered us to, and we will do nothing to jeopardize his trust in us, ever,” said Evan.

A silence overcame the room while Mauro inhaled what he'd just heard.

Mauro just looked at him. "I understand," said Mauro. "That's not something you need to tell me twice. I understand."

Evan walked to the elevator and pressed the down button.

"You are all so high in life. The only button you have goes down. I will not allow myself or my family to do so well. I will do as you've requested, and I will be here at noon tomorrow to let you know who you need to set these things up for, who will be involved," said Evan. "We've said all it is that we need to say."

Mauro walked to him and extended his hand.

"I appreciate your coming here, and I respect you and your family. We've done much together over the years, and I want nothing to come between us. We must view this as simply protecting my brother," said Mauro.

"That's the only way I'm viewing it. Please just do not ask me to do more than this," Evan said.

The elevator door opened, and Evan walked through the door.

"I will see you," Evan said, as the elevator door closed.

Mauro stood and watched the door shut. He then turned around and walked back towards the window, looking out, and wondering what Helen Wilson was doing right now.

"Readings, fucking hocus pocus bullshit," he said to himself.

CHAPTER TWENTY-ONE

Merton Howard sat in his car, pondering the enigma that sat inside the home he was parked in front of. He didn't know whether or not to get out of his unmarked vehicle, or just sit there and think some more. Like a Rubik's Cube, Detective Howard attempted to twist every possible explanation that would make what he had just experienced make some sense.

This woman, Helen Wilson, sent him to North Andover, Massachusetts to check out the residential area that surrounded a plastic wrap manufacturing company. This woman, Helen Wilson, knew about a case that had been driving him nuts. This woman, Helen Wilson, knew exactly how many kids were being held captive. This woman, Helen Wilson, made him question everything that he had learned about life.

This woman, Helen Wilson, was a fucking psychic.

And yet, there was no one he could tell. His captain, Captain Frank Delaney, would never believe him. He was never able to explain to the FBI in Boston what had occurred, or how he came by the information he would never have been able to learn had it not been for her. If it were not for Helen Wilson, those kids would likely have ended up like the two elderly people their captive murdered while taking over their "vacant" home. She saved their lives, and made him question his own. She solved the disappearance of two older people thought to have moved to Ft. Lauderdale to retire. Little did anyone in North Andover know that this man had been responsible for two murders in North Andover, held three kids captive, and was wanted in the disappearance of three other young girls and the murder of four other people in Kihei, Hawaii. The man who did these horrible things was just sitting in a vacant home, so the neighbors thought. And it wasn't until a woman, a woman named Helen Wilson, gave him a reading, uninvited, that these facts came to light.

Word was going to get out about this at some point. Reporters were beginning to ask questions, and even reporter Anderson Cooper of CNN, it was learned, was putting together a segment on police psychics. "Facts or Fiction?" it was to be called. Helen was going to be featured as one of those psychics after a CNN news editor, unbeknownst to everyone, sat in the high school auditorium during the talk that Helen gave at Naugatuck High School.

Sitting in his car, still debating whether or not he should proceed to talk to Helen about what had happened in North Andover, he continued to consider whether or not he should let this one go, or if there was some other haunting cases that kept him up at night that she might be able to help him with. His job was to be patient, even though the families of most victims never thought his police force was ever doing enough. The victims' families never realized how difficult it was to find them justice. To them, the address of the murderer would always be in some database where they could just go pick them up, provide them justice, and schedule an appointment for that electric chair.

He put his hand on the door handle as a car passed slowly in front of him, prompting him to just sit in his car for a moment longer so as to not be seen. What he didn't expect, however, was to see who would get out of that car.

Detective Merton Howard just sat there, watching in shock, as Luigi Nicolo pulling up to the wrong side of the road to park, as ordered by AC, and got out of the car. Merton slumped back in his seat, beginning to piece together in his mind just how big a find this woman was. If Luigi Nicolo and AC Nicolo were showing up at this woman's house, then it could only be bad news. This woman was in way over her head if the likes of the Nicolo family were showing up at her front door. There were other people in that car, but he couldn't make out who they were. This family knew when they were being followed, so the timing was just bizarre. You don't get this far, you don't build the empire they did, if they weren't very sure when they were being followed. Like meeting Helen, he felt as though he had lucked out, because they didn't even notice his car, a car that was just parked along the side of the road with everyone else's vehicle. So he watched, from a distance.

The illegal parking job gave him the right to approach their car, but if they knew he was watching her house, he knew she could be in more short-term danger than Helen might have thought. His best tactic, at least so he thought, was to sit and watch. Do nothing. This was a frustrating situation. The temptation was to just get out of the car and pull those assholes out one by one, but he knew he'd be unable to watch her forever, and there was no way anyone at the police station would believe his story enough to assign 24-hour patrol of this home. They would think he was crazy.

But this was opening up a can of worms, and he was witnessing something that could not have any happy ending, no matter how he spun it to himself.

"Fuck," he said to himself. "Fuck, fuck."

Three other men he didn't recognize got out of the car, and one of them lit up a cigarette. Clearly, they were just there to watch while Luigi went in the house. He couldn't be spotted. She wouldn't last another night if he was.

Detective Howard had to talk to someone about all of this, but he hadn't a clue where to start. Who could he discuss this with that would believe him? Who could he talk to that would even give what he had to say the time of day? Relatives from the biggest mafia family in the nation were walking into the home of a psychic that had just solved numerous cases during one half-hour visit, and he had nowhere to go. If Detective Howard didn't have his own team in place, one that believed him, then he would be just as gone as Helen would be if any of these thugs saw him sitting there. So he just sat there, and the Rubik's Cube in his head began turning once again.

"What am I going to do about this?" he whispered to himself.

He leaned his arm up against the driver's side door and sustained his head with it. This entire situation seemed impossible. Half an hour went by, and Luigi walked back to his car. The men with him got back into the illegally parked vehicle and drove off.

Merton stepped out of his car with a small paper bag in his hand. Walking to where they parked, he leaned over and picked up the cigarette butt that was now on the ground as a result of being smoked by one of the men.

DNA. He was going to find out what was going on. He had to find out, because if this woman, Helen Wilson, was as he now believed, then this could be bigger than anything he'd seen in his lifetime, and the most bizarre. It could be a crime he couldn't solve, especially given his only back-up would be fellow officers who would think he was crazy if he dared tell them this story, or even worse, start looking into Helen more than the crimes she could solve. Part of him thought they may even suspect her of involvement, given how specific her knowledge seemed to be, how precise.

He was a believer now, though. He knew damn well that AC Nicolo wouldn't be having his men pay visits to her unless it was for something sinister. If her talents were as real as he thought, then getting involved with this crime family was the wrong place for her to be. It was too late, though. She was on their radar now. Clearly, she was now more than on their radar. He was figuring it out as he sat there. This didn't take a detective.

This was a problem.

After putting the cigarette butt back into his car, he decided to talk to Helen. As he began to walk to the house, eyes on the ground, he lifted his head to see Helen standing in front of the gate of her home. He was a bit surprised, not having seen her even walk down the long pathway from her front door to the gate.

He smiled, and walked towards her.

"Hi, Helen," he said. "How are you?"

Helen walked towards him, expressionless.

"I'm glad you found the kids, but you need to leave now. I know what you know," she said. "You don't need to tell me anything you think. You already know what you're right about."

Merton wasted no time replying. "Helen, these people will take you out in a second," he said.

“Or, they take out everyone on this block,” she said. “I’m doing what I need to do.”

Helen turned around and began walking back to her home.

“Helen, it’s my job not to allow certain things to happen.”

Helen stopped and turned around.

“Detective Howard, what you don’t understand is, it’s already happened. Just not yet.”

CHAPTER TWENTY-TWO

"Typically, when someone is sitting in a car that I didn't invite, it's not good news. In fact, I can't say there has ever been an occasion when such a thing has occurred, especially in a location such as this, in a city I can barely figure out how to pronounce," said Jens, as he sat in his car next to his new travel companion.

Mauro just looked at him, sipping a drink from a glass that was not in the car as Jens drove to Helen's house.

"Well, let's just say I am a man who is full of surprises. Your excursion here to see Ms. Wilson is of little importance to me. You likely went in there to talk about your family, what the future holds for you, bullshit like that. Let me assure you, however, it's bullshit. These psychics are mostly unemployed older women who couldn't find a real job," Mauro replied. "But you have been a very hard man to nail down, and I'm not really the type to dilly-dally, as they say. That feeling you've had that you were been being watched was correct, but it wasn't meant to intimidate you or scare you. If it did, then you have my apology for that. I'm here in a manner that is strictly business," he concluded.

Jens wasted no time replying. "Wait a minute; you're Mauro Nicolo," he said, surprised.

"Yes, I am. But that name shouldn't instill fear in you, only the potential for profit," Mauro replied.

"Well, I'm out of the game, sir. I came here to do one last deal, and extended the trip out of nothing more than curiosity after I saw that woman pull off a stunt at a baseball game. It was nothing more than curiosity," Jens said defensively.

"That's fine. If you're not discussing me or my family, I couldn't care less what you talk about. I am, however, concerned with her innate ability to guess things correctly. This trickery, whatever it is…and I don't want her delusions or paranoia interfering with reality. I've seen her do it to my own brother," said Mauro.

"AC Nicolo believes in this stuff? I'm not sure if *I* even believe in this stuff," he said.

"Let's do each other a favor, and not discuss AC. Let's discuss why I stepped into your car, because that's the only reason I invited myself. This trip you're about to take to the airport, it's on me, as was your trip to see the astrologist inside," said Mauro. "It's a gift for my impolite intrusion on your day."

"Well, I'm going to the airport right now, and I won't be stopping anywhere along the way," said Jens.

Mauro seemed a little irritated by the statement, not because he had any intention on stopping anywhere, he just didn't like being told what would be. That was *his* job, but in the interest of calming down Jens, a Belgian businessman who likely wasn't used to having someone hop in his car uninvited, he let it go.

"I'm not here to interfere with any of your plans, Jens," said Mauro.

"How do you know my name? What exactly is this?" asked Jens.

"What this is, simply put, is that my family has an interest in doing business in the Asian markets. As you know, we're not a family they like dealing with, *especially* ours," said Mauro.

"Well, they choose not to associate with drugs, or violence," said Jens.

Mauro paused, looking at Jens with a little bit of disbelief.

"If you think that no one has ever died during one of your transactions in Europe, then you're not basing your opinions in reality yourself. You can call it denial, if you will, but no money exchanges hands in the way that yours has without there being some blood on it. So let's cut the charade and put aside the nonsense. You have a wife and children who are oblivious to reality, and that's fine. I get it. You don't want them to know some of the things you've seen, and I know this trip is your last to actually be involved in. I'm all for it. You go back to Belgium. I've already seen to it that you've been upgraded from business class to first class. You go home and begin your retired life. I already know your plans as a consultant, and that's all you'll be doing for us. It will be under the radar. You know who I am, even though you hail from Belgium, for a reason. One day, I will be the head of this family, and when I am, I will remember the help you provided to us. I can assure you that you will earn more from these consultant fees than you have ever earned flying all over the place. And what the fuck are you doing flying commercial? I know you've done far better than business class," said Mauro.

"I was just trying to join the real world," said Jens.

"I'm afraid it's too late for you to join the real world. You can retire, you've earned it. All I'm telling you is that you have your first client. You will set up a corporate entity in the United Kingdom that separates our family from the radar of the Chinese, and they will never know that we are the clients you are consulting," said Mauro.

"And what if I don't want to get involved in this masquerade?" said Jens.

Mauro just looked at him and smiled.

"Jens, you've lived a masquerade your entire life. It's in your blood. You're just getting out of the physical aspect. And to be honest, it's a pretty smart thing to do, to get out while you're on top. The bottom line is, you have your first client, and you will always have our protection. We are everywhere, and no one will mess with you or your family. And you won't mess with ours by making me return to my brother with any news that isn't pleasant," Mauro said.

This was about the nicest way you would ever hear a mafia figure engage you into his world. It was the nicest way to tell you how it was going to be. It was so nice, Jens might actually have considered him a friend if he hadn't known how much blood the man had shed over the years.

Jens just looked at him as the vehicle headed for the airport.

"Well, you're going to have to spell out exactly what it is you're intending to have me consult you about," Jens replied.

Mauro wasn't typically into questions such as this. You did as you were told; but in this case, there was more money to lose than to let ego get in the way of this situation.

"What do you think it is?" asked Mauro.

Jens didn't hesitate. "Asia," Jens replied.

“See that? You are a very smart man. That’s why I did my research, and knew you were the guy to go to. I’m looking for someone like you that can help my family enter a new phase for ourselves. Sure, what we’ve done got us this far, it’s why you know who I am,” said Mauro.

“With all due respect, Mr. Nicolo, I don’t know your name because of your charitable contributions to the world,” Jens replied.

“Ah, but that’s not true. We donate many millions of dollars every year all over the world to different causes. But at the end of the day, if we aren’t making millions, we can’t give away millions. It’s hard to broadcast a large donation to anyone who would report it, and announcing our generosities would only have the wrong people asking more questions. I’m sure you can understand that we receive enough questions as it is,” said Mauro.

The car was closing in on the airport, as signs began to pop up with “AIRPORT” as they got closer.

“Mr. Nicolo, I’m retired,” Jens said. “I’m not a messenger, and I don’t do errands. And what happens if things go south with you? What happens if I cannot give you what you need? Do you wipe my family out? Do I get a bullet in the back of my head?” Jens said.

“First of all, we never shoot anyone in the back of the head,” said Mauro.

“Well, that’s refreshing to know,” Jens replied.

“We do it in front of the head, that way the person knows who it’s coming from. We don’t believe in doing things chicken shit,” Mauro replied.

Silence.

Suddenly, Mauro laughed out loud in a roaring manner.

"I'm kidding with you, Jens! Come now. Listen, if things don't work out, they don't work out. You're not the only man over there that we can approach about such things," said Mauro.

As much as Jens didn't want to engage in business, he was always interested in making more money, especially if all he had to do was sit at home with his family and act as a Rolodex. If this worked out, the Nicolo family could end up being his only client.

"Okay, Mr. Nicolo," said Jens.

"Call me Mauro," he replied.

"Okay, Mauro. I will help you do this. But I have conditions," Jens said, never typically the brave one to have any.

"I'm listening to your conditions. Go ahead," said Mauro.

The car pulled up to the airport departures and parked. A police officer approached the vehicle, ready to tell them that they couldn't park there. The window in the back seat rolled down as the officer looked eye to eye with Mauro.

"It's okay, Mr. Nicolo," said the officer with a smile.

"Thank you, friend," Mauro replied to the officer, who walked away.

Mauro looked back at Jens.

"Neat trick," said Jens.

"I've got a few friends on the force," Mauro snickered. "About your conditions; go on, I know you've got a flight to catch."

"My conditions are simple. You, your family, anyone on your behalf, are off limits in Belgium or anywhere you know me and my family are. I will set up an international cell phone that is between me and you alone. No third parties. No visitors. If you haven't heard from me, it's because I have nothing to tell you. When your phone rings, it's because I have something to tell you. And when you want to talk to me, you call me every Sunday at 9:00 p.m. Belgium time. That's the only time we speak. You'll tell me what you've got in mind, I'll research it, and then I'll get back to you," said Jens. "You need to know, I'm retired. This is just something I'm going to do for you on the side. You will reward me with what you believe my efforts warrant. However, I will not play messenger boy. You will have a person set up a home, an apartment, whatever suits your fancy, in London. You will have that person set up a bank account there. I'm not doing any of that kind of work. I've already promised a woman who has already put up with far too much that I am a retired man, a consultant. If we speak for an hour every Sunday, if I make a few calls while she's out shopping, then it doesn't interfere with what I've promised her. I am serious though; no calls. Any breach will stop everything, and I will no longer exist to you," said Jens, realizing he likely wouldn't if he ever fucked over Mauro Nicolo.

Mauro just looked at him. That was a lot to ask of a man who had no patience.

"Okay," Mauro said. "You have yourself a deal. If your consultations provide my family with what we seek, then you will want for nothing."

"I've been doing this a long time, Mauro. I haven't wanted for anything for quite a while now. I'm sure I've made enemies in my line of work that have little to do with you at all, so don't be surprised if it's me who calls you with a request from time to time. I want to know my family is protected from all of this, and not just this, but my own past," Jens said.

"My friend, we all have large fences around our homes, or live in high-rises, for a very good reason," Mauro said.

"Yeah, and why is that?" Jens replied.

"It's to keep all the people we've fucked over from getting inside."

Jens just looked at him. He'd heard that somewhere before, perhaps in a song. He couldn't put his finger on where he'd heard that before, but he was sure he had.

"You will be receiving a phone in the mail, and your calls will begin to me the following Sunday after you receive that phone," said Jens.

"Do you even know where to send this phone?" said Mauro.

Jens looked at him as he opened the door to exit his car.

"You are not the only one with resources, Mauro. You'll get the phone within three days. As for setting up one of your associates in London, that is all up to you. I will have no part in anything that tracks back to me. And if asked if I know you, I will deny it. I am simply going to have a meeting with your associate as if he were any other client, but it's going to be such a great client that I needn't have another. I will leave that to you to make certain," Jens said.

Jens looked at the driver.

"Hold on a minute. Give me a pen, please," Jens said to the driver.

Jens wrote something down on the hood of the car as the door remained open. Mauro just looked out at him, wondering what he was doing. Jens then handed the card to Mauro.

"This is my routing and account number of my bank, which I've written on the card. I want you to wire me an acknowledgement of our new association," said Jens.

Mauro took the card with a smile on his face. The door closed to the car, and the car drove away.

Jens walked into the airport holding his shoulder bag and looked back at the car. About five minutes later, his cell phone buzzed as he stood in line at security.

It was a text message that read:

From: 44-001 MESSAGE

Jens opened the message.

CONF# 455400221Z transfer from BNY to GB BANK - $500,000 USD

Jens shut the phone off, and whispered to himself, "Acknowledged."

His smile quickly turned into fear.

"Acknowledged" had just become a very dangerous word.

CHAPTER TWENTY-THREE

New York had never seen the likes of the crime wave that began to take over the city. Banks were being robbed, even investment firms that held nothing but the power to transfer funds from one place to another, none of them having actual physical cash in them. Robberies thought to be impossible were happening at record pace, and despite New York being one of the most monitored cities in the world, with a camera at every stop light, there seemed to be no records of anything. Tapes revealed nothing. There wasn't a single criminal caught on tape, and yet more than thirty-three million dollars, combined, had been swiped from company after company, bank after bank, barge after barge. It appeared to be an unstoppable crime spree, and the only man on the planet who had a feeling for what was going on would be considered a laughing stock if he ever opened his mouth.

Detective Merton Howard was frantic. He should have stayed in Haverhill, Massachusetts, where he was born. Why on earth he ever moved to Naugatuck, Connecticut was beyond him. Never in his life had he heard of a bank robbery in Naugatuck. Who robs Naugatuck? And yet in the past two weeks, the same bank had been hit three times without even a snapshot from an onlooker, who for some reason never had time to onlook.

His next move was to contact Helen Wilson again, but not by phone. He was going to drive over and speak to her face to face. This time, however, he had company, as a vehicle tailed him from a distance.

"What the fuck, what the fuck?" he said, as he drove to Helen's house in an unmarked vehicle. "This is insane, completely insane," he said, as he continued talking to himself.

He was about to turn the radio on, then stopped himself. He instead chose to just think. He wanted to think about what he was doing, how he was going to explain this to Captain Delaney, who he already knew thought he was an overzealous detective who shot first and then said, "freeze." It's a reputation he got when he once raided the home of someone he thought was chaining his wife to the inside of her house. He obtained a warrant by a judge who he was buddies with, who allowed the warrant to include "video tapes, bedding, and numerous other items," that even a court-appointed attorney could get tossed out. The warrant was to seek out a bad check that was written for an eBay item that was valued at $38. Yes, there was a woman chained inside of that house, but there was no way to prosecute the man responsible because of how Merton obtained the warrant. He pulled a favor, and it was the only time he ever did so, and it blew up in his face. A $38 eBay item that required video tapes and bedding? The case was dismissed, and Detective Howard was reprimanded at the time.

He slept at night, even still, because he had saved that woman's life, a woman who was being chained for months and fed nothing more than a can of tuna fish and pickles every day. She looked like a skeleton when officers crashed through the front door. It was also the only reason he was able to keep his job. Had there been no woman in that house chained to a radiator, being treated worse than a dog, Detective Merton Howard would have just been known as Merton Howard. He should have received an award; but instead, was just able to keep his badge and gun, which for months had been taken away from him at the time while Internal Affairs decided what it should do about the mess. The local newspapers were all over it at the time. Not a cop in Naugatuck would partner with him for several years over the fiasco.

Now he's got a psychic to explain. *Good luck*, he thought. How on earth would he explain this situation to his captain? He decided the only way would be to bring him to her, and to let her tell Captain Delaney a few things about himself that would do the talking for Detective Howard.

New York had become a city held captive by a family that was plugged into everything. Detective Howard was out of his jurisdiction. New York had seen enough insanity that it couldn't believe; adding a psychic to the mix was just going to insult the city more than offer it a way out.

Pulling up to the home of Frank Delaney, on his captain's day off, to bring him to see a psychic named Helen Wilson, seemed a daunting task.

He walked up to the patio. Captain Delaney clearly saw his vehicle pull up and came out onto the patio.

"What's the problem, Mert?" asked Delaney. "Who died?"

Merton smirked at the remark, having never driven to his captain's home before.

"I need you to come with me, right now. I know we don't see eye to eye on a lot of things, but I put my career in your hands right now, it's that important. You need to come with me, and you need to listen to someone, because if I try to tell you, you'll think I'm out of my mind," Merton said.

"What is it, honey?" a female said as she walked behind Frank Delaney onto the patio. It was Frank's wife, Cynthia. "Oh, hi, Merton. Is everything all right?"

“Yes, Cynthia, everything’s fine. I just need to speak with your husband about a case. I am very sorry to be intruding like this,” said Merton.

Captain Frank Delaney wanted to be pissed off at this visit, but he just couldn’t be. He knew Merton. He knew how Merton would expect him to react if he’d ever just shown up unannounced at his home. Detective Merton Howard wouldn’t dare, and yet here he was, daring.

“You’re the only one I can come to about this, Captain. There’s no one else,” Merton said.

Captain Delaney looked at him, his arms built like bowling pins. If you put a sea captain’s hat on him you might mistake him for Popeye.

“All right, Merton. I’m not even going to argue about this. I’m sure you’ve got your reasons for dragging me out of my home on my day off,” said Delaney.

Captain Delaney said something softly to his wife. Merton was unable to hear what it was. He walked to Merton’s car and got in the passenger side. Merton walked around the front of the vehicle and got in.

Both men just stared at each other for a second, but it felt like minutes.

“All right, damn it, I’m here. What the hell is this all about? What’s going on?” said Frank.

“This is something I can’t tell you, Captain. This is something you need to see for yourself. You’d never believe me otherwise, and you’d likely throw me off the force if I did,” Detective Howard said.

"If this turns out to be a waste of my time, you can count on that. And I don't give out no fucking pens, either," Captain Delaney said, clearly irritated. "Do you know I was watching the game in there?"

"You just need to trust me on this," said Merton.

The ride to Helen Wilson's house was a very quiet one. There were no pleasantries on this drive, and Naugatuck wasn't big enough to make any destination become boring enough to begin a conversation just for the hell of it. As they pulled up to Helen's house, Captain Delaney looked at the front gate that said "Psychic Readings" and then gave Merton a look, that if it could kill, would have dropped Merton Howard on the spot.

"I hope you heard what I said about the pens. Not even a pen," Captain Delaney said. "Now, I gotta tell ya, especially before I kick your ass off the force, I am frigging dying to see what happens next here."

"Captain, you know me. You've known me a long time. When was the last time I ever showed up at your home on your day off? Do we barbeque together? Do our kids play?" Merton said.

"I don't have kids, but I do have a game on at my house that I'm missing while you're driving me to some fucking crazy place I really don't even want to know about, I mean…this is some sort of joke, right?" Captain Delaney said.

"No, this is not a joke. If I hadn't brought you here, I'd already be sitting in my recliner chair at home without a pen," said Merton.

This garnered a little chuckle out of Captain Delaney, the first Detective Merton could recall in years.

"OK, Merton, let's do this. I don't know what the hell is going on, but let's do it," he said.

Meanwhile, a car was parked about sixty yards behind the both of them as Evan Yastrzemski sat in his vehicle and watched what was going on, texting AC all the while.

"This is not good," Evan said to himself.

Both Detective Merton Howard and Captain Frank Delaney walked up the walkway to Helen's house, where she stood waiting for them, despite neither of them advising her that they were on their way.

"I've been expecting you both," Helen said. "Come inside."

Captain Delaney nodded to her politely as both men walked into her living room.

"Captain Delaney," said Helen. "I know why your detective here has brought you to my home, and what I'm about to tell you may be something you do not believe, or understand. He didn't tell me he was coming here, so what you're about to hear is coming from me. He and I had no conversation about your visit today, and up until about ten minutes ago, I didn't even know I'd have visitors today," she said.

"Okay," he said. "But how did you know we'd be showing up ten minutes ago?"

"Ah, yes, well, I gather that answer is why Detective Merton Howard has brought you here, to understand these answers. And more importantly, so that he does indeed get that pen."

Merton smiled as he put his head down.

"Pen?" said Captain Delaney, trying to understand how it was that Helen knew about the conversation that Merton and he had just had about how, if fired, Detective Howard wouldn't even get a pen.

“Captain Delaney, please come and have a seat at my table here. There are some things I need to tell you, and for whatever reason, I’m apparently going to need to be the messenger in this situation,” she said.

Helen looked at Detective Howard.

“This was the right thing to do, Detective Howard. You’re a good man,” she said.

Captain Delaney was losing his patience. “Wait, what the hell is this? What is going on right now that I’m not registering?” he said.

“Please have a seat here, Captain Delaney. Let me get you a drink, and let’s talk. I promise you’ll be back at home by the third inning. Your team is winning; you should be happy,” Helen said.

Captain Delaney wasn’t thinking about the game anymore. He was more interested in the next thing this woman, Helen Wilson, was about to say to him.

“Take all the time you need, Miss Wilson. You’ve got my attention,” Captain Delaney said.

Merton exhaled in a way that seemed to indicate he had a lot of breath stored in him, far more than he had breathed in.

CHAPTER TWENTY-FOUR

"You need to understand, Mauro, that this has been a collision that has resulted in nothing but success. I mean, this woman has literally earned us millions of dollars in just a matter of a few weeks!" said AC, looking and sounding like a little kid as he stood in front of his penthouse window. "It's the most unbelievable thing that I have ever seen!"

Mauro wasn't smiling.

"Oh, you're such a prick," said AC. "Can't you see what's happening here!?"

"What's happening here?" said Mauro. "Can I answer that question as your brother? Or can I answer it in a way that won't have me floating down the fucking river?"

Silence overcame the room, and the giddiness of AC had turned into a stoic look. He was no longer in a happy mood.

"What?" AC said. "What is it? You have something against making money? I mean, we go to guys every day that give us predictions on whose gonna win the fucking football game, soccer games, games we don't even give a shit about. And we let them bet our money on that shit. What is the difference here?"

Mauro walked up to his brother.

"AC, the difference here is that those guys know the inside and out of everything. They pay attention to details. They know the weather, they know if the players are in a feud with their wives, and whether that's gonna have some effect on their game. That's the difference here. What you're doing is walking in blind faith with a woman whose advice you fucking take, who is routinely visited by police. That puts us at risk," Mauro said.

"What cops are talking to her? I haven't heard any cops were visiting here," AC said.

"Well, I'm telling you now that they are. That's what you have me for. I'm the guy who makes sure you get to stand up here and look out your window pretending you're gonna see a fucking tree from six hundred damn stories high. I'm that guy. I'm the guy who makes sure your nights go smoothly while you play your instrumental fucking music or whatever the hell that is, and pretend you're not who you are. That's who the fuck I am," Mauro said. "It's my job to watch my brother's ass, it's my job to protect it. I do things you've made it very clear to me in the past that you do not want to know. That's my job, and I think I do it pretty fucking well."

AC seemed to compose himself a little, transitioning from gleeful to realistic.

"I feel like my arm is on fucking fire, been feeling like that all day. Anyway, go ahead, what do you got? What is it about this woman that is getting you upset like this? Normally when people make us money, you're all for it," said AC.

"I am, and Jens Maes of Belgium is that way, not some fucking psychic from Connecticut who charges $25 for a damn reading about your future. I mean, she sits at this table with all sorts of creatures and shit engraved into it like she's fucking Nostradamus, and people buy into this shit. Well, I'm telling you, I am not going to be one of these people, and we are not going to be one of those families who have worked their asses off to get to where we are to have this woman set our asses up. I mean, you tell me, AC; do you want to end up in fucking prison over this woman? Do you know anything about her? Do you really think we should put the fate of this family in the hands of someone because they called a few baseball games right? Because she told us days to rob banks, banks we've robbed before and look…here we still are, and we didn't even need a psychic to do it?" Mauro said. "This is your brother talking. Remember you have one, will you please?"

It had been a very long time since AC had been spoken to like this, by anyone. AC was not the type of person you preached to, and he certainly was not the kind of person who changed his mind when he had it made up. However, in this situation, hearing the words come out of his brother's mouth like this, he had to remember why he assigned Mauro as his right-hand man. It was, indeed, to protect him. Here Mauro was, protecting him, and he just wasn't listening at all. It was disrespectful.

AC walked over to his couch and sat down.

"Sit down, Mauro. Talk to me. Tell me what is on your mind," said AC.

"I'm just gonna level with you, AC. I've got some guys watching her," Mauro said.

"I've got no issue with that," AC replied.

"And I've spoken to our friend in Belgium, because I just wanted to make sure he was going to play ball with us, and I think I've got that all lined up nice for you," Mauro said.

"Well, so far I'm not seeing a big problem," AC said.

"So far there hasn't been one. But my intention is to keep a problem so far away that it's never one we need to deal with. That's what you pay me for, and as your brother, that's my duty," said Mauro.

"As well as your own ass," said AC.

"Should there be something wrong with doing that, too? I mean, you're the snake's head. You go down, we all go down. It's with every breath in my being that I make sure that you don't go down. And I am worried about the fact that you are walking into situations because of what some two-bit psychic says to you. I think it's dangerous, it's unchecked. You don't know if she's telling you the truth, or if she's just setting you up for a fall. Do you know she's had detectives going to her house? Police? They think she's got some fucking ability to solve crimes and find missing people," Mauro said.

"And what's the problem with her doing that?" said AC.

"The problem with that, AC, is that we commit fucking crimes every day," Mauro replied sternly.

And there was that pause again. AC pondered. His head leaned to the left, and while it appeared he was about to say something, he didn't. His head just switched to lean to the right.

AC stood up, now clearly in deep thought. Deep thought was never a place he liked to go. It's why he had the men working for him that he did, for the many years they had.

"I stopped looking for the trees, smart ass," AC said, not facing his brother. "OK, well, put some more people on her. I'm sure you've got a small army doing that already, but just in case, just watch her. You're gonna bug everything. Her house, her fucking clothes. Everything. I want to know her every move, and then you'll be more relaxed, and that'll relax me."

Mauro stood up.

"Boss, it is my recommendation that you no longer associate with this woman," said Mauro.

"I have received your recommendation, and *I* will decide when that day comes, not you, do you understand me? I have run this family for many years and I know what I'm doing, in case you have not noticed," AC said.

"Yes, but you are comfortable now. That's when they get you," Mauro replied.

AC threw a glass against the wall.

"Who the fuck is *they* Mauro? Who the fuck is *they*? I own *they*. *They* answer to me, I don't answer to them. And in case you haven't noticed, this family has survived everything they have tried to throw our way, isn't that true? For decades. They don't win against us. Now you do as you're told, and you go put buffers all around us by flying in men and bringing people over, and whatever it is you gotta do. But do not ever come up here to my suite and talk to me the way that you have this day, do you understand me?" said AC.

Mauro wished he'd shut his mouth. He didn't recall seeing his brother like this. He understood that it was he who brought up his concerns about Helen Wilson, but AC snapped, and snapped right in front of him. Mauro was his brother; he felt he was supposed to be looking out for him. At this moment, however, Mauro felt as if he was an outsider being told what to do, in the same manner that Luigi had. Suddenly, Helen Wilson had become the underboss, and she didn't even know it. Mauro just didn't know what to say.

"Listen," said AC, as he put his arm around Mauro. "Everything is going to be fine. You do what you need to do, and you let me have my own conversations with the psychic lady. I have yet to fail this family," said AC.

"Well, I heard some TV shows are doing segments about psychics, and yours is about to be a national face," Mauro said.

"Ah, fuck that. Big deal. I'm already a national face. Let people think I'm crazy. They'll think I've lost my mind and then they won't take me serious. Let that happen, and then they will all see how serious I am," said AC.

AC sat back down on the couch. His face suddenly looked wet, almost gray.

"Are you all right, AC?" said Mauro.

"Yes, I'm all right. Just go get me a drink of water real quick, and not from the sink. Bring me that shit the maid brings over," said AC.

Mauro walked over to the kitchen and poured water from a bottle of Evian, adding a few cubes from the refrigerator's ice dispenser. With his back to AC as he prepared his water, Mauro continued to talk.

"You know, boss, I know you think I'm a big pain in the ass, but you're my brother first, and I need to look out for you. That's all I'm trying to do. Isn't that what you want in a brother?"

No answer.

No answer.

Still…no answer.

Mauro turned around to see his brother, AC Nicolo, flopped over the arm rest of his couch, his tongue hanging out.

"AC!" Mauro yelled, as he ran over to him.

Grabbing the phone, Mauro called 911.

911 quickly responded to the call, but AC wasn't responding at all.

CHAPTER TWENTY-FIVE

"There is a fucking storm coming if he doesn't make it," Mauro said to Dr. Elmer Drake, an emergency room doctor at Mount Sinai hospital in Manhattan. "You'd best make sure he comes out of this."

Dr. Drake knew exactly who his patient was, but he also knew that he wasn't God.

"Mr. Nicolo, I can assure you that I know the importance of this man, especially to you. Your culture is one that believes in God; so does mine. So you need to let me do what I can, and the rest you need to leave to the God you believe in," Dr. Drake said, stretching to save his own skin.

"Good save, Doc. Do what you can; he means a lot to a lot of people," said Mauro. "I don't blame you for this, just do what you can do."

"Thank you. There's a waiting room that I have made arrangements to be especially for you and your family, as dozens of your family members are flooding the lobby. We're doing our best to accommodate your needs, and if there's anything you need, please do not hesitate to come see me personally," said Dr. Drake.

Mauro stood in the lobby, for the first time in his life feeling completely and utterly lost. Yes, he had many members of his family, but his brother was his entire family. AC was all he knew. Sure, he didn't like some of the things he would do, his fantasies about this psychic, all of it seemed a little sketchy to him. This, however, was not part of the plan. His brother lay on that bed hooked up to tubes and wires, and his face was unrecognizable to him.

"What the fuck happened to him? That's not my brother in there," Mauro said. "That is not who I was talking to just two hours ago!"

"Mr. Nicolo, your brother has suffered a heart attack brought on by what appears to be undiagnosed high blood pressure. It hasn't been treated, because he hasn't had a checkup in years. The last doctor that there's any record of him seeing died nine years ago. Your brother isn't 18 anymore; even twenty-year-olds have high blood pressure and don't even know it. We are doing absolutely everything we can do, and I know who you are, so believe me, if it can be done, it's being done."

Celebrities and even politicians swarmed the lobby of the hospital, eager to learn whether or not AC was going to make it, dreading the reality that if he didn't, it would be Mauro Nicolo at the helm of "The Family," and that, to all of them, was a very frightening thought.

Mauro walked out to the lobby as everyone there turned their head to him, awaiting some sort of word on what had just happened.

"Everyone, there's a room at the end of the hall that the hospital has set up for us to wait this thing out. I know some of you have kids, and for those of you who do, just go home. Someone will call you if anything changes. But right now, all we can do is wait. I am in command of this family while my brother is incapacitated, so any business questions should be directed to me. No move is to be made without my approval, and no one is to assume what AC would want you to do. You do nothing, no matter what instructions AC may have given you, unless you run it by me first," said Mauro.

This was important for Mauro to make clear, because if AC didn't make it, any given family member or associate could lean on the crutch of "AC told me to," and think they'd get away with it. Mauro was way too smart for that bullshit, and made it perfectly clear that no move would be made without his say-so.

A few of the rougher-looking family members got the hint, and their facial expressions certainly conveyed that they knew what Mauro was getting at, loud and clear. Self-preservation would dictate that they would all do exactly as Mauro had instructed them to do.

"The boat dock," said Luigi to Mauro, seemingly coming out of nowhere. "That's tomorrow night. AC said he was going to decide what to do, but now, what do we do?"

Luigi was clearly shaken up by this. He wasn't his uncle's favorite, but AC was all he knew; he was his god on earth. Every action he'd ever taken was an instruction from AC since he was 14 years old, and now he didn't know what to do, even with himself. Mauro, usually quite stern, tried to calm Luigi.

"Get a grip. Eyes are on you. Not everyone in this lobby are friends, and a few of them are here for reasons other than to shed a tear. I know who they are, and you do, too. You need to man up, and get ahold of yourself. Go down to that waiting room they set up for us, and I'll keep you posted. They are gonna bring down a few cots for those of you who intend to spend the night," said Mauro. "But listen, Luigi. I need you now. I need you to keep together for me, and we'll discuss the boat later."

The boat was a cargo ship that held millions in gold medallions shipped from a Swiss bank, along with antiquities and paintings, some Picassos and a Van Gogh. The contents were known, although Mauro didn't know it, because of a prediction provided by Helen. AC made Luigi swear he would not tell Mauro how he knew of the contents of the cargo ship, afraid that Mauro wouldn't believe it, and might refrain from assembling the right team.

"And the woman, that lady, she gave me an envelope. I don't know what I'm supposed to do with it. AC swears by her, and I don't know what I'm supposed to do with the envelope. AC made me go get it from her before he'd make a decision about what to do with the ship," said Luigi, clearly frantic, but trying to hold it together on some level.

"I know you love him," said Mauro. "Just go do what I said, and we'll talk about the psychic after I learn whether or not my brother is about to die in there. Sound okay to you?" said Mauro, a bit frustrated himself.

Taken aback by that reply, Luigi seemed to snap out of it himself, realizing, after all, that despite everything, Mauro was AC's brother. They grew up together, they loved one another.

Even though they were both murderers.

Luigi did as he was told, and rounded up the crowd of family and friends who stood in the lobby. Giving them all a hand gesture to follow him, they all followed like a herd into the room that had been set aside for the family of one of the most notorious mobsters in US history.

Mauro had a lot on his mind at the moment, and for the first time in his life, seemed torn between his brother laying in that room appearing lifeless, and the barge that would pull up to the dock the next day carrying a king's ransom. What would be floating into New York was worth far more than even a king.

Mauro picked up his cell phone about to make a phone call.

"I must be going out of my mind," he said.

Mauro walked down the hospital corridor, and as he saw Luigi steering the crowd into the room, walked up to him.

"Do you have this fucking envelope?" Mauro said.

"I do," replied Luigi.

"Is it on you now?" said Mauro.

Luigi reached into his pocket and handed Mauro the sealed envelope marked "AC" on its face. Not even Luigi dared open the envelope, consistently torn about whether or not he was dancing with God whenever he was given one to bring to AC. For the first time ever, he was now handing the envelope to Mauro, who he knew had no faith in Helen's abilities. Luigi, like AC, knew that there was something about Helen Wilson that was not of this world. Helen Wilson had powers beyond anything he'd ever seen, and was definitely a book not to judge by its cover. Her face lit up a room, and put at ease people who made careers out of never being at ease.

"That's all, Luigi. I'll take care of this," Mauro said.

Luigi nodded and turned around to walk towards the room that had been set up for his family.

"Luigi," said Mauro.

Luigi turned around, startled by what appeared to be the beginning of Mauro actually caring about his opinion.

"What do you think about what's in this envelope?" asked Mauro.

Luigi looked down, trying to inhale the question, as well as everything that appeared to be happening in the hospital. With a heavy sigh, he replied, "Mauro, I don't know much about this world. I know what we do. I know AC swears by this woman. If you're asking me if you should follow the advice in that envelope, if you're asking me as family, I say you should. You and AC are very different people, and we both know that who is in that room right now isn't AC. You gotta do what you gotta do, but I'm telling you, this woman is not like anything either one of us have ever come across, and this family has shown me a lot," said Luigi.

Mauro just stared at Luigi, a bit numb by the fact that Luigi answered him that way. He thought for sure Luigi would tell him to just tear the thing up and take that ship down.

"Okay, Luigi. Get back to the others. The cavalry has arrived and are on post," said Mauro, referring to about twenty "security" people he'd contacted to watch the hospital. You'd have thought the president had been brought in. Every health professional in this hospital knew they could be a target if they fucked this one up. Absolutely everything would be done to make certain that AC made it through this, even if it meant that he was drinking his dinner out of a straw. AC could not die on their watch.

Mauro walked to the lobby, now empty of those there to see how AC was doing. He sat down and looked at the envelope.

Sitting back in the chair, he looked at the envelope which was simply marked in black ink "AC."

"Fucking insanity," Mauro whispered to himself.

He tore the envelope open slowly, so as not to rip its contents, and pulled out an index card.

The card was blank, until he turned the card on its other side.

"No."

That's all that was written on the index card, a card that would have provided AC with his instructions as to whether or not his family would take down a barge worth potentially hundreds of millions of dollars.

"No?" Mauro said. "No?"

Mauro stood up and looked at the card and the envelope it arrived in.

"I don't fucking think so, bitch," he said.

Mauro's cut in this barge takedown would be in the millions as the underboss of the Nicolo crime family. And he didn't like the word no from anyone.

Mauro walked to the hospital garbage can and took one more look at what he was about to throw away.

"You may have got him, but you don't got me, honey. I'm no believer in your hocus pocus bullshit," he said, as he stuffed the card back into the envelope and threw it into a trash container.

Mauro turned away from the garbage can and began to walk away from it as he heard a loud thud, like the sound of a stick hitting a pan.

No one was there.

At least, no one that Mauro had the ability to actually see.

Mauro joined his family, and tomorrow he had a big day ahead of him.

CHAPTER TWENTY-SIX

Helen Wilson was feeling the pressure in a manner that she was not accustomed to. She went from being the psychic down the street who would tell you your future for $25, to now being on the hook to the biggest mafia figure in American history. Her neighbors, her friends, and everyone else she knew could be wiped out during a lunch hour by this powerful, well-dressed group of nothing more than thugs.

Helen was given a gift. She could see the future, and she could feel it. She knew that in this current situation, she was being forced to use a celestial gift for negative, and there was simply no way she could avoid doing as she was told if she valued her life and those she cared about.

"Just a mustard seed," she said to herself. "I have much more than a mustard seed," she repeated. "God, point me correctly. I don't know what to do. You didn't give me these abilities to do this. I know you didn't bestow these abilities on me to hurt people. Tell me what to do," she said, as she sat alone at her table.

She'd stopped giving readings at this point. There was nothing she could offer anyone while knowing she was being forced to aid criminals in conducting horrific acts of violence and theft. It was now about self-preservation, and the preservation of those in her life. Sandy Finnigan and her son were the closest people in her life. Standing up and looking outside of her window, she realized that she'd become somewhat of a spectacle.

Typically at 8:00 p.m. there wasn't a car parked on her road, just the typical cars parked in their respective driveways. Now, there were cars everywhere. And there were people in every single one of them. They had one purpose: Watching Helen Wilson.

"How did this happen?" she said to herself.

How it happened was an easy answer: she was real. It dawned on her that she was given a gift she'd never asked for, and it went from a gift she didn't ask for, to a fun trick at parties, to now being something she was forced to use if she wanted to live. It wasn't feeling like a gift anymore. It was feeling like she had to, and she wasn't sure how accurate her readings could be under these circumstances. She had a very bad feeling about several members of this family that she didn't know, or had even met. But she knew. Something was happening that shouldn't have, she just couldn't put her finger on what it was.

Helen was a bit startled as Sandy Finnigan walked up behind her. Helen jumped a bit, regardless of the fact that Sandy would also come and go as she pleased into Helen's house. Helen's house welcomed everyone who wanted to come over. She'd spend hours on that porch just smiling at anyone who walked by, an actual angel among them. She was good. She'd always be good, and yet this pressure that had taken over her had her acting in ways she didn't recognize. She was beginning to not know herself.

"Relax, Helen, it's just me," said Sandy.

"Sorry, Sandy. I'm just a little stressed out," Helen replied.

Sandy sat next to Helen and held her hand.

"Helen, you need to talk to me and tell me what's going on. You're not acting right. There's something you're not telling me," said Sandy.

Helen shot up straight in her chair, looking only forward. Slowly, her head turned to face Sandy.

"Sandy," she said.

"What, what?" Sandy replied.

"Don't ask me anything, please. Just take your son and leave. I need you to take Brett and get out of this state for a while, at least a few months," Helen replied.

"What? Wait, what about you? Why don't you come with us Helen? Let's get out of here for a while," Sandy replied.

"I can't. I can't go. I need to stay here for a while. It's not something I can tell you about, and you really just need to listen to me on this," said Helen.

"Helen, you're scaring me now. What the hell is going on?" Sandy said, clearly becoming frantic.

"The less you know, the better. Just go, tonight," she said.

Sandy shook her head. She'd seen this look of determination in Helen's face before. This wasn't a joke. It was time to get out of town. Sandy had seen enough from Helen to know when she was serious, and it was time to leave.

"All right, Helen. We'll go now. You call me on my cell if you change your mind," said Sandy.

Sandy turned and quickly hurried out of the house.

"Goodbye, Sandy," she said softly to herself.

Helen got up and walked over towards the living room sofa, a sofa that she'd had for years. It was far too comfortable to ever give up, and she slowly sat down on it, her dog Zeus laying in the corner as he always had. She grabbed the remote and turned on the TV.

Little House On The Prairie came on again, and once again, Michael Landon was crying about something.

CHAPTER TWENTY-SEVEN

The fog rolled in like the waves did during the day. It appeared that everything surrounding the barge that pulled in was soaked. As men who were employed by Carson Shipping scrambled for its arrival, there were men scrambling who didn't belong there.

And it was those men who intended to make certain that anything of value on the arriving barge belonged to them, at the direction of Mauro Nicolo. Sixty men had been assembled with the task of taking the twelve men hostage whose responsibility it was to protect that ship, along with various crew members, some armed. It was unknown to Mauro's crew the exact number of men on that ship, but most of the men onboard had been at sea for months, and were more concerned with seeing their families than whether or not the goods on that ship ended up arriving at their destination. None of them were paid enough to die for someone else's belongings, and it was that way of thinking that turned several barge arrivals into successful scores for the Nicolo family.

Mauro remained at the hospital, awaiting word on his brother's condition, and made a call to Luigi on his cell phone.

"Yes, boss," answered Luigi.

"Update," replied Mauro.

"Everything seems in order," Luigi replied.

"Listen, Luigi. I want you to be extra careful on this. I don't want any fuck-ups. You know what this means to me, and what it means to AC. So this is something you need to pay very close attention to, more than the others," Mauro said.

"Can I ask what the message from Helen was?"

"No," Mauro said, though he'd just told him what that message was, unbeknownst to Luigi.

"Okay, I understand," Luigi replied.

"I just want you to be paying close attention. I don't know how many guys they got over there, and at 3:00 a.m. it should be pretty quiet. There's a lot of noise over there, so if you stick to the plan, this should go nice and smooth, like it did last year," said Mauro, referring to the last barge heist his family was behind in Florida, that netted the family about $13 million euros, beautifully packaged in €100 bills

Most of the crew had never been privy to the contents of the containers, but the captain of this barge, a man named Juni Ortiz had been on the take for years. The problem was, whenever there were shipments of this size, or value, even the captain himself was kept in the dark. The arrival of security forces from Switzerland and several family members of the late Howard Hughes, who accompanied the paintings by Picasso and Van Gough, had all but spelled out its contents.

There was a lot of money on this barge, and Carson Shipping had become a little too comfortable.

"I'm going to go check on how AC is doing, but it's not looking very good so far," said Mauro.

"OK, Mauro. So this is a go?" Luigi said.

"Go," said Mauro.

Mauro ended the call and walked up to a doctor standing in front of AC's room, two nurses standing by his side.

"What's the word, Doc?" asked Mauro.

Dr. Kyle Evans stood with his clipboard, on call as the hours grew later in the evening. Mauro's mind was in two very different directions at the moment. One was on what was about to go down at the shipyard in about an hour, and the other was whether his brother was going to last another one.

"Mr. Nicolo, at this point, all we can do is wait. We've taken him off all medications that would prevent him from waking up, while we've attempted to give his body rest," said Dr. Evans. "There's nothing preventing him from opening his eyes at this point. All we can do is wait for that to happen. But rest assured that we've done everything, and I mean everything, to make him comfortable and to give him the opportunity to come back to us."

Mauro looked tired and helpless. Dr. Kyle Evans, well aware of who he was standing in front of, found himself a bit lost himself as he tried to comfort a man likely responsible for many of his past patients, some of whom were not so lucky to even have the fighting chance that AC was being given.

"If you'd like, I can set you up in a room where you can get a little sleep," Dr. Evans said.

Mauro just looked down towards the floor, shaking his head in disbelief that he was standing where he was.

"I just can't believe this, any of this," said Mauro.

“A lot of people don’t go to the doctor enough, Mr. Nicolo. If he makes it out of this, and I’m not sure he will, his entire lifestyle is going to have to change.”

This was hopeful advice from Dr. Evans, even though Mauro was smart enough to know these were likely standard speeches this same doctor had likely told many people who’d come through the doors of that hospital.

“I understand, Doc,” said Mauro. “And yeah, I’ll take that room.”

“I’m going to give you a little something to help you sleep, if you’d like,” Dr. Evans said.

“Yes, that would be fine,” Mauro replied.

“You’re no good to anyone unless you’ve got your strength,” the doctor replied.

The doctor walked Mauro over to the nurses’ desk and said a few words, the nurse shaking her head in response. The nurse walked around the desk and approached Mauro, placing her hand on his shoulder, and walked him to an empty room.

Mauro went to sleep, the darkness of sleep that became a welcome friend.

Mauro dreamed of his brother, laughing and smiling, as he recalled the both of them playing around in the yard of their long-passed parents. In the dream, his father was approaching him with a smile. Then suddenly he reached inside his pocket and appeared to be pulling out some sort of gift, with a smile on his face, a smile one’s dad gives their son. His father pulled out a gun.

Mauro woke up.

Banging and thrashing throughout the hospital, screaming voices came from outside of his room as rolling bed after rolling bed flew by the view about his feet, as he looked down from his bed to see what all of the ruckus was about. He shot out of the bed.

"Whoa, what the fuck?" he said to himself, wiping his face off, and the seeds that accumulated in one of his eyes in what felt like a nap, that was actually about four hours.

Four hours. It was now 6:00 a.m. Three hours had passed since Luigi and the clan were to take down the barge. Three hours had passed, and he hadn't a clue as to the latest prognosis of his brother, who continued to lay down at the end of the hall.

Mauro walked to the door of the room provided to him by Dr. Kyle Evans, and opened it to see what looked like a war zone in the hospital.

"What the hell is going on?" Mauro said to Dr. Evans, who quickly approached him.

"Chaos; but your brother is awake, and I'm going to send a nurse over in a few minutes to bring you down to see him. He's looking good," said Dr. Evans.

"Chaos? What's going on? What happened?"

"A shipyard robbery gone bad," said the doctor. "Dozens dead, dozens coming in, something awful. I gotta go. I'll be back to check on you and your brother later."

"What shipyard?" said Mauro. "WHAT SHIPYARD!"

Dr. Evans couldn't hear him as he ran to treat a patient, but Mauro already knew what shipyard. He knew the shipyard very well. Whatever happened while he slept wasn't as had been planned. Mauro had an alibi for whatever did happen, as an entire hospital knew the underboss of the Nicolo crime family was asleep in one of the hospital's rooms. That, however, was of little consolation to the rest of his family, who were now being distributed to numerous hospitals in the area. There was nothing that Mauro could do, and he'd slept right through it.

"Fuck," said Mauro.

A nurse walked up to Mauro and began talking to him, but the words sounded like another language to him. He couldn't hear her, and the lights of the inside of the hospital became brighter and brighter, spinning out of control.

"Sir!" said the nurse, snapping Mauro out of his daze.

"What? WHAT?" said Mauro.

"I'm here to take you to see your brother," she said.

Mauro shook his head.

"All right, all right. Yeah, bring me to him," he said.

Mauro and the nurse looked like they were walking through a crowded nightclub as multiple doctors and nurses scrambled to treat patients that were screaming, some making no sound at all. They both zigzagged through the hospital beds that seemed to be avoiding them as if they were in the middle of a highway with cars zooming past them.

"My God, this place is fucking crazy," he said to himself, though the nurse assumed he was talking to her.

"We're just beginning to figure out what happened. Apparently there was some sort of heist at the Carson shipyard, though you didn't hear that from me. A lot of fatalities, gunfire, just a terrible scene," she said.

Mauro, realizing she had thought he was talking to her when he was in fact speaking under his breath, looked at her and put his hand on her arm.

"Who? Who were the fatalities?" he said, startling the nurse.

"Sir, I have no idea. All I know is what I've just told you. Now will you please let go of my arm?"

He looked at his own hand, and the firm grip he'd had on her arm, and released her.

"I'm sorry," he said. "Where's my brother?" he said.

She walked him over to a room, and there was AC, sitting up. He looked as if he could have been in his own penthouse suite, in his own bed.

But he wasn't.

"Mauro, Mauro. Come in, I'm okay," he said. "Nurse, would you please give us a moment?"

The nurse nodded as she walked backwards out of the room, something immediately attracting her attention that had her running off to another patient.

"Do you know what happened?" asked AC.

"I have no idea. I've been here all night. The boys have been watching you, they made me grab a few hours of sleep, and I woke up to this place looking like a fucking zoo," said Mauro.

"Well, it is a fucking zoo in here right now, and I want to know why," said AC.

AC looked good for a guy who looked like he was on the door of the celestial just hours ago. But here he was, looking like he had just gotten out of the shower. He looked fresh, alive. He looked just fine.

"I have a pretty good idea about what's just happened," AC said. "I want some fucking answers. Did she contact you?"

"Did who contact me?" said Mauro.

"DID HELEN WILSON CONTACT YOU WITH A MESSAGE FOR ME!" screamed AC.

"Yes, yes. Fucking Luigi brought it to me in the lobby. I told Luigi to do what it said," Mauro said, fearing his own survival had he told his brother the truth.

"What did the fucking note say, Mauro? Tell me what the fucking note said," said AC.

Mauro looked shocked, in utter disbelief that this psychic had turned his brother into such a believer.

"AC, I did what it said. It was just some fucking white envelope with an index card, just a damn index card is all that was in it. It just had one word on the card and I told Luigi what it said!" said Mauro, as defensive as anyone would have ever seen him had it not been just his brother and himself in the room.

"What was that word?" demanded AC.

"It said yes. The card just had the word yes on it."

AC looked at him. For Mauro, it felt like he was being looked through. Mauro didn't dare say another word, resting on the lie he'd just told, and not wanting to feel as though he was being in any way defensive, regardless of the fact that this was exactly what he was being.

"She said yes? She said yes? How many people are fucking dead? Did nobody get away with nothing?" said AC, sounding like a cast member of *The Sopranos* despite the years he'd spent cultivating the image of a businessman. It was if someone had flipped a switch in AC, and pushed him back through time about twenty years. The AC of the streets was suddenly in this hospital bed, and he was livid.

Dr. Kyle Evans quickly stuck his head in the room.

"Is everything okay in here, gentlemen? I'm sorry, we're just inundated at the moment with multiple people flooding in, some police officers, some from the boat, the dock, the thieves…just everyone is coming here, and about three other hospitals. You're just gonna have to give us a little time. But I'm glad to see you awake, Mr. Nicolo," Dr. Evans, relieved, said to AC.

"We're fine, Doctor," said AC.

Dr. Evans nodded his head "OK" without saying the words, and off he went back to the chaos that engulfed the hospital.

AC looked back to Mauro.

"Mauro, you're telling me, right now, that she said yes. Is that what you're saying? Just a card with one word?" said AC.

AC had reason to believe Mauro, despite the lie. First, it was his brother. Second, Helen did only typically send him an envelope with a one-word answer on it whenever there was a prediction he sought. There was simply nothing other than Mauro's word to go by, especially since Luigi, who delivered that envelope, had never opened it.

Mauro looked his brother straight in the eyes.

"Yes, AC. The card just said yes," lied Mauro.

AC looked down towards his legs, suddenly feeling an overwhelming sense that he had been fooled all along by this psychic who turned out to be a fake, embarrassed by his own stupidity.

Even though Helen Wilson provided the correct prediction.

AC looked back to Mauro with fury in his eyes.

"I want that bitch taken down. Do you hear me? I want her taken down. I want that entire fucking street to feel like it just got hit by a fucking atom bomb. Everything we got, you use it; but I want her first. I want her to know what we're about to do to everyone she loves, and then you take her out," said AC.

Mauro just stood there, knowing that for the rest of his life he would have to live with this lie, and hope that there wasn't an afterlife at all where he'd one day have to see his brother again where that lie would be exposed.

"Yes," said Mauro. "Yes."

"Now get outta here, go get some information for me," said AC.

Mauro walked away to the door. AC yelled to him.

"And Mauro!" said AC.

Mauro turned around.

"Yes, boss," Mauro replied to his brother.

“Thank you for looking out for this family while I’ve been away, and for the record, I didn’t dream of shit.”

Mauro just looked at him and nodded his head, walking out of the room.

AC just sat there, a rage in his face that could give him another one of the heart attacks that put him in that bed.

“You’re done,” he whispered to himself.

CHAPTER TWENTY-EIGHT

Detective Merton Howard hadn't slept at all. He didn't even know the woman, and yet felt an overwhelming sense of concern about her well-being.

It was at 8:00 a.m. that he'd received a phone call from Captain Frank Delaney.

"You need to get up, right now, and come down here. The Carson Shipyard in Manhattan, it's a fucking massacre, Merton," said Delaney.

Merton shot up out of bed. He had a feeling something was wrong, but he didn't know why he was feeling the way that he did. He just knew something wasn't right. His feeling was that it somehow involved Helen Wilson.

"Captain, I need to go see Helen Wilson," he said, expecting the captain to freak out on him for even mentioning her name. But he'd met her too, and somehow he had not thought Merton to be the crazy person he previously had thought he'd become.

"OK, Merton. Go talk to her. But then I need you to get down here and help us out. See if she knows anything about this," said Captain Delaney.

Merton was surprised by Captain Delaney's response to this; it was unlike him. If Delaney hadn't met Helen himself, Merton would have been told to drop off his badge and weapon on the way.

Captain Delaney hung up the phone, obviously consumed with the events that had taken place at the shipyard. The tally had been taken, and what occurred in that yard had been assessed.

Seven crewmembers were dead. Two Swiss security guards were killed, two others wounded. Six US citizens just accompanying their valuables were wounded, and the Nicolo family had just lost six family members, while their friends from Poland and Bosnia lost twenty-three in an attempted takeover of a ship that carried, it was learned, more than $100 million in valuables. This was not necessarily any different from any other barge ship carrying cargo. The difference was that these valuables could be carried away in a single U-Haul, while the remaining cargo was a shipment of vehicles from various ports around the world by various foreigners moving to the United States. Antiques, Picassos, a Van Gogh, and euros made this shipment something that could have gone down in history as one of the largest barge thefts in America.

Someone had tipped off the cops, because they were waiting at that barge for this attempted heist. It wasn't Helen Wilson, who was more concerned with the ones she loved than a Picasso painting. Whoever it was would eventually be found out, and if they weren't already dead as part of the heist, they would be when AC found out who it was.

Merton Howard pulled up at Helen's house at around 9:00 a.m., this time with a patrol cruiser with him as backup. Once he'd seen that the Nicolo family had been to her house, he'd requested more coverage of the area. It wasn't illegal for any member of the Nicolo family to roam about Connecticut, and unless they actually took some sort of illegal action against Helen or anyone else, all they could do was watch. The city of New York was up in arms on this attempted heist, and the death toll was enormous. While it was not in the jurisdiction for Connecticut to investigate, it was only an hour and a half drive to Manhattan, and the two states were generally pretty cooperative with one another if they had any tips on illegal activity taking place. Helen Wilson had yet to really impact New York City outside of a baseball game, and besides the Nicolo family and Jens Maes, no one else really knew much about her.

There was a lot of action in Naugatuck, as it had planned to have a county fair on this day. But for Captain Delaney to call Merton in to his office, it was obvious that New York was looking at every angle. Could Captain Delaney have told New York officials of this psychic? How was it Merton would have been laughed out of the office for bringing up Helen, but not Captain Delaney? How was he able to explain Helen Wilson in a way that would have made Merton Howard unemployed if he'd done the same thing?

CNN was all over the attempted heist in New York City, and while anchor Anderson Cooper was in Naugatuck intending to meet with Helen as part of a show that would discuss psychic phenomena and its use in law enforcement, what happened at the shipyard had him doing live interviews via satellite with onlookers at the crime scene. Still, he had been preparing to interview Helen, his third psychic of the week. While Cooper or CNN had no information on whether or not Helen's services were being utilized by law enforcement, word of mouth had gotten out that she was for real, or he wouldn't be in Naugatuck at all. CNN intended to have a camera at the fair, which Helen Wilson would be attending to give readings to fair-goers for her usual $25 fee.

Helen had learned of CNN's interest in having her be a part of the piece Anderson Cooper would be doing when she was contacted by Boston-based medium Joanne Gerber. Gerber had been in communication with Helen several times, and she had attended events held by Gerber. Gerber's expertise was communicating with the "other side," and all psychics who shared similar abilities seemed to connect a little better with each other when they weren't working, as it was oftentimes difficult to have "normal" friends who weren't pleading for some sort of information. It's why most celebrities only marry other celebrities. It's hard to find something in common with an electrical engineer if you're being nominated for an Oscar.

Merton knocked at Helen's door, and she answered with the same smile that so many had become accustomed to.

"Can we talk, Helen?" said Merton.

"Yes, come in, come in," she said. "I was just watching TV, trying to relax a little today."

"I doubt you find a lot of time to do much relaxing, from what I hear," he laughed. "You're the talk of the town, with your appearance at the fair tonight."

"I doubt you drove over here to ask me about the fair," she said. "Why don't you have a seat?" she invited, as she sat at the table that no one seemed to realize had history beyond belief, as it was once the table where Nostradamus himself has written many of his prophecies.

Merton sat down.

"Would you like some coffee, Detective?" asked Helen, already knowing that he did. Helen had put on a fresh pot about ten minutes before Howard arrived, never pouring herself a cup.

"Yes, Helen, that'd be great," he said.

Helen brought his coffee, three creams, two sugars, exactly the way he always enjoyed it, without him ever actually telling Helen so. It seemed to be a habit of hers.

"Helen, I'm sure you've heard about the barge incident in New York City today. It's been all over the news. And I also know you're being interview tonight by Anderson Cooper at the fair as part of some segment they're doing over there. I've also, personally, witnessed Nicolo family members visiting you. Given our history, and frankly, my belief in your abilities, as well as my captain's, I wanted to know if you knew anything about this."

Helen was hesitant to talk about the matter, but she already had believed she'd been using her abilities in the wrong way, even though by the threats and intimidation tactics of the Nicolo family. She wouldn't lie as well.

"Detective, you have pretty good instincts yourself, and you know who these people are."

"Yes, I do," he said.

"The fact is, I find myself in a situation that I don't think I can get out of. These types of people are ruthless, violent, and have no love in their hearts. They profit through ego and criminality, and we live in a neighborhood that has never known the atrocities that they make a living doing," she said.

"Go on, Helen," he said.

"Merton, you're close to retirement, and these people are beyond our abilities to fight. There's an entire neighborhood here at stake, innocent people. There were also innocent people at that shipyard, and when AC Nicolo sent one of his nephews over to talk to me, I told them not to do what they intended on doing. If I told you about their visits, it was made clear that everyone on this street, everyone that I love, would be killed. I don't know what to do," she said.

Merton was rather shocked by her honesty. He'd expected her to be evasive, because it's what most people did when he showed up at their door. This sort of blatant honesty was just not typical to him.

"Helen, I want to bring in some people to protect you. I don't think you should be appearing at some fair. I think it's very dangerous for you to be doing, and now you're getting ready to go on national TV with a very well-known journalist, and you're inviting trouble," he said. "To you."

"Merton, the moment that you start doing that, people will die. I knew people were going to die at that dock today. It's why I conveyed the message to those people that they needed to stay away from this latest venture. No one had been hurt before, but someone in that family took a gamble despite my warnings, and the outcome is now known," she said.

Merton just sat there, drinking his coffee, unable to really respond to this in a manner that would make any real difference. Helen wasn't the problem here. The problem was the Nicolo family, and how a cop in Naugatuck, and now his captain, could make a difference. She was right about everything she had said to him. It was hard to protect federal witnesses in murder cases involving the Nicolo family; there was simply no way he would ever be able to make a promise to Helen that he could say with a straight face.

"Well, what are you going to do, Helen?" he said.

Helen stood up and looked at her table, running her fingers across the wood.

"I'm going to do what I do until I don't anymore. You can't stop this, Merton. These people are going to keep doing what they do. They've become a corporation of sorts, and they've got their supporters, even in law enforcement, who are very much inspired by monetary gain. It's hard to compete with it."

Merton just looked at her, unable to say much else on the subject.

"You know, Helen, I could make you go into protective custody," he said.

Helen stood up. "I need to get ready for this evening," she said. "I'm sorry that I can't tell you more. What I can tell you is, this is where I need to be if you really want to save lives. Putting me in protective custody, even me leaving by myself, would put many people at risk. I need to stay here, and you need to work with New York to bring that family down. I am no threat to you, but I gather you already know this," she said.

"I do know this, but you're a threat to yourself," he said, as Helen opened the front door for him.

"Merton, I'm not worried about me, and you shouldn't worry about me, either. I'm an adult, I can do what I want," she said with an adorable smile. "Now, have a good day, and try to get some sleep. I feel you haven't been getting much lately."

Merton smiled back at her, knowing she knew everything about him without him ever divulging anything to her. It was no use trying to convince this woman. She was unlike anyone he had ever met in his career, and as he stood in her presence, he knew that he was watching someone extraordinary.

"You are an enigma, Helen. I don't know what to make of you," he said. "But okay. I'm still gonna have a little patrol watching the house for a while, and there will be some presence at the fair tonight."

"Do what you have to do, Detective," she said, as she extended another smile before closing the door.

Merton just stood there, looking at the closed door. To its right was a sign hanging on the house that said "In my home, love grows."

He put his head down and walked down the stairs, back to his unmarked car.

CHAPTER TWENTY-NINE

"There is no death. There is no dying," said Helen Wilson, as she spoke with a group of about eighty people, some in the back eagerly trying to hear her every word. One of those people was CNN journalist Anderson Cooper, listening in with a cameraman to his left.

"The concept of a printed obituary has never been something I've believed in, because there is no conclusion date to a person. Once that person exists, they always do. Life does not end, it only changes. We are the universe, all of us, manifesting through a human nervous system that will one day deliver us to a new beginning. It is our goal to do all that we can to be the best we can, learning from our mistakes, and shaking the Etch A Sketch, if you will, of our pasts, in order to deliver our life lessons to those who might be able to avoid the pain we've all experienced in life," Helen said.

This was a little deeper than had been expected at a fair, but she had the attention of everyone who gathered around her, as other fair display tables all looked upon her, some a little irritated that she was receiving all of the attention.

"I am going to walk through all of you who have gathered, and if I tap you, you are to sit in the chairs to my right and wait for me to call you. The rest of you, please enjoy the rest of this fair, and one day we may meet again. There's simply no time to speak to you all individually, but I hope you all take what I've just said with you," Helen said, as she began walking through the crowd who gathered to see her.

Tapping several people, Helen also tapped Anderson Cooper, who wasn't expecting that at all. He was there to interview her, and never was it discussed that he could possibly be obtaining a reading himself.

"Really?" Anderson said.

"Yes, please have a seat with the others."

Helen got behind her table, which she had brought from her home to the fair. She never did a reading outside of its presence. She sat at the table with her stack of tarot cards that were held in a blue Asian-styled pouch. In addition, the signs of the zodiac were in front of her as she looked down to the engravings on her table. She had various small bags of powders that had meaning only to her, for her own reasons, including Sister Sage. The Latin word for sage, *Salvia*, means "to heal," and in French, it means "all is well." American Indians have Sister Sage in every ceremony. The smoke of Sister Sage will cleanse, purify, uplift, and carry prayers to the Great Spirit. Helen spread a little of it on her table.

A blue notebook with her handwritten notes also accompanied her at the table.

Helen, however, was not ignorant to the fact that out of every booth at the fair, uniformed police officers stood near hers. Anderson Cooper himself saw the officers, and could be seen whispering something to his cameraman, who stood next to him. This made the cameraman suddenly take a shot of the officers, who turned away when they noticed they were on film.

"Interesting," said Cooper.

Helen sat at the table and looked at it, rubbing her hand across it as the Sister Sage powder ran through her fingers, the powder remaining on her fingers as she called out to the first person she'd give a five-minute reading to. All totaled, six individuals were chosen by Helen.

"I'd like to ask that Nancy Gentile please approach the table," she said.

Nancy stood up and walked over to Helen's ancient table, sitting down across from her.

"Hi, Helen, I appreciate you choosing me," she said.

"You were chosen for me, Nancy," Helen replied. "I never choose anyone."

Nancy smiled and awaited Helen's next word.

"Is there something you'd specifically like to know?" asked Helen.

"No, I was just sorta hoping for a general reading," replied Nancy.

Spreading her tarot cards across the table, Helen pulled three of them. The cards were The World, The Page of Wands, and the Death card.

"A death card?" questioned Nancy. "What is that about?"

"It's not what you think, Nancy. It's actually just telling me that something that has been bothering you is about to end, and that you are about to begin a new chapter in your life, with love and hope. You are a good person and have been generous your entire life. It is appreciated, and you are always being looked after from this world and the next," said Helen. "I see many good things happening for you in the future, but you need to stay the course. You're also being offered something by someone, and you need to say no to it. It's not what you're going to want," said Helen. "Wait until the next opportunity, and give yourself more time to think. Don't be pressured by anyone to make a decision for yourself," said Helen.

Nancy smiled.

"Thank you, Helen. I appreciate hearing that from you," said Nancy.

Nancy stood up, and Helen called the next name.

"Kathy Vaccaro, will you please come up to the table?" Helen asked.

"You're going to be an easy read, Kathy. I'm assuming you're friends with Nancy, closer maybe," Helen said.

"We're cousins," Kathy said.

"I feel connected to the both of you," Helen replied. "Your concerns, the ones you've had recently, are all non-existent concerns. You are a mighty soul, and you are strong. Don't waste your money on something you were about to spend money on. It's not going to have the return you expect," Helen said.

Kathy seemed surprised by the reply, as she was about to do just that. She didn't even need to get into what it was with Helen, just accepted the answer.

"And you're worried about a family member. You need to know that our paths are made individually, and for a reason. Sometimes things happen that we do not expect, or do not want. When you get a weird feeling, don't blame yourself for it. That's why it's called a 'weird feeling' and not an '"exact feeling,' said Helen. "Don't beat yourself up about things you have no control over. When we think we can change certain things, we forget that we are not the One who calls the shots," she concluded.

“Thank you, Helen, I appreciate that,” Kathy said with a smile, then walked away.

Helen nodded to her. “I’ll be thinking of you and your cousin,” Helen said. “I’ll see you both again.”

Helen then looked to her right, and eye-to-eye contact was made with CNN journalist Anderson Cooper.

“You,” she said.

Anderson walked over to her, his cameraman following.

“No, leave the camera. This isn’t about television,” she said.

Anderson looked puzzled and sat down.

“Hello, Ms. Wilson. You want to ask me something?” he said. There was little doubt that attention was being brought upon them all, as a famous journalist such as Anderson Cooper was being read by Helen Wilson. But the mere fact that Helen wouldn’t allow it to be filmed gave him a certain amount of comfort. She wasn’t looking for a plug here, or media exposure; she actually had something to say to him.

“Anderson, it’s OK to tell everyone. You’ve had concerns about it, but I’m telling you that it’s not a big deal,” said Helen.

“What are you talking about?” asked Anderson.

“Just put out a statement and let it go. Don’t even dignify the topic with an on-camera discussion. You’re a journalist, and a great one, and when you’re not being one, that’s your life to live, and you should live it. Just put it out there in a classy way, and move on. No one will care about it. You’ve got a spark that exceeds society’s issues, and they’ll eventually get over those, too,” said Helen.

Anderson just sat there and didn't say a word.

"Is that all?" asked Anderson.

"That's all," she replied.

Anderson stood up slowly, eyeing Helen as if she'd been onto something, though he wasn't prepared to respond to the reading, or even lead her on to make her think he knew what she was talking about. He did know, however, but it would take him time to inhale what he'd just been told.

"Have a good life, Anderson. You're a good man."

Helen then went on to read the remaining three people, a man and two women who just wanted their horoscopes read and a tarot reading. Each lasted about five minutes, except the last one, which went for about twenty. A man named Emerald had a little more to discuss about his home life, and Helen gave him the extra time.

There were no negatives today, and Helen felt good about that. Following the readings, Helen gave Cooper, who acted as if he'd never been given a reading just minutes before, a ten-minute interview where she discussed the topic of what it was like to have the gifts she had, and she explained that the gift wasn't always a gift.

"It's never a curse," she said. "It is, however, sometimes exhausting, depending on who I'm talking to," she said.

The fair was a success, and as the darkness rolled in, the younger generation came out to throw baseballs at bowling pins to win Xbox games and ride rollercoasters. Helen was packing up to return home. Two men carried her table and chair into the back of a small pick-up truck that had brought it there in the first place, and off Helen went.

The uniformed escorts followed, and as one officer opened the passenger side of his cruiser, Anderson Cooper approached him.

"Off the record, why are you following her? Why are you watching her? Nothing she said seemed to indicate that she was working with law enforcement," Cooper said.

"Just following orders, Mr. Cooper," he said. "And by the way, we love the show at the station. You're great," the officer said.

"Thanks, man, appreciate that," Cooper replied.

Cooper just stood there and watched the patrol car follow the pick-up truck. Off they went.

"Weird," said Cooper.

Cooper got back into a small minivan using the passenger side to do so.

In the parking lot, however, were seven vehicles, all unmarked cars, but none of them police. Slowly, they began to follow Helen Wilson's vehicle, but far enough away as to not cause suspicion by the police car that followed the truck that was bringing both Helen's table and Helen back to her home.

At her house, the men brought the table back into the house, and Helen sat on her couch, exhausted from the day. Exhausted from everything.

Officers sat in front of her house for about an hour. One of the officers' cell phone rang. Merton Howard was on the other end of the call.

"Is everything good over there?" he asked.

"Yes, everything looks fine. Quiet out here," the officer, Chris Bourque, said. "Should we leave?"

"Just get out of the car, and each of you take a walk a few blocks around the house. If everything looks okay, then you're free to go," said Merton.

"OK, Detective," Bourque said.

So Officers Chris Bourque and James Boraczek both strolled the street, and after about twenty minutes, decided it was a little too quiet to hang around much longer. Boraczek sent a text message to Detective Howard with the update, and all assumed it was OK to leave the area. Everything seemed fine.

The street was darker than normal, given two of the street lights had "somehow" gone out in front of the home of Helen Wilson. It was no power outage. The street lights weren't just out, they were made to be out. And with the coast clear, eleven men walked towards the front gate, slowly entering the pathway. They walked up to the front door, and Evan Yastrzemski opened the door.

Helen was sitting in a chair that startled Evan, due to the fact that the chair was not where it normally was. It was literally sitting in front of the door, about four feet in, as the door opened. Helen had been expecting them.

Helen looked at Evan with a blank look on her face that suddenly displayed fear; fear and worry.

"You should be scared," he said with a heavy accent.

Helen shook her head. "Oh, Evan. I'm not scared for me. I'm scared for you. All of you," she replied.

Evan, startled by the fact that she knew his name, composed himself to do as AC asked, to rid this enigma from the situation.

The outside of the house was dark. A light on in the house came only from a small lamp on her reading table, so it appeared quite dark inside from the outside.

But then four flashes could be seen from the outside of the home, as men stood outside as lookouts.

There was silence as Evan was the first to walk out of the home, removing a silencer from his gun.

"It's done," he said. "Go."

They all walked away from the property and drove away. Across the street, and unbeknownst to them, sat Nick Riccio on his porch. He saw the flashes, but had no idea what they were. Seeing the men, he thought it best to not make a move, and was unable to make out a single face from anyone. As the men got into their car and left, he remained seated, looking into the home.

"Helen," he whispered to himself.

Suddenly, every light in the home turned on and began to blink. The front porch light also began to blink, and became so bright that it exploded on the patio door. Nick got up from the porch and walked down his front porch stairs and onto the sidewalk. Slowly crossing the street, he looked both ways just to make sure the vehicles those men were in were gone, and there was no traffic to speak of.

“What’s going on?” a voice yelled from behind Nick.

“I don’t know, but something is,” he said to Kevin Guard, a neighbor.

“I think we should go over there though, make sure everything’s all right. Her electrical just lit up, and something is not right.”

CHAPTER THIRTY

Captain Frank Delaney rang the doorbell at Merton Howard's home at around 5:30 a.m. Merton, slow to answer the door, as he was waking from what was a rare sound sleep, knew that no one knocked at his door that early for something good.

"What is it, Captain?" asked Merton.

"You didn't feel that?" responded Captain Delaney.

What Captain Delaney was referring to was a 6.0 earthquake that had rocked Connecticut, an occasion that rarely occurred.

"There's a lot of damage. I've never seen anything like this before," said Captain Delaney. "It's really unbelievable. You should see City Hall, it's just thrashed."

"Sure, sure," said Merton. "Come on in and let me wake myself up. Do you want some..."

Both Captain Frank Delaney and Merton Howard stopped in their tracks, as they saw that every piece of furniture in Merton's house had been turned upside down. All of the drawers to anything that had them were open as far as they could be without falling on the floor. The contents of those drawers remained intact. Every framed picture on the wall perfectly hung.

Upside down.

Both just stood there. Neither knew what to say. This was hard to process.

"Uhm...everything all right at home, Merton?" said Frank, trying to get a sentence out. "So, what might you make of what we're looking at, Mert?"

"I haven't a fucking clue," said Merton.

Both continued to just look at everything in his house.

"Gravity wouldn't exactly allow this sort of thing, I mean, right?" questioned Captain Delaney.

Merton just looked at him. He was at a complete loss for words.

"Helen," said Merton.

As Merton said the name, the contents of all of the drawers that somehow remained intact dropped to the floor. Both men ran out of the house like children afraid of the boogeyman.

Captain Delaney grabbed his cell phone and called headquarters as Merton just stared up the stairs of his own home.

"All units, I want all units over to the Helen Wilson's home, the psychic lady in town, all units. I want everyone available over there to see where she is," said Captain Delaney. "Everyone."

Captain Delaney looked at his weapon, something he hadn't done for a very long time, just to make certain that it was functional. It had been a long time since he'd unholstered his weapon except to be cleaned.

"Don't say anything," said Captain Delaney. "We'll both end up without jobs," he said. "Let's just get the hell over there and see what's what."

"I already know what's what," Merton said. "You go. I'll be over in about an hour."

"What are you talking about? I need you over there!" replied the captain.

"Frank, we're in over our heads here on this one. I'm not going over to that house, because I already know what you're gonna find. I just saw her, and I can't do it," said Merton.

Captain Delaney just looked at him.

"You don't know if you're right about this, Merton. You don't know if you're right about what you're thinking," Captain Delaney said.

"Captain, we just saw the contents of everything in my house completely intact, upside down. The moment I mentioned that lady's name, those contents fell to the floor. They didn't fall after I greeted you, they didn't fall when you knocked at the door. They didn't even fall when they were upside fucking down. I'm telling you, what I just saw…I know, I just can't see it."

Delaney just stared at the front steps for a moment, then turned back towards him.

"Okay, Merton. I'll go check it out. Either way, I'll see you over there in an hour. Maybe make it two if you want. If you're right, I'll still be there," he said.

"I'm right, and I'm sorry. That woman is an angel. I know I sound crazy saying it, but I'm saying it," said Merton.

Captain Delaney walked to his car and got in. With a last glance towards Merton, he drove away. Merton walked back upstairs, ready to fix his house of which the contents were completely turned upside down. Instead, he walked back into his home to see that all of its contents had been correctly placed. The drawers intact, their contents back where they belonged.

"I hear you, Helen," he said. "I hear you. And I'm sorry. We'll get those motherfuckers."

As police began to arrive at Helen's house, cars swarmed the street. Neighbors all poured out of their homes to see what was going on.

"She didn't cause the earthquake, did she?" said one old lady on the sidewalk.

"Just get back in your home, ma'am; and no one can cause an earthquake," said an officer.

Captain Delaney pulled up in his own private GMC pick-up truck as officers began approaching him.

"What do we got in there?" asked Captain Delaney.

A young officer looked at him and deadpanned the words.

"Nothing good. Whatever happened in there didn't happen long ago, but this was a professional hit," said the officer, who, judging by his paleness and tint of green, appeared to have just been to his first homicide scene.

"All right, well, do the rounds and get CSI over here," he said.

"They're already here," he said.

Neighbors who were getting wind of the news had begun to cry as reality was setting in that the sweet woman who read their fortunes was no longer there. The sense of loss on the street could be felt all the way down the road, as literally hundreds of people began to gather outside of the house. An officer began roping off the area with "CRIME SCENE" tape while other officers slowly moved back neighbors and other wandering eyes.

Captain Delaney just stood there, looking at the house.

"I'm sorry this happened to you, ma'am," he said to himself. "We will get these bastards."

A news truck pulled up, but was approached by officers and told to stay clear.

"What happened?" asked a female journalist.

Captain Delaney approached the woman.

"Captain Delaney," she said. "Can you comment on what has happened here? Isn't this the woman who was just at the fair? Isn't this the woman who does the psychic readings here in town?"

"I don't have a comment just yet. We just got here ourselves, and you obviously have those police scanners running full swing in your trucks. When we have something to tell you, we will. Right now we're at a scene that's just been declared one, so there's nothing to tell you yet," Captain Delaney said.

The woman nodded her head and walked back to her truck, a male cameraman by her side.

"Bastards," Captain Delaney said to himself.

Detective Merton Howard pulled up to the home a few hours later, waiting until the occupant he'd just spoken to had been removed. He was clearly shaken as he approached his captain.

"It was her, Captain. It was her who found those kids in Massachusetts, caught that guy. It was her," he said.

Captain Delaney nodded his head.

"I gathered," he said.

"Can I go in now?" the detective asked somberly.

"Yeah, you can go in there now if you want," Captain Delaney replied.

Merton walked up the pathway to the home, up the front stairs, and walked into the home. Looking at that table, he slowly walked towards it. On it sat a notebook, apparently notes of readings; but some pages appeared to be simple poems she'd written, simple notes to herself. He opened it from the middle of the book:

"A piece of me's in everyone that I have ever known, and they're in my heart. But after all is said and done, we hope we've saved the best, to make us all so happy because of those we've met."

He turned to the next page:

"The thing that makes me happiest is the radio all day playing all that country."

He turned to the next page.

It was titled "The Brat." It read:

"He came along before I was ready

That headstrong little boy

So full of fun & mischief

My little bundle of joy?

The one who never slept at night

Who scared the neighbors & everyone

With tales of those whodunits

And yard sales that left me with none

No dishes, knickknacks radio

No pans or Tupperware

No Daddy's guitar or Mommy's nightgowns

But you had eight dollars to spare

I learned in quite a hurry

To watch you closer till

You grew into a handsome man

Who drives me crazy still."

Merton was visibly moved as an officer came in.

"Everything all right in here, Detective?" the officer said.

"Yes, leave me be, please. I'm reading."

The officer nodded and walked back out the front door.

Merton flipped the page again to find another piece written by Helen called "Sometime."

It read:

"It sucks to be good at a lot of things

And to never excel in none

To always be in the running

But never the person who won

I wish in my life that at least sometime

I do something better than most

And at least do better than almost the best

And maybe the most of the most

I think I feel A #1 coming on.

It's only a matter of time."

Merton put his head down towards the table, not realizing that he was more upset than a seasoned police detective should be. A tear had welled up in his eye, and dropped slowly to the wooden table he sat at, the tear dropping directly into the eye of the engraved Taurus sign, the bull.

Composing himself, he opened a drawer to see notebook after notebook with various writings.

He was going to be here for a while.

Captain Delaney walked into the house.

"How are you doing?" he asked.

"I'm fine," Merton said. "Do we know if she has any family?"

"We're working on that now, and just contacted Sandy Finnigan, who worked with her. She was staying out of town for a while, apparently at the caution of Helen," he said.

“Really? She told her to leave town?” replied Merton.

“That’s what she said, and her son,” the captain replied.

Merton stood up from the table.

“This table, I want it secured. I want it placed in police custody until it’s properly claimed. This table, what she did here, it’s who she was. I won’t see it auctioned off if the stuff here goes unclaimed, or in some yard sale,” said Merton.

“I’ll take care of it,” said Captain Delaney.

Merton looked down at the table.

“I won’t retire until these bastards are brought down,” said Merton.

Captain Delaney walked closer to Merton and put his hand on his shoulder.

“Neither will I, detective. Neither will I.”

CHAPTER THIRTY-ONE

All eyes were on AC and Mauro has AC was wheeled out of the room that most in the hospital thought he'd never leave. A crowd of about twenty family members packed the hallway to see The Boss out, who was all smiles and shook hands with those who came to wish him well. Some were a little disappointed that he'd made it, but most were relieved that they wouldn't have to answer to Mauro.

Luigi stayed behind in the room to pick up a few things left behind in the emergency room that had almost taken his uncle. It was a miracle that AC had even made it through it. Luigi grabbed a shirt that was on the floor that appeared to be his uncle's, and a small leather bag that was either his uncle's or someone who had visited him, he wasn't sure, but took it anyway. He was used to taking things regardless of who it belonged to, anyway.

As he walked out of the room he was approached by a small Mexican man who appeared to be in his sixties. A stocky fellow, he extended his hand. Instinctively, Luigi began to extend his hand to shake it, but realized that the man was trying to hand him something.

"Mr. Nicolo?" said the janitor.

"Yes, what can I do for you," Luigi replied, sounding as if he'd just come out of a business meeting.

"I'm the janitor, and I was opening the lid on this can over here, and on the top of it was this envelope. It has your uncle's name on it, and everyone knows him around here, so I just wasn't sure if this was meant to be garbage or not," he said.

Luigi looked at what the man had in his hand, and was stunned by it. It was the envelope with Helen Wilson's instructions that was meant only for AC's eyes, but apparently was thrown away by Mauro. It was the specific instruction on whether or not AC should move forward with the barge heist. It was an envelope that could destroy a relationship.

"Thank you," said Luigi, taking the envelope. "I'm sure this just got mixed up with some other items we've been throwing away. I'll see to it that he gets it. I appreciate you coming to me with this," said Luigi.

Luigi felt his heart race as he held in his hand something that could potentially find Mauro in a river. He stuck the envelope in the inside of his jacket pocket and hurried to catch up to the entourage that followed AC out to a waiting SUV. Mauro looked at him running towards them.

"What are you doing?" said Mauro.

Luigi extended his hand out with the shirt and leather bag.

"Oh, there that is," said Mauro, indicating that the leather bag had actually belonged to him.

"That's not my shirt though," said Mauro. "And it's not AC's. Just leave it."

Doing as he was told, he put the shirt that apparently belonged to no one on one of the empty visitor chairs as he exited the hospital.

In the SUV sat Luigi, Mauro, and AC sat in the front passenger seat as Carl "The Bean" Giordano took to the wheel. It had been a long time since Carl had played chauffer to anyone, as he spent most of his days doing the hit-man work for AC when someone needed to be removed from the world as we know it. Tensions were high at the hospital, given that word was getting out that AC had survived, so Luigi had decided it would be best to have Carl pick his uncle up to make sure it stayed that way. Two cars in front of AC's SUV and seven vehicles behind it were now delivering AC back to his penthouse suite.

"We really need this many cars? It looks like a fucking procession," laughed AC. "Doesn't everyone know I survived?"

Everyone laughed.

"Next thing you know we're gonna pull into a fucking cemetery," continued AC, seeming in very high spirits for a man who just realized the shipyard heist was a bust, and that several of his family members remained in that hospital's morgue as a result of it. It was as if nothing had ever happened, but when AC was settled again and began to think, the barge would be on the forefront of his mind.

For Luigi, he just sat there, not really hearing anything at all. The conversations in the vehicle seemed to be just noise as he wondered what secrets were held in the inside pocket of his suit coat. How would Mauro react if he knew he had it? What was on the inside of this envelope that he himself had yet to read? If it said something contrary to Mauro's instructions, how would AC react to it? Did Mauro lie to AC? He just didn't know, and he wasn't sure that he wanted to know. There was just a sickening feeling in his stomach.

Realizing Luigi was being a bit quiet, AC leaned around his seat and looked at him.

"What's wrong with you? I wasn't paying you enough?" asked AC, as again the passengers of the vehicle burst into laughter.

"Nothing, boss, it was just a little scary, that's all. A lot was up in the air. I wouldn't want to feel that way again," said Luigi.

"Well, someday you will have to for real, all of us will. Consider that a rehearsal," AC said, which strangely again had others in the vehicle laughing at the comment.

"Well, I'd just as soon you were in your penthouse running things," Luigi said.

This comment brought silence, and a direct look by Mauro. Mauro wasn't about to comment on the remark, but was clearly offended by it.

"We're all just glad you made it outta there," said Mauro. "We're glad you're back. Fucking technology these days, eh, boss?"

AC looked at Mauro, just giving him a smile.

"Yeah," AC said, then looking to Carl. "Carl, I'm fucking starving. Call the building and tell them I want some food brought up there, some seafood. Every kind of seafood."

Luigi actually had something to say.

"AC, I think you shouldn't do that."

For the first time during the drive, the car went silent. AC leaned over to see Luigi in the backseat again.

He didn't say a word, simply expecting Luigi to follow up from that remark.

"I'm just saying, AC, you just dodged a bullet. I read some stuff about seafood, and it's got that cholesterol shit in it. It's not good for you, that's all I'm saying," said Luigi.

AC looked at him and smiled. It had just occurred to him at that moment that someone actually gave a fuck about him. Despite his inner feelings, he was still the boss. What he would respond with to Luigi's comments were not what he internally inhaled from Luigi's remarks. Compassion had been foreign to AC for quite some time, and it wasn't anything he dished out often, either.

"Hey, I'll eat whatever the fuck I want. It's my life," said AC.

Carl looked at AC. "Ah, give the guy a break. He's looking out for you, shit," he said.

"Yeah, well, I don't need nobody looking out for me. I can look out for my own fucking self. I don't need no nutritionist in the backseat, all right?"

AC turned to Luigi again and gave him a wink.

Luigi just sat there, deciding that for the rest of the ride he'd keep his mouth shut. Mauro gave Luigi a quick look as well, not quite sure what to make of him. Mauro still wondered if Luigi might have taken a look at Helen's prediction before handing it to him, but he was giving him the benefit of the doubt that he hadn't. The envelope was, after all, sealed when Luigi handed it to him, and he felt he had Luigi pretty much in check enough to instill enough fear in him to not dare open something that wasn't addressed to him.

Unfortunately for Mauro, Luigi had just become the underboss due to a letter addressed to AC that sat in his jacket pocket, a fact that could lead Mauro to off him just for not telling him the janitor handed it to him. That time had passed. It had been about twenty minutes in unusually light traffic from the hospital that Luigi could have, or should have, alerted Mauro to that fact already. Just Luigi having an opened envelope that he hadn't even read the contents of could have him killed. Luigi had a decision to make, and if it was ever his intention to hold that envelope over the head of Mauro, he'd best do it from far away. And the prediction had better not have said to go through with the heist. Even if it did, the moment Luigi took it upon himself to "forget" to give that envelope to Mauro would be the end of the line for him.

On the other hand, Luigi knew that the fast track to the high suites in AC's building could lay in that envelope.

But it would also lead to the end of Mauro, and AC had proven in the past that blood was not thicker than water when it came to betrayal. Mauro knew this as well, and the only one truly disappointed by AC's survival was him. They were brothers who remained loyal, but that heist cost many lives, was a complete failure, and all of the lower, but still competing crime families knew that it was the Nicolo family behind that heist. They were not happy to have mud on their face, but that's exactly what they had on it now.

At AC's building, his security team had been alerted long before they left the hospital that he was coming home. As the SUV pulled up, AC was escorted back to his penthouse, where he just sat on his couch and reveled in the view of the seafood that was spread across his living room table. It had everything. Calamari, lobster, crab legs, scallops, and every dip one could think of to enjoy with the delectables.

"Hey, Mauro, go get the keys to Luigi's car, and give it back to him," he said.

"Absolutely," said Mauro. "You got it."

AC looked at Luigi as Mauro left the room. Mauro was still a little uneasy about leaving the two of them alone until he knew for sure what, if anything, Luigi might know about Helen Wilson's prediction. AC hadn't a shred of thought as to whether or not Luigi had any knowledge of it. Why would he? It would be Mauro's call, not one of his nephews collecting money from the local mom and pop shops who would be responsible for such actions, like for instance, attempting to heist $100 million off a barge.

"Anything you want to say to me, Luigi? Anything bothering you?"

"No," said Luigi.

Mauro returned to the room with Luigi's keys, dropping them on the floor as Luigi said the word 'no.'

"Here you go, Luigi. Have a good night, and thanks for your help. We'll remember it," said Mauro.

"We will," AC agreed.

"Of course," Luigi replied, as he stepped into the elevator that would bring him back to his beloved Mercedes Benz.

Mauro looked at AC as the elevator door closed.

"I got a call from the lawyers, and we're gonna have to talk to some pigs at some point," Mauro said. "You got yourself an alibi, as do a few of us. Some of our family members don't."

AC looked at Mauro with a slight glare of uncertainty himself.

“Some of our family members don’t have an alibi because they’re fucking dead, and I want to know why that is,” AC replied.

“You don’t need to worry about that. We will find that out,” said Mauro.

“And I got a text on the way here. Our friend in Belgium is setting up a meeting with the Chinese over there in Chinatown. We’re gonna need to do something nice and low-key to make that all happen. I think you’ve handled that well, but you gotta keep me a little more in the loop on this stuff. I have ears everywhere, and I don’t want to have to use them when it comes to my own brother, understand?”

“Absolutely, boss. I always tell you the truth,” replied Mauro.

“I know you do,” AC replied. “I know you do.”

CHAPTER THIRTY-TWO

Merton Howard just stood in front of the house, feeling a sense of sadness he had never felt in his entire career as a detective. He'd seen many crime scenes, but this was just one that he couldn't bring himself to be present for. He knew that the Nicolo crime family was behind this, and he also knew that trying to interfere with an investigation that involved New York was going to be a challenge. Sure, New York State and Connecticut had been amiable to one another, not having any real issue with sharing information. This, however, was different. New York was up in arms over the attempted heist, and the frustration only grew for the New York City Police Department knowing that the head of the snake had been sitting in a hospital room with an iron-clad alibi. Mauro Nicolo had that same alibi.

Detective Merton Howard was very angry about this case. This woman had saved the lives of many, and her reward was that a bunch of cowards took her from this earth. There wasn't a person who lived on her street who hadn't been the beneficiary of one of her smiles, and those smiles made your day. In many ways her innocence was like a child, but she was gifted in many ways. As he recalled many of her writings, he pondered upon the remarks she wrote that seemed to insinuate that she hadn't done enough in her life. Merton thought of this absurdity as he pondered the many lives she had changed, the lives she had saved, and how this woman would ultimately help bring down a corrupt organization if it was the last thing he ever did, while knowing it could indeed be the last thing he ever did.

Flipping an ink pen over and over while standing in front of Helen's house, he ground his teeth at the thought that AC Nicolo, who he'd learned was now sitting back at his fat penthouse condo, was likely behind this entire thing. CNN aired the piece on Helen, who was interviewed by Anderson Cooper at the fair on that evening. The entire situation had just depressed him like no other case that he'd ever been involved in.

Looking up to the sky, he was struck by how the stars appeared brighter than he had ever recalled seeing. They seemed closer than he remember them being. Some stars had what looked like spikes that never ended, their ends disappearing into the endless space above him.

Sandy Finnigan approached him, having returned home after the news of Helen. Brett, her son, stood by her side.

"This was a crying shame, sir," Sandy said.

"I know it was, ma'am, and we'll get those responsible for this," he said.

Brett looked up at him.

"Yeah, but it doesn't bring her back," he said.

Merton looked down at the young boy.

"No, son, you're right. It doesn't bring her back. But you know, I never really believed life ended, only that it changed. I think she's right here watching us all, right now," he said. "This woman was special, like no other," he said.

An unexpected wind blew by the three of them, a gust that seemed to come from nowhere. Sandy just looked at Merton Howard with a mixture of sadness and anger.

"You know, I know who did this. I know it was those Nicolo hoodlums. They'd been harassing her for weeks now," she said.

Merton just nodded his head up and down.

"That seems to be the general feeling. But proving these things is always a different matter," he said. "But we will."

Merton looked up at the sky. "Look how bright those stars are tonight. Have you ever seen the stars so bright? Some of them just look like little patches all stuck together. It's really something out here," Merton said.

"It's Helen," said Brett. "She can do things."

Sandy just looked at her son, then at Merton, and decided it was time to leave Merton to his work, if you could call what he was doing work.

"I miss her," said Sandy. "You get these bastards."

She turned around with Brett, holding him close to her by his shoulder as she somberly walked back to her home. Zeus, Helen's dog, walked alongside them, back to his new home after they'd taken him in. Merton just watched.

"I will," he said softly to himself, out of the reach of their ability to hear him.

Pulling up to the curb was Captain Frank Delaney, who had been unable to reach Merton by phone for the last several hours. While various patrol cars lined the street, his intention was just to watch Helen's home.

He had no expectation of anyone pulling up to scope out the place, he just wanted to be there. He just felt like he wanted to be there.

"You're out late, Mert. What are you still doing here?" he said.

"Oh, I'm just watching the place. It's just hard to believe. I was just talking to her, and everything seemed fine," he said.

"Typically things do before they aren't," Delaney replied. "This is what we do, Merton. I try to tell most of the guys not to get emotionally attached to people for this reason."

"No," Merton said. "She wasn't one of them. You saw my place; there's something going on here," said Merton.

"Are you suggesting she caused an earthquake, Merton?" Captain Delaney queried.

"I'm just suggesting it's the beginning of what we had the privilege of witnessing. I think that family has been running New York for a long time now, and it's time that someone went after them," Merton said.

"Yeah, well, most of those who have didn't really live talk about it, Merton. Those people wipe out someone every day, and there's even judges out there afraid to piss them off. Technicalities that have been tossed aside in random burglary cases were the same technicalities I've seen those judges let them walk on. They have a lot of people scared out there, because they don't just go after you. They go after everyone, and there just aren't enough witness protection programs out there that could possibly fit all those we'd need to make vanish in order to nail these guys," said Frank.

"Yeah, well, I appreciate you coming by. I'm going to do what you've just said, and I'm gonna get out of here. Going back to that house is a little strange for me. I keep hoping I'll see her. It's the strangest thing," he said.

Captain Delaney looked a little concerned by that remark, and reached into his pocket to pull out what appeared to be a prescription bottle.

“Go home, take these when you walk through the door, have yourself a drink, and try to get some sleep,” said Delaney. The pills were a prescription medication known as Clonazepam, which was an anti-anxiety medication.

Merton grabbed them. “Dealing drugs, are we?” smiled Merton.

“Yeah, don’t tell no one,” Captain Delaney said. “And ya know, Merton…I had you pegged wrong. I’m sorry, truly. I know you’ve taken a lot of shit from me over the years, and you probably would have taken a lot more if I hadn’t seen what I’ve seen with my own eyes,” said Delaney.

“You know, there’s something I didn’t tell you. When I walked back into that house, everything was right-side-up again. Even the papers that fell on the floor were perfectly placed back in the drawers as if they had never been moved,” Merton said.

“Truth be told, Merton, I’m gonna be just fine pretending I didn’t see it for myself. I enjoyed life a little more when I just thought you were-”

Captain Delaney stopped as he looked to the sky, twelve streaks of light slowly heading towards earth. Merton, too, looked in amazement.

“What the hell is that?” said Merton.

“I have no idea,” Delaney replied.

Flipping out his cell phone, he made a phone call to dispatch. A female voice answered the phone.

“Cindy, it’s Captain Delaney. I want you to have a few units check out…” he stopped. “Hold on a second.” Cindy was a dispatch operator for more years than Captain Delaney had been a captain. He looked to Merton.

“What do I tell her to have a few units look for?” pondered Delaney aloud.

The patches of stars seemed to be brighter than the others that surrounded them. The patches formed twelve streaks of what looked like very slow-moving lighting, as if something were aiming at the earth beneath it. The Constellations. Celestial. This was something else.

“What do you make of that?” Delaney said.

“Meteors? Satellites?” replied Merton.

“That many at once?” the captain replied.

“I don’t know. But it sure is something, whatever it is,” Merton said.

Captain Delaney got back on the phone with Cindy.

“Hi, Cindy. Contact the Air Force to see if they’re picking up any incoming debris, satellites or something. Call me back,” he said, as he hung up the phone. As he did, you could faintly hear Cindy’s voice say, “Debris?” as the phone call was ended.

Merton and Captain Delaney knew that something was happening in Naugatuck the likes of which neither of them had ever seen. There was no way of explaining the events of the past several days, and no one that they could speak to about it besides each other, or they’d both end up in a nuthouse.

“I think I’m gonna take these pills and try to pass out,” said Merton.

Captain Delaney shook his head. "I think I'm going to get home as fast as I can and pretend that all this isn't terrifying the shit out of me," Delaney replied.

Merton smiled. "Yeah, well. Good luck with that. If you find out what any of that is, I sure would be interested. Hope it's not some shuttle that's gone to shit," Merton said.

"Whatever that is, twelve is a lot. I'm betting on a satellite. Take it easy tonight, Merton," said the captain, as he walked to his truck.

Merton just stood there and looked at the lights. They were endless streaks.

"Hey, Captain!" said Merton, as his boss got into his pick-up. "That table, where is it?"

"I put it in the evidence room, in its own cage at the precinct," he replied.

"I want to come look at that tomorrow, if that's all right. Might be something to it," he said. "And her writings, there are some questions I have about them."

Captain Delaney just looked at him. "Merton. Clonazepam. See you tomorrow," he said. He pointed to the streaks of light. "That's all probably some balloon or military test."

"Probably right," said Merton.

Captain Delaney got into his truck and drove away. Merton also got into his vehicle and just sat there, looking at the beautiful streaks of lights, some of them appearing to be different colors.

He started the car and drove off.

Frank Delaney's cell phone vibrated, and he answered the call. It was Cindy from dispatch.

"I just spoke to Lieutenant David Athens, and he stated there's been nothing on radar that would indicate there is anything out of the ordinary coming from the sky. I've also not received any 9-1-1 calls, which I usually get a dozen of when anything remotely blinks from up there, especially from the old ladies," she said.

"Really? Nothing? They don't even have a visual?" Delaney.

"Captain, I just went out there and looked myself, and I don't see a damn thing. Sounds like you guys need a little sleep," laughed Cindy. "Trust me, I'm all about UFOs. I watch all the stories, and this one time I saw a show..."

Delaney had heard enough, and wasn't about to allow Cindy to do what Cindy is known for...talk forever.

"Thank you, Cindy. I've got to go right now, but thanks for the information," the Captain concluded.

"OK, I'll speak with you later, Captain. Take it easy, you two," she said.

CHAPTER THIRTY-THREE

AC and Luigi sat at an old Chinese restaurant located in Chinatown. None of the mobsters who arrived to meet with Michael Zhang Wei had any intention of eating the food there. The appearance of a dead chicken hanging in the window, head intact, was enough to curdle the stomach of AC Nicolo on its own.

Michael Zhang Wei knew he was taking a risk just speaking with the Nicolo family, but Jens Maes had a way with words. They all decided that meeting was not an issue, so long as it didn't get back to Michael's counterparts in China. If word did get back, it could always just be chalked up to the Nicolo family visiting the restaurant. Still, Michael didn't believe it would be a believable excuse, knowing the lavish lifestyle of the Nicolo family in general. It would be one meeting in order to coordinate an individual in London to act as an intermediary between the Nicolo family and the Zhang Wei organization, without either of the two knowing who the client was. Mauro stayed home for this meeting, feeling as if his concerns were paranoia as it related to whether or not Luigi knew something he shouldn't, but also because AC wanted to do a little digging himself by talking to Luigi alone. AC was great at making Mauro feel like everything was fine.

This was all going to be a bit tricky, but tricky was the line of work they'd all been in for years. In fact, they had all pulled many tricks over the years, tricks that had cost hundreds their lives, and built them an empire that no law enforcement agency had ever been able to penetrate. Of course, having control of law enforcement and politicians from every country they conducted business with made that issue much easier to deal with as well.

Evan Yastrzemski had had a busy last couple of days. He'd rid the world of the psychic, per the instructions of Mauro. His entire network had been surrounding the hospital as AC sat inside, not because they cared, but because AC signed the checks. No one is eager to have Mauro Nicolo take over this family. Evan sat at the front of the restaurant, keeping an eye out for whoever may be disappointed about AC's survival. A few of Evan's compadres stood outside of the restaurant, chatting it up with a few of AC's men and one of Michael's men. This restaurant wasn't typical, given any cook could grab a machine gun as fast as a knife to make Kung Pao chicken. AC had no problem with the Kung Pao part, he was more disgusted by the chicken part, hanging in the window.

Each, however, respected one another's culture. No one would ever say a word about their disgust for one another, and Evan's clan didn't seem to have an opinion, much less an emotion, about anything at all.

AC just stared at Evan as he sat at the table, as Evan nodded to his buddies outside of the window. AC was looking at the man who ended it all for a psychic that he really believed in, and his general feeling about the entire situation, all of which occurred while he was in a coma, was that something didn't feel right about what happened. He knew Mauro didn't like her, and the first thing that happens when he's not in control is she suddenly provided a prediction to Mauro that got a bunch of people killed, and the FBI was now sniffing around his ass, despite his alibi of having been in a coma. That's generally a pretty good alibi.

Luigi sat at the table and watched AC looking at Evan, feeling guiltier and guiltier about the fact that the original envelope that came from Helen still sat unread in the glove compartment of his recently retrieved Mercedes Benz. Luigi himself knew that once he opened that envelope, everything could potentially change within his family. Something told him it would say something he didn't want to read, and brought back the memory of him asking Mauro in the hospital if Mauro would tell him the prediction. He remember Mauro told him 'No,' but now wasn't sure whether or not Mauro was answering his question, about whether or not his uncle would tell him what the prediction was, or if 'no' was in fact the prediction itself. What Luigi wholeheartedly believed, because he'd witnessed it with his own eyes at the ballpark, was that Mauro had made a very bad decision that cost everyone their life.

"Hey, Evan," said AC, getting his attention from his through-the-window conversation he was having with one of his friends. "Come here a second."

Evan walked over to AC, who was sitting at the table with Luigi, awaiting Michael to come on out from the kitchen so that their meeting could begin.

"How you doin'?" asked AC.

"I'm all right. How are you doing? Ticker working better?" said Evan.

AC smiled at him. "The ticker's working fine, my friend. I want you and your boys to go check out the psychic's house, make sure there's nothing there that could come back to us," said AC.

"We never leave nothing behind," said Evan.

"Still, it'd make me feel a lot better, and the request is on the clock," AC said, making it clear that he didn't expect Evan to do anything for free. "And your payment for that thing you did for us a few nights ago, it's where those payments go."

"Those payments" go to a locker at Union Station, and his payment was for $150,000 in cash.

"Thank you, appreciated as always," replied Evan.

Evan walked out of the restaurant, clearly gathering up his associates, who headed off. AC's three men remained outside of the glass door.

"Luigi, I wanna ask you a question, and I don't want you to lie to me. You'd never lie to me, right?" AC said.

Luigi felt the fear in his stomach. It was the question he'd been dreading since the janitor approached him in the hospital with the envelope that he himself didn't dare read.

"How do you feel about the decision to move forward with the thing that happened at the water?" AC asked. The water clearly meant "The shipyard," but AC never knew when he was being tapped, and wanted to be as vague as possible, though he might have done a little better than "the water" in referencing the shipyard heist.

Luigi just looked at the table, readying to answer. AC could see he was having difficulty answering this question.

"Never you mind, Luigi. I already know. What I'd really like to know is what Helen gave you, what exactly she wrote in response to the question I had you ask her before that all went down," said AC.

"I never read your mail," said Luigi. "I would never do that unless you told me to. You ask me to pick something up, I never know what's in it."

AC nodded his head "OK" without saying the words, but mouthing them.

"OK, well, let me be more direct, because I don't wanna play any fucking games. What happened to that piece of mail?" AC said.

Luigi was now in the position he feared most. This was not a question that he wanted to answer.

"That, just being honest, was thrown away. Mauro read it and he threw it away," Luigi said, hoping that'd end the topic.

Fat chance.

"How do you know it was thrown away?" his uncle replied.

Luigi heard the word "FUCK" in his brain without saying the word. At this moment he was feeling as if he was being grilled by police. AC, he thought, was interrogating him. Lying to AC could mean something very bad. For all he knew, AC could have had his car completely checked out while he was sitting in the restaurant. It was a really stupid place to put it, because Mauro could have done the same thing. The mere fact that Luigi was still alive meant that it just wasn't something Mauro had thought of, or at least, thought Luigi would be stupid enough to leave in his glove compartment.

"Listen, boss, I can't lie to you. But what you're asking, if what you're thinking is true, and I have a pretty good idea of what you're thinking…it could kinda change things. Very bad things could happen, and I'm wondering that, since what's done is done, if we should just let this one go. No answer is gonna be a very good one. Still, to answer your question truthfully, a janitor approached me with it when he saw your name on it, and told me it was sitting at the top of a trash can he was cleaning, cuz that's what he does, he empties trash and shit," said Luigi.

AC didn't share the same feelings as his nephew. He liked Helen. Yes, he intimidated her and made her do things she didn't want to do, but he liked her.

"Go get me the fucking envelope, Luigi. I need to know who I can trust. I am not here today because I just take someone's word for it, and I don't care who the fuck that is. I worry about the direction this family goes in, you got that?" AC replied.

"Yes, I'm sorry," said Luigi.

"Don't be sorry, you got nothing to be sorry about. You were honest with me, and I appreciate it, and ain't nothing gonna happen to you, so don't worry about that shit; just go get it."

"All right, I'm on it."

Luigi stood up and walked out of the restaurant, to his Mercedes across the street. One of AC's security men nodded to him, keeping an eye on Luigi as he walked over to his car.

"Fucking phone died, gotta get my damn charger, these fucking things," Luigi said.

Running across the street, which appeared as wet as the one at the shipyard, Luigi was beginning to get that feeling again that he had to be in numerous places at once. Only now it wasn't because he was watching over the shipyard heist and bouncing back and forth to the hospital; now it was the numerous ideas flowing through his head over what giving AC this envelope could mean to all involved.

AC grabbed the envelope from his glove compartment and walked back into the restaurant. Michael Zhang Wei, seemingly coming out of nowhere, was seated next to AC.

Luigi just handed him the envelope. AC looked up at him.

“Why don’t you go home, take the night off. Get laid or something.”

“OK, boss. You know where to reach me if you need me,” Luigi replied.

“Goes without saying,” his uncle replied.

Luigi leaned over and gave him a hug, something AC clearly didn’t expect, as he just sat there, not even putting the coffee he had in his hand on the table to return the hug.

“Go on, go home. Now you better get laid, or I’m gonna start thinking some shit,” AC laughed.

Luigi smiled, turned around, and walked out of the restaurant.

Luigi stood briefly outside of the restaurant as he watched Michael Zhang Wei begin talking to AC. AC was listening, but he slowly opened the envelope.

“No,” the message read.

AC sat up straight with a sudden jolt, and looked at Luigi standing outside, both of them making eye-to-eye contact.

“Go home,” AC mouthed to him. Luigi turned around, and did just that.

AC was listening to Michael, but he wasn’t hearing very much of what he had to say.

CHAPTER THIRTY-FOUR

Merton Howard sat on a patio chair on the back porch of Helen Wilson's house, twirling an elastic band in his hand. He didn't even remember where he'd found the thing, but he was spinning it around his fingers regardless. He sat there, remembering the conversation he'd had with Helen, and how she seemed to know something he didn't about her own future. He just couldn't see her the way she must have looked after the Nicolo family had done to her what it had. She didn't want a fuss if something like this were to happen, but it was Merton's goal to make certain that the years they took from her were going to stand for something.

Looking around the yard, it seemed a property out of place for the neighborhood. It looked a little like the only thing it was missing was a farm. A lot of grass, and a small garden in the backyard that Helen obviously maintained. Merton stood up and grabbed a hose that was linked to the house and began watering it. It was something he was going to do until her family could be notified, but so far there wasn't any that he could locate. Recalling a few of her poems, one indicated that she might have a son, or wrote about someone's son.

Going through her house, there wasn't a lot of information to go by. She seemed so singularly individual, and her family were the neighbors and the friends around her that kept her company. She had owned the home for years. It was her oasis from a world gone mad, until the world got inside her living room.

Merton watered the garden, and then sat back down. He didn't care that it was evening; it was the least he could do for her. Seeing there were some vegetables growing, he decided to pick them, sticking them in an empty can he'd found on the ground.

"I'm sorry," he said to the garden, hoping that somehow she could hear him. He really believed that she could. "I'm going to get every last motherfucking one of them, Helen. I know you don't like me talking like that, but I can't help it," he said, suddenly hearing a door slam.

Slowly Merton walked around the back of the house and peeked towards the street to see who was closing the door. As one man got out of his car, a car behind him pulled up. Another four men got out of that vehicle, which looked to be a Lincoln Town Car. Given the neighborhood had been up in arms over what happened to Helen, not many onlookers dared peek through the curtains as they normally did. They were scared, and at this moment, even Merton was a little concerned. Reaching for his phone, he realized that he'd left it in his car.

"Shiiiit," he said softly to himself. The one thing he did have on him was his .38, but up against the likes of what he was seeing in front of him, he didn't think he'd have much luck in a gun battle.

Meanwhile, Evan leaned up against his car and pulled out a joint and lit it up. Those accompanying him gathered around him for instructions. David, Peter, Seth, and Vince surrounded him, all family members from Poland.

"So, what now?" asked Seth.

All of the men dressed very European; tightly fit clothing, a couple of them looking like Mike Myers' character on Saturday Night Live when he portrayed the role of Dieter. Whoever they were, Merton could see they weren't local.

"Go check out the house, see if anything looks out of place," said Evan.

"But the police tape; what if neighbors call cops on us?" said David in a thick accent. "I think we can see there's no one here. Let's just get the fuck out of here. I don't think it's good for you to be here, anyways."

"Hey, we get paid for this. This is what the man told me to do, so this is what we do. So go check the yard and the backyard and just make sure it's all, how you say, copacetic," said an irritated Evan. Evan wasn't someone like AC, but he sure wanted to be. He didn't like being questioned by his crew. He had high hopes for himself one day, and that's why he involved himself with the Nicolo family to begin with.

"Fine," said David. "Seth, let's go check it out."

The two men walked towards the house, bending down to get beneath the police tape. One of them turned on the flashlight function of his iPhone in order to get a better look around.

"I guess bringing a flashlight wasn't a bright idea," said Seth.

"Shut the fuck up and let's just do this," said David.

Merton was in a bit of a panic, trying to find a place to hide, when the only thing in the backyard was a garden that had about seven plants in it.

The two men split up, one going to the left of the front of the house, Seth to the right.

"I can't see shit," said Seth.

The lights of the home were all off. As they got closer to the front of the house, what appeared to be security lights brightly blazed the front of the house, sending both men into a panic.

"Fuck, let's get the fuck out of here, there's nothing here!" said Seth.

David looked around, seeing the movement of curtains in a window across the street.

"Yeah, we better get outta here, there ain't shit here," he replied.

Both men walked back to Evan and the men.

"I don't see shit out there, man, and those lights are giving the whole damn neighborhood too good a look at our faces. We need to get out of here now," said Seth.

Evan looked at the house, concerned a little himself that the security lights could cause an issue down the road.

"Okay, guys, you go on. I'm gonna stick around and check out what's what," Evan said.

The road looked quiet. Cars were all parked in their garages. It looked like something similar to the neighborhood Henry Thomas rode his bike through when he portrayed Elliott in *E.T.*

Leaning back on his car, he looked to the left and saw not a sign of life on the streets. It was so quiet he could hear the faint sound of TVs from some of the homes, unable to see anyone but the back of the head of some neighbor watching an episode of what appeared to be *All In The Family* on a massive television. It had to be a sixty-inch, Evan thought.

"Fucking Americans," he said to himself.

To his right he watched his partners driving away, a long stretch of road that appeared to end because of the shape of it. In actuality, it was a sort of hill that then veered down and went on for about a mile longer.

Merton just stayed put, but his attention was caught when he looked up at the sky to see something that appeared to be falling. It wasn't lit up in any way, it just looked like this large black mass that was falling to the earth, and it seemed very close to the area he was standing in.

He couldn't tell what it was. Seeing the visitors were all apparently leaving, he slowly sat back down in the chair. Suddenly he heard a thunderous *bang!* that sounded as if a bomb had gone off, and distant screams. He was unable to understand what it was he was hearing. It sounded as if a jet had crashed, but there wasn't a flame to be seen. His first instinct was to run towards it, but was prevented from doing so until Evan got back into his vehicle, the crash clearly getting his attention, as well as every car alarm on the street. Still, as the sounds of the car alarms stopped one by one as residents clicked their clickers, no one wanted to walk out of their homes until whoever that guy was parked in front of Helen's house was long gone.

Rather than getting into his vehicle, Evan slowly closed his car door and just stared at the street in front of him. Something appeared to be flying down the street, airborne. Whatever it was, it was happening so quickly that it took a moment for his brain to register what he was looking at…

The bottom of the car his counterparts had just driven away in was flying towards him at what appeared to be light speed. It bashed into a tree, the bodies of his family members dangling out of the windows, every one of them dead. The car crashing into the tree resulted in an explosion of the vehicle, as Evan just stood in shock. What the fuck was going on? That car flew towards him as if it had been placed in a sling shot. Some neighbors walked out to the porch, but couldn't get back into their homes fast enough, one neighbor holding a phone in his hand.

Evan was frantically looking for signs as to what the cause was of a vehicle holding four of his family members appearing to have been "thrown" down the street and into a tree, but the drop-down road in front of him made it impossible.

The street lights suddenly went out. All of them.

"Whaaat the fuuuck," Evan said as more of a statement than a question. The road was pitch-black, the lights from the homes also apparently impacted by the vehicle being introduced to a tree, a tree that had electrical wires running through them. None of those wires appeared ripped, but Evan had no idea what to make of what he was seeing, which so far, was nothing.

In the center of the street that looked suddenly wet, Evan walked towards the road that became a sort of hill, seeing nothing in front of him. He just stood there, speechless.

Suddenly, what appeared to be two small red lights appeared in the middle of the road about one hundred yards from him, just beneath where you couldn't see past the downward slide of the street. At first Evan jolted back when he saw the red lights, thinking they may be guns aiming for him, and he took cover behind his car.

The red lights went out, and Evan slowly moved back into the middle of the road. Not a neighbor dared come out of their homes as the vehicle smoldered and thick, black smoke wafted throughout the street, barely giving anyone the ability to breathe on this road, never mind see. It was thick, and Evan rubbed his eyes as he slowly walked down the road towards whatever it was that caused the car to fly past him, literally, the way that it just had.

Walking about fifty feet past the front of his car, which faced the right of the street if you were to stand in front of Helen's house and was parked on the opposite side of her home, Evan continued to walk slowly down the road.

Again, the two red lights came on.

Evan was speechless.

The red lights didn't move.

Evan slowly moved towards the lights.

Evan stopped as he heard a sound, which sounded like something digging into the ground. It was gritty, like a shuffle of an object against rocky dirt, or broken granite.

He slowly extended his head to try to make out what it was that he was looking at, only what he was looking at he couldn't possibly be seeing.

Suddenly, two large streams of what appeared to be smoke shot out of…nostrils.

Very big, very round, nostrils. Nostrils of a beast that made Evan freeze in his shoes as shock and disbelief overcame him. The head of this beast slowly revealed itself as it rose from behind the downside of the street, growing larger and larger until what appeared to be in front of him was a beast. A bull. A bull whose face you had to look up at to see.

And he was looking directly into the eyes of Evan Yastrzemski, the man who introduced Helen Wilson to the other side.

Suddenly, Evan felt it was an introduction he was about to have himself.

Snapping back into a reality that provided his body with the function to move again, he looked in horror as this beast just stood there.

Evan took a step back.

Five seconds later, the bull took a step forward.

Evan took another step backwards.

And again, the bull took a step forward.

After about ten seconds of standing still, looking at one another eye to eye, the bull was no longer waiting for Evan to step backwards, and began a slow trot…directly at Evan.

Evan turned around, running to his vehicle, and jumped into the car as the bull trotted faster towards him. Struggling to find the car key in a massive ring of them, he started the engine and without even looking in front of him, did a 180 degree turn in his attempt to escape towards the other end of the street. As he did, he came to a complete halt as the bull stood in front of his vehicle, its size making the Mercedes he was driving appear to be a toy vehicle.

Evan sat there as the bull, the Taurus, walked to the car. As he heard a large bang, his eyes shut instinctively. Opening his eyes back up, the speed of the impact of the bull's horns had made Evan unaware of what had just occurred, until he realized the roof of his vehicle had been ripped right off.

Evan leaped to the back of the newly created convertible and fell off the back of the trunk. He stood up to see…nothing. The bull was gone.

Evan breathed a sigh of relief as he turned around, eye to eye with a beast which he never knew existed. A beast with a look of anger, a beast with a look of revenge, and a beast who then swiftly impacted Evan's face as he injected his horn through Evan's head between his upper lip and nose, lifting him into the air and bashing him into the car he'd just tried to escape from, slamming him from the car to the ground, whipping the corpse off his horn like a Frisbee across the green front lawn of Helen's house, and through her front window.

Merton stood in front of the house in absolute disbelief of what he was looking at, and the bull stared at him, then slowly approached him.

The detective was unable to move, and was sure that he was about to meet his Maker.

It's face no more than two inches from Merton's, the beast grunted, then looked up towards the sky and roared a monstrous sound that the detective never knew existed. It was a haunting sound that no instrument could reproduce.

He looked back towards Merton, then turned around and walked away.

The neighbors didn't make a sound, and Merton just stood there, unable to move at all.

The beast walked away, the smoldering vehicle that surrounded the broken street lights making it impossible to see even across the street. The smoke blinded anyone looking out of their windows as it consumed the creature in the darkness.

Merton just stood there and watched the impossible happen right before his eyes. Again.

CHAPTER THIRTY-FIVE

Luigi ran into the Chinese restaurant as Michael and AC continued on what was now running into a three-hour meeting set up by Jens Maes. As the night was turning into the wee-small hours, the boss was surprised to see his nephew run into the restaurant, completely out of breath.

"Boss, I gotta get you outta here right now, something is going on," said Luigi in a huff.

Confused, AC looked at him.

"Didn't I tell you to take the night off?" demanded a perturbed AC.

"Boss, I am telling you to get the fuck up, and come with me now," said Luigi. "Right now."

No one spoke to AC like that, especially in front of someone else. This meant either two things. Luigi either wanted to die this fine evening, or there was something seriously wrong.

"Evan, all of them, they're all dead, right in front of her house, all of them are dead," Luigi said.

AC looked dumbfounded, and Michael just sat there, knowing that whatever was happening wasn't his battle.

"Can you see why my family might be hesitant to do business with your family, Mr. Nicolo?" said Michael.

AC looked at Michael.

"What we're doing here is as good for you as it is for me, Michael. Now let me go see what the fuck is happening and I'll…"

AC was unable to finish his sentence as he heard a thunderous smashing sound that emanated from a distance, but was loud enough to give credence to Luigi bursting into the restaurant the way that he did. All of the cooks in the Chinese restaurant dropped their utensils and replaced them with machine guns.

"I don't think this is about me, Michael," AC said, trying to take the heat off himself. "This is something else."

AC looked to Luigi. "What's going on? What is this?"

"Boss, we can figure that out when we get you out of here. But one of Evan's cousins went down to check on him when he wasn't responding, and the place was crawling with cops. I went as far as I could get to see what was going on, and all I saw was…"

"What?" replied AC.

"I saw a vehicle impaled on a tree, and the cops were just swarming the place."

"Why don't you come with us?" said AC to Michael.

Michael nodded his head yes, and told everyone else in the restaurant to evacuate in his foreign language.

The sound from the distance was getting closer as a crab that appeared to be three stories high and about 40,000 pounds slowly walked down the street towards the restaurant. The street was littered with different Chinese food outlets, and the crab, the Cancer, slowly walked down the road, veering his head left to right. The Cancer was in search of something. People ran for their lives as they saw what they could not possibly be seeing walk right by them. The Cancer was on a mission to find something, or someone, and nothing was going to get in its way. Looking from left to right, moving full-steam ahead, the Cancer stopped only when it walked past a restaurant that had a water tank filled with about a hundred crabs piled onto one another as they waited to be dinner for some patron. Looking at the crabs in the tank, the Cancer swiped its claw right through the window of the restaurant, slicing the tank clear in half as the crabs found freedom on the streets of Chinatown, all heading for the sewers. It wasn't gonna be a beautiful sandy beach, but for the crabs, it sure did beat being next to a salad.

AC, Luigi, and Michael, along with a few of their men, walked outside of the restaurant to join their family members who were all staring up the street, to the right of the door as they exited.

"What the fuck is that?" said Michael, speaking in very clean English, his accent suddenly disappearing.

"What that is, is time for us to get the fuck out of here," said Luigi. "Now!"

"Agreed," said AC. "Go get the car," AC said to one of his men. The man nodded his head and ran across the street. Frank Nicolo had worked security for AC for years, and did his best to do as his boss had requested. Unfortunately for him, a claw that appeared to be about 20 feet long grabbed him before he could get into the vehicle, completely swallowing the man.

"The back, the back!" said Michael, as the men ran from the front of the restaurant to the back, hoping that nothing was on the other side of the entrance that led to the alley.

"Is there a fucking roof on this place we can get to from down here?" AC said to Michael.

"Yes, yes, there's a roof," Michael replied.

"Then fuck the back; let's head to the roof. How many floors are in this building? What is the number and the street address to this place?" AC said as fast as he could.

"There's nineteen floors in this building and no elevator, so we must go up the stairs, 245 West 19th Street," Michael replied.

"Then let's go up the fucking stairs, let's go, let's go!" AC commanded.

The men waited for Michael to use a key to open a padlock to a green iron door in the kitchen. The door led to a stairwell that appeared to go on forever, as they all looked up from the ground. The men all ran up the stairs as fast as possible.

"You understand what we're doing, right, Luigi?" said AC.

"I sent the text the moment you mentioned the word roof," Luigi replied.

"Good. Let's do this. Then we can figure out why fucking seafood is walking down the street eating my security team," said AC.

"There's something more to this, AC. You gotta tell him, you know," Luigi replied.

The men huffed and puffed up the stairs. Michael, being the first to arrive, waited for the rest of them to catch up.

"Hurry, hurry, I can hear it out there now!" Michael said, referring to a helicopter that was fast approaching the top of the building.

The pilot was Matthew Waters, an African-American pilot who served in Vietnam. Waters had nothing to do with any crimes, and fancied himself as just a helicopter pilot who was where he needed to be, when he needed to be there, for those who could afford him. He just wanted to get paid; who paid him was none of his business, and he didn't want to know any details about anything.

The men ran to the chopper and hopped in while they watched as the giant crab's first claw crashed upon the room as it climbed up the building. As the Cancer scrambled onto the roof, it burst into what appeared to be thousands of small crabs that headed towards the chopper.

The swarm of crabs fell over each other as they took aim at the chopper that would carry AC Nicolo and the rest of them to the penthouse suite that was only about two minutes by helicopter.

"Holy shit!" said Matt. "This is some fucking *Harry Potter* shit; we're outta here!" And he raised the chopper into the dark sky. The crabs leaped towards the chopper, several of them attaching themselves to one of the chopper's landing legs. Luigi began kicking them off, watching them fly back to the roof of the building they'd just departed. The thousands of crabs formed back into one and it gazed at the helicopter it had wanted so much to annihilate.

The men just sat in the chopper, their backs pressed against the inside interior so strongly that if they had pressed against it any more they could themselves risk breaking its walls.

"What was that, what was that? Someone needs to tell me what the fuck we just saw because I just saw it. I mean, what the fuck was that?" said AC.

No one answered. No one could answer.

"I know this," said Michael Zhang Wei. "I've heard about this before, not here, but I've heard of this before."

"What the fuck are you talking about, man? What did we just see that you could have possibly heard about before?" said AC. "That was a giant fucking crab walking down Chinatown, and it wasn't in a tank. It wasn't gonna be cooked. It ate my security guy right in front of all of us."

"This is something else," Michael said. "This is bad, this is very bad."

The occupants were silent as they attempted to cerebrally process what they had just seen.

"Someone in this helicopter has done something very bad, very, very bad," said Michael.

"I've been doing some pretty bad things most of my life, Michael. I've never had a giant crab try to get me as a result of the things I've done," said AC.

"That was no crab, AC. That was a sign of the zodiac. The thing that killed your friends, it was this, it was that crab, or it was something like it. That thing turned into thousands of themselves, and this was not a random," Michael said.

"Y'all need to just get the fuck off my chopper, because I don't want any part of this shit," said Matt. "This is all you."

The chopper landed on the heliport of AC's building, its occupants leaping out one by one.

Michael followed the rest of the Nicolo family into the elevator, and they all entered AC's condo.

"Can I get you all a drink?" AC said.

"Yes," they all said simultaneously.

"I will need to make some calls about this incident. Not to my family, and nothing about our business, which we will proceed to arrange for you as requested. I need to do more than make calls. I need to visit a relative of mine who resides in Jakarta, because if this is what I think it could be, you are no match," said Michael. "They will get you; there is no way out of this."

AC looked at Luigi. Mauro arrived to AC's unit and stepped out of the elevator.

"Fuel the jet for this man, and get him where he needs to go. Mauro, pack your bags. You're going to China," AC said.

"China? When?" Mauro replied.

"Now," replied AC.

"I don't understand. Why don't you send Luigi? What is this all about? Who's the chink?" said Mauro.

AC had a pissed-off look on his face as he slowly walked over to Mauro, a look rarely aimed at him.

"The *chink* is from the Zhang Wei family, and you can apologize to him right now for saying what you just said, especially since you're about to share a very long flight with him. And Luigi isn't going because I didn't tell him to go. I told you you're going, so pack your fucking toothbrush, put some shit together, and get ready to go to the airport. Now," AC demanded.

Mauro looked to Michael Zhang Wei.

"My apologies," said Mauro. Michael nodded back without a smile, but knew the flight would be a little more comfortable if he wasn't pissed off the entire time. The more important thing on everyone's mind was how and why a giant crab had just chased them through Chinatown, climbed up a building, exploded into thousands of crabs, and then returned to being just one giant crab.

AC looked to Luigi.

"Luigi, go to my office and grab my brown briefcase," AC said. "Go."

Luigi did as he was told, running into his uncle's mahogany-filled office and grabbing a briefcase that always carried emergency cash. He picked it up from under the desk, and stood up to find Mauro standing directly in front of him.

"You know. You know, don't you? You know," said Mauro.

Luigi just gave Mauro a blank look.

"Know what? I don't know what you're talking about. I know what I just saw, what we all just saw. That's what I know, and if you saw what we just did, you wouldn't be giving a shit about what anyone knows," replied Luigi. "A giant fucking crab just tried to kill us."

Mauro just gave him the same sinister look he'd given many he was about to kill, but he couldn't take out his nephew, not while AC still liked him. That sinister look then turned into a smile.

"Okay, Luigi. It's all okay. I'll see you when I get back from fucking China," said Mauro.

Luigi just stood there as AC walked in.

"A problem in here? Give me the fucking briefcase," said AC.

Luigi walked over to AC and handed him the case, who in turn handed it to Michael.

"If you need more than this, you tell me. There will be a credit card in your name in the plane by the time you get there; use it for whatever you need to, and find out what the hell is going on here," said AC.

Michael nodded a 'yes' to AC, and another one of AC's men walked him to the elevator, another Nicolo family member named Paul.

"Bring him to the airport, him and Mauro. See to it they get out of here safely," AC said.

"Yes, boss, you got it."

Mauro looked at Luigi as the elevator door shut.

AC walked back to the window. This time, he didn't care if he could see the trees below, and wasn't even going to try to.

"AC?" said Luigi.

"Shhhhhh," he replied.

CHAPTER THIRTY-SIX

"Well, you were first at the scene, and I don't see a report on my desk," said Captain Frank Delaney. "New York has been in an uproar over some pretty bizarre shit from what I hear, and I have no doubt I'll be getting a call from them. So, do you want to tell me what happened last night?"

Merton just sat in the chair in front of his captain's desk.

"Captain, I have seen everything in this line of work; at least, until last night. You've seen some strange things as well over the last few weeks. All I can really tell you is that you do not want me to write a report on this one. For one, I'd be out of a job, and it's not the job I care about; it's the ability to bring that family down, or at least to help New York do it," he replied.

Captain Delaney had seen some strange things, but protocol was that the officer on the scene, especially the first officer on the scene, had to turn in a police report. Captain Delaney continued.

"I mean, I can't get a word out of anyone who lives on that street. These people are terrified, some even moving out of state because of whatever has been happening on that street. So, why don't you tell me what happened, off the record, knowing that I know all of the strangeness that has occurred on that street. I met the lady, and let me be the judge of whether or not you should write a report that's actually on the record. You know how this works, Merton. Five people were killed last night, and there needs to be an explanation, no matter who it was who died."

Merton Howard just sat there.

"What I'm about to tell you is the most ridiculous thing that I have ever said in my life, but, you want the truth? If you want the entire truth, off the record, you can ponder whether or not I should be putting this all on a piece of paper…a piece of paper you'll have to sign, then OK. I'll tell you exactly what happened," said Merton.

"I am all ears, Mert. Shoot," said Captain Delaney.

Merton took a deep breath, because he just wanted to put it out there for his captain and go on about his day.

"I went to Helen's house to see if I could find something that could shed more light on what happened to her. While I was in the backyard, I turned a hose on and watered her garden, because it looked like it needed to be watered, and I was there, so I figured what the heck, I'm here, I can water the garden. There was barely any light in her backyard, and what light there was came from the neighbor's house, that Sandy Finnigan's place, so yeah…I watered the garden.

"Then a few cars show up. A guy gets out of one car, and four out of the one parked behind him. The one guy sends the four guys to check out the place, but fortunately the security lights come on in the front of the house. That spooks them, and fortunately for me they didn't make it to the backyard, or I likely wouldn't be here right now. Anyway, the one guy in the first car tells them to leave. Moments later the car comes flying down the road, right-side-up, at a speed I couldn't clock if you asked me to, where it proceeds to burst into flames when it crashes into a tree.

"Then a bull the size of a bus comes out of nowhere, and I mean a big bus, not the bus you likely think I should be a passenger in at this present moment. It sticks his horn through the guy's head, bashes up his body pretty good, throws him off his horn, and the victim flies across Helen's lawn and lands in her front window. The bull then comes up to me, looks me in the eye, turns around…and walks back to the street, where it disappears. That's what happened. So…do you have a blank report you'd like me to begin writing? Or can I get back to investigating the case?"

Captain Delaney just looked at him.

"So, where is that paperwork, Captain? I'm ready to write all this out," Merton said.

Captain Delaney swung around in his chair, facing the window behind him.

"Are we sure we can't tone that down a little?" the captain replied.

"Frank, I'm not the only one who saw what happened over there. Neighbors in the area saw some of it themselves, and given the rumors about what happened in New York City, I'd venture to say that whatever I write in some report isn't gonna mean jack-shit," said Merton. "The word is out that there is something out of this world on the loose, and we need to figure out who opened the cage."

"I have a feeling you already have a feeling about what opened that cage," said Frank.

"I didn't say it, you said it, and we both know that neither of us are wrong. None of this happened until they took Helen."

Captain Delaney swung back around to face Merton.

"I will admit, your house was a bit, upside down…"

"Frank, it was entirely and exactly upside down. The paperwork in the drawers didn't even fall out of them until I said her name. When I went back into my house to fix that mess, everything was exactly in place. The pictures on the wall were upright, the furniture was upright, even the mess on the floor from all that paperwork was neatly organized in the drawers again, as if they had never been touched," Merton said.

"An illusion of sorts. Maybe none of it was even upside down in the first place? Maybe our minds were playing tricks on us?" Frank replied.

"Ordinarily I'd agree with you, if it weren't for the fact that I just saw a bull the size of an army tank stick its horn in the head of one of Nicolo's men and toss him through a window about fifty yards away," replied Merton. "So sure, I'm down to go with the idea that David Copperfield has somehow escaped Las Vegas and is torturing the city of Naugatuck. But those people are dead. That was no illusion. Those people are all gone, and not even Copperfield is gonna be bringing those people back to life. I saw that Evan Yastrzemski guy, and that wasn't done by any man."

Captain Delaney just breathed in heavily, and then let it all out in one deep, exhaling breath.

"I want to go see that table in the evidence room," said Detective Howard. "It's there, right?"

The captain nodded his head yes.

"Well, then let's go look at this thing. Let's see if there's anything about it we've missed," said Merton.

Merton called the evidence room, speaking with a man named John Spiro, a detective who on occasion racked up some extra-duty hours logging evidence in and out. Merton let John know that he was on his way.

"The mayor wants answers," said Captain Delaney. "I don't know what to tell him."

The mayor, James Fiorentini, was a former attorney who had turned the city around in his many years as mayor. Born in Groveland, Massachusetts, he had moved to Naugatuck after working as a police officer in the city for twelve years. His wife had convinced him to move to Connecticut to be closer to her aging parents, and Fiorentini reluctantly agreed.

Still, the mayor wasn't someone who was easy to bullshit, and his tolerance level on huffing and puffing the truth out of his officers was not something he had a lot of.

"Well, tell the mayor we'll talk to him soon. Who knows what he'll see on the news between now and then? Maybe it'll be an easier conversation than we thought if he catches some of this on TV," replied Merton.

"So far I haven't seen anything on the news about it, but they did run that interview with Helen a few times. Apparently that Anderson Cooper really took a liking to her, and seemed a bit upset by learning about what had happened to her," the captain replied.

"Well, I'm pretty fucking upset myself, Captain. That woman didn't deserve this. She was just a cute lady who had fun doing psychic readings," Merton replied.

"Yes, well, the problem is that she wasn't a carnival act. She didn't get on the radar of the Nicolo family because she was an inexpensive psychic and they were somehow in the market for inexpensive intuitives," Delaney said with a smirk. "You found those kids; there's no way you would have. That woman saved their lives, and probably many we don't even know about. The Nicolo clan is about taking them, not saving them."

"Well, my guy tells me they took the wrong life this time," said Merton.

“That would seem to be the case. But I think we’re getting ahead of ourselves. We don’t know whether or not any of this is really anything more than strange. You start talking about after-life and ghosts and goblins, and I’m telling you right now that you’re gonna look like a nutbag,” Captain Delaney replied.

“I’m not sure what to do on this one. But what I’m gonna do is go down to the evidence room and see if there’s anything there I’m missing. There’s gotta be something. She had a lot of very intricate writing on some confusing stuff, even for me. I mean, I’m no Harvard professor, but this lady was truly into what she does.”

Captain Delaney stood up, preparing to walk Merton out the door.

“She was charging $25 for a reading in her living room, and at fairs and festivals. I don’t really get the feeling that she was Nostradamus,” Delaney replied.

“Personally, I never saw a prediction or an event that Nostradamus ever did that would make me believe he was legitimate at all. What I do know is what I saw, and with this person, I saw what I saw, with my own eyes, and I believe what I see,” said Merton.

“Including a bull that no one else saw impaling a man and throwing a vehicle down a street,” Delaney said.

“You don’t know if I’m the only one who saw that, Captain. Give YouTube a chance.”

Merton walked out of the office as the captain sat back in his chair.

“YouTube. Shit,” Delaney said.

The table was about to have a visitor.

CHAPTER THIRTY-SEVEN

The Macy's Day Parade in New York City was as historic as the city itself. The annual parade would bring the biggest stars out, and the inflated cartoon characters such as Snoopy and Garfield became a wonder to the children who stood on the sidewalk watching them slowly drive by. The mechanical technology had Snoopy and Garfield waving to the thousands who stood along the street. Parents held their children in their arms, and the music blared over several blocks.

Mauro had been in China the past eight days, and AC was contemplating how exactly he intended to deal with a betrayal of his orders as it pertained to Helen Wilson. He was very upset about this. Of all the havoc he had caused in his life, he wasn't familiar with the world "guilt" before, but was consumed by it during his alone thoughts, as rare as those were. His guilt wasn't about how he was feeling about his brother, but the psychic he'd come to know, and whom his brother had betrayed, a betrayal that cost the lives of several of his family members and associates.

AC Nicolo was meeting at the Sixth Avenue Café in Manhattan with several members of the Nicolo family as Luigi walked in carrying a small box.

"What is it?" AC said to Luigi.

"It's a package from England. I didn't open it," he said.

"Give it here," AC said, as he extended his arm.

Looking at the box, he sensed that despite his conversations with Jens Maes, maybe the Belgian gem dealer wasn't as eager to do business with him as he had agreed. One of AC's men, Marcus Nicolo, a man of about 45 years who acted as an accountant for the lower-tier mobsters in the family, looked at AC.

"You want me to open that for you?" asked Marcus.

AC just looked at the box, and given the events of the last few days, decided that if a giant crab wasn't going to get him, he wasn't too worried about a little box. He began to open it when he heard a ringing from inside of it. Marcus grabbed the box and began running out of the café.

"For fuck sakes, Marcus, get back here. It's not what you think!" AC said.

Marcus stopped and looked at AC.

"Boss, it's ringing," Marcus said, as other customers in the café looked on, some of them appearing a bit fearful themselves.

"Just bring the damn box over here. It's a phone, and I should be answering it," he said. "Bring it here!"

Marcus walked back to AC and handed him the box.

"Fucking paranoia in this family," he said.

AC ripped open the box to find a European cell phone in it, and it was indeed ringing.

"Yes," AC answered.

"It's Jens."

"I know who it is, glad to receive the phone. It arrived a little late, yes?" AC replied.

"Well, there were a few delays in getting your guy set up in London. But apparently it's all coming together, and we can proceed," said Jens.

"Good, because I've got…"

Screams came from outside of the café that stopped AC in his tracks from finishing his sentence.

"Go see what that is," AC said to Luigi.

Luigi walked out of the café as the Macy's Day Parade rolled down Sixth Avenue, the crowd enthusiastically cheering to his left, but screaming to the right as a large figure seemed to be flying in the sky. Perhaps not so much flying as dropping.

"What the hell?" exclaimed Luigi.

Suddenly the large mass landed on the Snoopy float, exploding it into what seemed like instant confetti. It rocked the entire block as onlookers ran for cover.

A massive Scorpion had landed on the float, and it wasn't a balloon. It was a massive creature that arrived at its destination, and that destination was right in front of the Sixth Avenue Café…Macy's Day Parade or not. The massive creature circled the float as television cameras focused on the monster. There was simply no scorpion that could possibly be the size of what he was looking at. It was the size of a school bus, and as it checked out the crowd, it looked directly at Luigi.

And then it stopped looking, and began approaching.

"Hooooly shit!" said Luigi, as he ran into the café.

"Let's get the fuck out of here! Now!" said Luigi.

This time AC wasn't going to second-guess the reason as he had the last time Luigi crashed a meeting. All of the men ran out the back door. There were six men, including Luigi: AC, Luigi, Marcus, and three of Evan Yastrzemski's goons all ran out. Christian, Anthony, and Frederic were eager to seek revenge for the death of their uncle. Christian, following Evan's death, actually suggested the crab could have been part of some sort of genetically manipulated weapon that was created to kill AC, which his cousin Anthony quickly responded to with a smack to his face at the time. That ended that absurd discussion. Still, the men didn't know what they were running from until, from the top of a building, the Scorpio leaped into the back alley.

A flash of its tail completely beheaded Frederic Nicolo. AC was not a man in top form, and police cars suddenly screamed down both sides of the alley.

"Mother of God," said a young police officer. "All units, we're in the alleyway behind the Sixth Avenue Café, and there is what appears to be a large animal that we need to control back here; it's just killed a man."

AC ran back into the building with Luigi, as Christian and Anthony started firing their .45s at the monster. Once again, a whip from its tail completely split Anthony directly down the middle, his organs splattering on the cement as officers, too, began firing. Typically when a police officer saw armed men shooting at anything, it was those armed men the police were firing at. Not today. Today, all armed men were welcome, as the men began firing upon the beast before them. Christian attempted to get back into the building, but the door was not opening. Christian began banging on the door as yet another strike from the Scorpion completely severed the arm that was banging on it.

Christian screamed until its tail impaled his chest, putting a whole the size of a bowling ball directly through the iron door.

An animal control truck pulled into the alley as the Scorpio was fending off the officers, and despite its ability to do so if it had wanted, it did not kill a single officer that had been firing at it, especially given the bullets shot at it seemed to have no effect at all.

A man jumped out of the animal control truck. As fast as he jumped out, armed with what appeared to be a noose on a stick typically used to snag the random loose dog, the man leaped back into his truck as if he had just seen his death.

Had he tried to put that noose around anything that was standing in front of him, he would have been.

Meanwhile, AC and Luigi ran out the front door of the café as their awaiting driver hurried them into the vehicle.

"What's going on?" the driver said.

"Just go! Go!" said Luigi.

"Do they have guns!?" asked the driver.

"No, fucking claws and stingers and shit. Let's get the fuck out of here, man!" he said.

The car sped off, but the Scorpion leaped from the alleyway onto Sixth Street, where thousands of onlookers ran for their lives. Little did they know that they had nothing to fear from the creature; but AC and Luigi were now being chased by something that they couldn't possibly be getting chased by, as they tried to avoid the floats and people that were in their way.

"Hit them! Hit them if they're in the fucking way! Just fucking go!" said AC.

People jumped to avoid the vehicle as it headed towards them, going from the street to the sidewalk as the car drove as fast as it could down a street that since 1924 had held one of the most celebrated parades in US history.

"Someone get Michael on the phone; get them on the phone and let's see what the fuck is happening right now," said AC.

The car was now at a speed of about sixty miles per hour when they looked behind them to see that the Scorpio had disappeared.

"Where'd it go?" asked Luigi.

"Oh, don't go by that shit. Keep your foot on the gas if you want to live," AC said to the driver.

The car flew down the road and took a turn down an alley, stopping in front of what appeared to be the rear exit of an Armenian restaurant.

"This is some fucking crazy shit, and this is personal," said Luigi.

"You just figuring that out now, Luigi? You thinking you don't know what this is about? Because I sure do, and that *stronzo* will never step foot back in my country. Mauro is no longer a part of this fucking family," replied AC. The word "stronzo" is Italian. It means "piece of shit."

"Are you sure about what you're saying?" said Luigi; even the driver looked back at his passengers.

"Did I tell you to look at us? Keep your eye on the road. We just dodged a scorpion the size of a truck, and now I gotta worry about you crashing into shit?" said AC. "Just get us the fuck home."

Luigi got on the international phone and called Jens. Jens answered.

"What is going on there? I lost ya," Jens said.

"I don't think you would possibly believe it if I told you."

The car parked in front of the building that AC had called home for decades. Jens wasn't sure about what was happening in New York City. It had been made clear that calls could only originate from Jens to AC, but AC made an exception given the call appeared to have simply dropped.

"I have seen a giant crab and a giant scorpion in the last two weeks," said AC.

There was silence originating from Belgium.

"I'm…I'm not sure I just heard what you said," said Jens.

"Neither am I," said AC. "But there is something happening, and we may both know from whom it originates."

"I'm really not sure what you mean. What is happening?" Jens replied.

"My friend, for the first time in my life, I do not know," replied AC.

CHAPTER THIRTY-EIGHT

Detective Merton Howard intended to visit the evidence room of the Naugatuck Police Department early in the morning. Captain Frank Delaney did as Merton had requested, and stored the table in the evidence room of the police station. The world at large now knew what just days earlier would have cost him his badge, and that was that there were creatures among us. It would be a little easier to write the report of the events he'd witnessed now that Macy's Day Parade attendants were uploading a giant scorpion onto YouTube by the hundreds, each angle just as amazing to view from whatever point of view the person had filmed it from.

The Macy's Day Parade had never been interrupted before, with the exception of government officials who constantly rerouted the parade to the protestations of businesses at Times Square, who once relied on the traffic of people who flew in from all over the world to visit the once-a-year event. For the world to see something like this brought into question just what could possibly have occurred to have a creature such as this appear from the sky? It seemingly hovered, then dropped, from thousands of feet above. Where did it come from? How could this creature be?

Merton had only one thought on his mind, and it was the table that Helen had first sat him down at when they first met. CSI had dusted the top of the table for prints, but came up empty in search for intruders with a record. Merton did his own combing of the house, which to date no one had come forth to claim as a relative or next of kin. As he arrived at the police station, John Spiro gave him a nod, and handed him a clipboard to fill out his name and badge number, acknowledging that he was entering the room to review the table more in-depth.

"Thanks," said Merton to John, as he was buzzed into the room.

Merton walked past what seemed a library, but instead of books there were numbered files and cases that were being stored to put many people behind bars. At the end of the hall was a room marked "K," though why it had this particular letter to mark it was a mystery even to Merton. Still, it's where Captain Delaney had ordered the item, given its size.

Merton opened the door to see the table in the middle of the floor, tagged "Wilson" on the leg. Merton walked over to it and gently removed the sticker from it, feeling as if it somehow disrespected it by leaving it there. This was not just some random woman, and this table was not just some piece of furniture. There was more to this table than CSI or any of the other police on site had understood. The one thing he did know was, it wasn't going to be safe in this room for long. He didn't know why, he just knew.

Kneeling down on the floor, Merton looked at the etchings on the legs, some that seemed from very long ago. He looked in awe at some of the etchings that surrounded even the top of the table and its sides, which at about an inch thick had to be painstaking to be able to create such detailed illustrations. He found it amazing, and felt that this table before him held more answers to life than he'd ever live himself.

A small bookshelf was the only other item in the room, and most of those held books and notebooks that Merton wanted stored, many that were writings Helen had written herself as she explained various elements of astrology and the tarot cards, and why horoscopes existed. She had various opinions on dates and the signs themselves, but would go from very articulate writings about the zodiac signs to simple poems about her mother. There didn't seem to be much written about her father, and there were poems about "a boy" and "a son" that he had been unable to confirm the identity of.

He stood up and put one hand on the table as he just looked at it, not really certain about what he was looking for.

"Come on, Helen. Tell me something," he said.

But then he noticed something, something he had not seen before. The Taurus, Cancer, and Scorpio signs had color in their eyes. He could have sworn, in fact, he knew, that the eyes of those wood-etched drawings did not have any color. He flashed back in his mind to the first time that he had seen the creatures on the table, and he was positive that there was no color in the eyes of those creatures engraved in that wood.

Merton walked back out to John Spiro, and he had a serious question.

"Has anyone been back to that room, to the K room? Has anyone touched that evidence back there?" said Merton.

"Absolutely not, why?" said John.

"I'm just asking. You haven't had anyone else attempt to look at the table or any of the contents of that room?" he asked.

Spiro looked puzzled, and even a bit perturbed that anyone would ever get into the evidence room on his watch without him knowing.

"Detective, no one but you has ever been in that room since those items arrived," Spiro replied.

"Ok, I'm just asking," said Merton.

"Is there something wrong? Something I should know?" John asked.

"No, it might be just me being too tired or something; maybe I saw something wrong," he said.

Merton walked back to the room, rubbing his eyes, as he tried to make sense of what had become international phenomena from a police evidence room in Naugatuck, Connecticut.

He walked over to the table again, this time slowly turning it on its side. The bottom of the table seemed to be quite old, almost peeling. However, it was one of the legs that caught his attention, as what appeared to be very old black tape covered the bottom of one of the legs. He looked closer at it, and slowly began to peel it off, but it wouldn't budge.

Pulling a pocket knife out of his front pocket, something he'd carried since he was a Boy Scout and always held onto for luck, he started picking away at the tape. Something was beneath this tape, and he wanted to see what it was.

He began to make out the last letter as his new approach with the jackknife began to work. The numbers "562" began to show themselves. He could tell there was more, and continued to peel it back.

"Man," he said to himself. "You got some secrets, don't you, young lady," he said, as if Helen was in the room with him.

Slowly the tape began to peel off even further, this time sending a jolt to his stomach, a jolt of nervousness, the kind you might feel if you were playing a slot and all three sevens came up. Part of the feeling was fear itself.

As he peeled the tape completely off, he froze at the realization of what was before him.

Michel de Nostredame – 1562

"This is impossible," he said to himself. "This can't be possible."

The focus on the table stopped at this realization, and for now, Merton was only consumed with whether or not what he was looking at was actually real. There was more to inspect, but he had just begun to see that he was in over his head on this one.

"My God," he said to himself.

Merton sat on the floor and just stared at the table. His mind raced. 1562? This table had to be from at least 1562. Was this even possible?

Merton stood up, and slowly placed the table upright. He had enough information to inhale for the day, and had to figure out what to do with this information. This table was already priceless in his mind, knowing what it had meant to Helen. Now it could actually *be* priceless, and he wanted extra precautions to be taken.

A bit shaken, he exhaled and a color caught his eye. It was a color that he did not notice before. He had just seen the color of three of the creatures' eyes colored in. Now it was the Capricorn, and its eye was suddenly blue.

Detective Merton Howard wasn't sure if he was seeing things, hadn't had enough sleep, or was simply losing his mind. That creature absolutely did *not* have a blue eye when he first walked into the room, and he was the only one in the room between the time he'd noticed the Taurus, Scorpio, and Cancer signs with colorized eyes. But now he'd witnessed the transformation of the Capricorn with his own eyes.

Merton stepped back, and turned to exit the room. Shutting the door, he headed to the front desk of the evidence room as a green glow suddenly emanated from the floor of the room. It was a bright, shining glow, but a glow Merton Howard didn't even notice.

Once again, Merton approached John Spiro. This time Spiro was ready for a question.

"What is it now, Detective? You all done in there?" Spiro asked.

Hardly, but he couldn't talk to the officer about this, and had to play down the potential discovery despite the fact that his heart was beating a mile a minute.

"Everything's in order, just checking on a few things," he said.

"All right, well, sign here for your outbound," Spiro said, referring to the need for Merton to check out of the evidence room.

Merton signed out and flipped open his cell phone, speed-dialing Captain Frank Delaney.

"Hello, Merton, how are ya?" he said to the detective, clearly having him on his caller ID.

"Captain, we need to talk about the table you put in the evidence room from Helen's house," he said.

"Why, what do you know?" Delaney replied.

"This table might hold some answers to questions we may not want to know the answers to, and I'll admit, I'm in way over my head right now," he said.

"I think we're all in over our heads, but what do you got?" he replied.

"Captain, what I think we've got is something I don't even think I should talk to you about over the phone," he said. "But what I had you put into protective custody, it needs to be moved to a more secure location, somewhere that it can't be touched."

"All right," the captain said. "I'm sure you'll explain this to me in person."

"I don't know if I'd go that far, but a bank, something secure, very, very secure, and somewhere we can have access to it, where we can have people who know something about this sort of thing have access to it," said Merton.

"I understand. I'll get on it the moment we're off the phone," said Captain Delaney.

Captain Delaney did just that, calling a friend from Bank of New York.

Kevin Guard, the bank manager that Delaney had known since college, agreed to place the table in a vault at his location.

"I'm not going to ask why, Frank, but sure, not a problem. You gotta have your reasons," said Kevin.

"I definitely do, and I appreciate your help here. I'd also appreciate it if you would please keep this request to yourself," the captain replied.

"You have my word."

Delaney relayed the message to Merton via text, and a relieved detective drove back to his house, armed with information he'd just obtained that would keep him glued to his computer for the rest of the night. He would begin to research the origins of the table, and he would try to recall if the colorized eye of the Capricorn was something he just didn't see at first glance when he entered that evidence room.

But then he remembered before he even opened his front door. He hadn't glanced.

He'd stared.

He most definitely stared.

CHAPTER THIRTY-NINE

Michael Zhang Wei sat with Mauro in the lobby of the Hotel Jakarta in Jakarta, Indonesia.

"So, where's the Great Wall of China here in Jakarta?" Mauro smirked.

"We need to meet someone here before we go there. I believe that you needed to be here to hear what it is he had to say," said Michael. "There are things you cannot control."

"All it takes is a gun," replied Mauro.

"I think you misunderstand the situation, Mauro," replied Michael.

"Well, I guess that's why you all hauled my ass to China now then, isn't it? I'm thrilled beyond belief to listen to more tales of crabs and bulls. Bullshit, is more like it," Mauro said.

"I think you are in for what is called a rude awakening," said Michael, as they got up and started walking.

Mauro stopped Michael in his tracks in the middle of the lobby, pointing his finger directly towards Michael's chest.

"Listen, you all may have my brother wrapped around this hocus pocus bullshit, but I'm no fool. I've been around a long time, and I've seen just about everything. What happened in New York proves that there was some experiment by some asshole that went south. If you think I believe there are celestial beings walking the earth that tell my brother what crimes to pull off, you've got another thing coming," Mauro said firmly.

"There's a lot you don't know, Mauro. But one thing I agree with you on is that such beings aren't here to help any of us, or anyone who helps you do the things you do. My family runs a clean business, and never has there been a death to those we do business with. My family has a history here that dates back a thousand years, and we do not shed blood to obtain the things that we want. We work for our profits; we do not threaten or kill people to get them. But I do agree with you on one singular point, and that is that what is happening right now is not meant to help you," Michael replied.

A hotel staff member approached Michael. Clearly the staff member knew who Michael was, obviously having him as a guest in the past.

"He has arrived. He awaits in our private suite behind the restaurant," the man said.

"Thank you," Michael nodded. "Please take us to him."

"Who's him?" Mauro replied.

Mauro didn't receive an answer, and proceeded to follow Michael and the staff member to the private suite. If one was eating in the restaurant, they might not even realize the suite was there unless they saw someone walking into it, hidden behind what appeared to be a thin, brown wall that slid from side to side, two pieces connecting with a slice of wood that connected both pieces in its center.

"This oughtta be good," said Mauro.

"This way, gentlemen," said the staff member.

Both men walked in, and there sat a man in a brown robe, a small Indonesian man who looked to be in his early 70s. He looked at both men.

"Come, sit," he said.

The man's name was Boodemun Budiman, and most of his day was spent at the Borobudur, where he would pray and seek guidance and wisdom. While the Nicolo family were committing crimes and obsessing about money, Budiman could always be found at the Borobudur, a Buddhist temple established in the ninth century.

"I understand that you have an issue in America," said Boodemun. "An issue that may require more than you are capable of dealing with by yourself," he went on.

The staff member of Hotel Mulia entered the room again, this time with a small roll-away table with a TV monitor sitting on it. The man plugged it in. It was AC on the screen.

"I thought I'd listen in on this conversation," AC said.

"AC? I'm glad someone sane has entered the conversation," Mauro replied.

"Shut it!" said AC. "It might do you some good to listen for once."

Mauro was stunned at the response that he'd just received from his brother. Rather than replying, he sat down with Michael on a small sofa to listen to Boodemun.

"You have awakened something that you cannot stop," said Boodemun. "What you have done is to remove a spirit that you did not have the right to remove. There are, I feel, many spirits that await your arrival to another side, but this one in particular was a spirit with exceptional force with which you interfered. You had no right."

Mauro looked at AC.

"Uhm, really, AC? Am I really here to listen to this shit?" said Mauro.

AC, again looking with anger towards Mauro, had no more tolerance for his younger brother.

"Mauro, let me tell you something. There's a code in this family, and there's a consequence for betraying that code," said AC.

"What the fuck are you talking about?" replied Mauro.

"Shut up! I know! I know it all. I have seen the envelope that carried Helen's prediction, and you fucking ignored it. How many people died because you didn't listen to me? How many of our own family are gone because you decided to do the opposite of what Helen Wilson told you? I know everything," AC replied.

"Luigi," said Mauro.

"No, Mauro, not Luigi. A fucking janitor who saw my name on an envelope and made sure that I got it. The next time you're going to lie to my face, use a shredder," said AC.

"Well, I was looking out for our family. No one knew what was happening to you in that hospital, and I had to take control of the situation," Mauro replied.

"Would you say you did a good job at that, Mauro?" AC replied. "Because I'd say you did the opposite of looking out for our family. You got our people killed and back on the radar of the FBI in a way they never have. And now I have twice been attacked by things I can't possibly be getting attacked by. And it's you, it's all you, who did this. You are the one who ordered the hit on Helen, and because of you, we are a family in chaos. Worst of all, you lied to me. Lied right to my face. So I hope you like Asia, because you are going to be there for a while so that I can figure out what I intend to do with you," AC replied.

"Are you joking? You think I'm going to just live in China?" Mauro replied, standing up angrily.

"Yes. That's exactly what you're going to do. You lied to me. Our own blood has been shed because of you. For this, you will stay there, and you will work with Michael and Mr. Boodemun to coordinate efforts to protect this family in the way that you couldn't when you were here," said AC. "If you accomplish this, I might see past your lie to my face and let you live. I might even let you come back to New York one day. But right now, you are not my brother; you are a man who has much to make up, if you even can."

"Gentlemen," Boodemun interrupted. "We need to focus on what is now at hand. I know of a man in Dali, a village where few homes exist in the southwestern Chinese province of Guizhou. He has an ability to bring to life the astrological signs of our country."

"The Chinese zodiacs? You're talking about, wait, you're telling me that you know 'a guy' who lives in the middle of nowhere, China, who can bring to life the signs of the Chinese zodiac? I mean, what is this shit, *Lord of the Rings*?" Mauro replied, then looking to AC. "Are you serious with this shit? I thought I was coming here to engage in the gem business, not to feed into your delusions, AC."

"Mauro, you haven't seen what I saw, what Luigi saw. Maybe when you do, you'll have a different opinion of all of this," said AC.

It just seemed impossible for anyone to convince Mauro of anything. He was stubborn. AC was positive of what he'd seen, what he knew. Michael and Boodemun didn't think; they knew. And yet Mauro seemed either in denial, or truly believed that all of this was some sort of hoax. Whatever his opinion was, the only truth at the moment was that he was about to become a resident of China for a while, and not the nice part.

Mauro put his hands on his face, resting his elbow on a table in front of him.

"Well, I guess I don't have much of a choice," Mauro said, as he looked to Boodemun.

Boodemun was the type of man who didn't give up what he was thinking. You couldn't tell by looking at him if he liked you or not. To Boodemun, this situation was strangely straightforward, which is how Boodemun reacted.

"You still think this is about your brother deciding to keep you here. You think this is about something within your family. You do not understand that you probably would not be alive right at this moment if you were still in New York. These are not powers that care where you are, but they are powers that can always find out. They have a birds-eye view, so to speak, and you won't be safe here for much longer either, if the man I am going to bring you to is unable to accomplish what your brother seeks. You must also understand, you can only do business if you are alive, and your gems will mean very little to you if one of these beings arrive at your front steps," said Boodemun.

"Well, take me to your leader," Mauro said, as if he were in a movie more than taking any of this seriously. Looking back to the screen, Mauro was about to say something to AC when the TV shut off, turned off by AC from his part of the world. He'd heard enough from his lying brother, and was now deciding whether or not he wanted to hear anything at all.

Michael stood up and bowed to Boodemun as the men prepared to leave. Mauro just looked at Boodemun.

"Yeah, what he just did," Mauro said, as he mocked the cultural respect that Michael was showing the old wise man from Jakarta.

They both left the room and walked to the lobby of the hotel.

"You're gonna just have to show me something, something that says this isn't all bullshit. What you, what my brother is saying, it's just crazy talk. I feel like I'm living in the fucking *Twilight Zone* with all this shit. I'm waiting for Captain Kirk to beam in next to tell me something about my ball sack."

"You mock everything, Mauro. But rest assured, I need not prove a thing to you. The proof you need is looking for you, right now. You are being hunted by something that you cannot shoot, you cannot beat up, something you can't have 'your men' deal with. What you need to do is take this very seriously if you want to live, because what Boodemun said is right. Your focus is on material things, when you are being sought after by things that do not care about cars or money or your fancy clothes. You took a member of their family by your decisions back in New York, and you know what you would do if such a thing were to happen to someone that you loved."

Michael walked away from him as they were to head back to the airport. Mauro just stood there, looking at Michael as if he was just as out of his mind as his brother.

"Are you coming, Mauro?" Michael said.

Mauro clearly did not want to be standing where he was, but as his brother said, he had no choice.

Mauro walked to Michael, and both men exited the hotel.

CHAPTER FORTY

Detective Merton Howard spent the night on his computer, just as he had planned he would, after visiting the table that Captain Frank Delaney had moved to a vault located in the Bank of New York. Through vast research and several tablets of Advil, as the screen began to blur his vision, he had come across a Dr. Gary Huberdeau, an archaeoastronomist who lived in Hilo, Hawaii, known as the "Big Island" in that state.

Captain Frank Delaney played yet another card when he contacted Governor Neil Abercrombie, an old golfing buddy back in college, who had worked his way up the ranks to become head of the Aloha State. Governor Abercrombie obliged Captain Delaney's request, and arranged for the detective and Dr. Huberdeau to meet in New York City, on the dime of the Naugatuck Police Department.

Huberdeau would arrive at around 2:00 a.m. He was a reclusive man in his early 50s, but still looked quite youthful at six feet tall and 180 pounds. His long brown hair made him look like an old-school surfer more than the archaeoastronomist that he'd become, and he'd spent hours just looking towards the sky. He had become so well known in his field that Virgin Airlines CEO Richard Branson had given him an invitation to be on the first commercial flight to space when his Virgin Galactic brand eventually launched. Huberdeau hadn't yet decided to take him up on the offer, as his belief was that the answers he sought from the stars couldn't possibly be reached with a machine.

“But it is a closer view,” Branson had said to Dr. Huberdeau, when they spoke several years back. Branson laughed at the response at the time, and the two men agreed to speak about it again at a later point.

Merton Howard wasn’t wasting any time, pulling in another favor that would permit him to drive from the airport directly to the bank vault at such a late hour in order to inspect the table that, at least to him, held many answers and countless questions. Dr. Huberdeau, despite the long flight, seemed as giddy as could be to see the item under strict secrecy. By now, the world had seen the events of a giant scorpion that had crashed the Macy’s Day Parade, then disappeared into thin air. His anticipation was unlike any he’d felt before.

As the plane landed, Detective Howard stood at the baggage claim, awaiting the arrival of a man that up until now he had only seen on the Internet. The brilliant archaeoastronomist spoke frequently at the University of Maryland, and had published several books on the topic of archaeoastronomy. This East Coast trip would also include a visit to the Museum of Science in Boston, Massachusetts.

The wait at the airport seemed to take a while. Yes, the Naugatuck Police were funding the flight, but that didn’t mean the good doctor was going to get a first-class seat. Seat 33A was where Dr. Huberdeau sat on the United Airlines flight that was a direct flight from Honolulu once he puddled jumped from the Big Island to Oahu.

Finally, Dr. Gary Huberdeau was in the sight of Detective Merton Howard, and he waved to get the doctor’s attention.

“Right here, Doctor,” called the detective.

Huberdeau approached Detective Howard with a smile that was a little unsettling for a guy who’d just spent about 16 hours in travel with the layover that Honolulu had to offer. He seemed just a little too awake to be normal, in Detective Howard's mind, but also figured the guy had to be a little off the wall to be an archaeoastronomist, which was still a word that even Webster's dictionary didn't recognize, despite the official title by various universities in the United States.

"It's great to finally meet you. Bring me to the table," said Dr. Huberdeau.

Apparently, the doctor wasn't very hungry. He didn't want to stop for a bite to eat anywhere; he just wanted to go to the Bank of New York, as described by Governor Abercrombie, to inspect this piece of evidence that was, in actuality, in the interests of national security, despite the fact that no one other than a couple of people knew that the table even existed. Even Governor Abercrombie was in the dark about the introduction, per the request of his old golfing pal, and had simply set it up as a favor. Abercrombie knew, however, that for Captain Delaney to make a phone call like that out of the blue, it had to be important. Delaney had never done so before, unless it related to a potential golf game, which rarely took place anymore.

Detective Howard drove in his unmarked police car for the airport pick-up in order to avoid the security measures of JFK Airport, enabling him to park directly in front of the baggage claim doors they now walked out of. In the vehicle, both men headed to the Bank of New York to see Helen's table, and see what to make of it.

"I've been watching some of the details on the news, and I knew right away that what I was seeing was a celestial event. Unfortunately you will find, as I have, that it's pretty difficult to bring in the scientific community on such things. Most of those old goats want their name in lights like a movie star, but not me. I just want to have some sort of physical evidence that shows the world that the sky is indeed alive. The sky holds secrets. The sky watches us, not the other way around," Dr. Huberdeau said.

Merton didn't really know what to make of the man yet, and despite finding the statement rather odd, decided to just play along. This man was for all intents and purposes…all he had. The doctor did have credibility, the Governor of Hawaii being just one example of the contacts that found his opinions quite intriguing, whether he actually believed in them or not.

"Well, I'm not really sure about all of that, but I'm hoping you can shed a little light on this situation. We have had several murders where I come from in Connecticut, and it was like pulling teeth just to be able to drive into this jurisdiction in my squad car to come get you. What I'm hoping for is more information about the woman who owned the table," said Merton.

"We do have our own purposes, and I'm more than happy to help you with yours. My purpose may differ from yours," the doctor replied.

"If you coming here gets us both what we need, then I'm all for it. You just cannot discuss what we're about to see with anyone, although there are influences out there who have the ability to obtain it no matter where it is," Merton replied.

Dr. Huberdeau laughed.

"What's so funny?" asked Merton.

"I just find that remark amusing. You know, influences out there who have the ability to obtain it," Dr. Huberdeau replied.

"It's true, lotta money and powerful people would like to get their hands on that thing," said Merton.

The car pulled up in front of the Bank of New York, its manager waiting out front for their arrival. Dr. Huberdeau turned to the detective as the car pulled up.

"Detective Howard, I assure you that the influences you believe would want to obtain custody of this table are no match for the powers that would prevent that from ever occurring, if this turns out to be even remotely of the value you put on it as a human being. You are talking about celestial beings, the horoscope signs, whose powers are proving to be beyond mere legend…but are walking through Chinatown here in your New York City."

Merton sat there as Dr. Huberdeau got out of the car and extended his hand to meet the greeting bank manager, who was doing Captain Delaney a special favor by permitting the men to enter the vault this late, something that was completely against every banking law. New York officials were equally eager to make certain that there was never a repeat of what had just happened at the Macy's Day Parade, and the manager did convey to Captain Delaney that he should call any contact he might have with NYPD to make sure that allowing them into the bank at that late hour wouldn't cause any sort of a stir, especially a jurisdictional one. The table had been brought there, it wasn't found there, so Captain Delaney's friends at the precinct didn't really have a problem with storing a piece of evidence. "The less they know, the better," Delaney had conveyed to Merton before he picked the doctor up from the airport. "But they know we're doing something over there, and they don't have a problem with it."

It was just a mutual respect that police departments had for one another. If you're coming to town, they at least want a phone call.

Merton walked over to the two talking men as the bank manager looked around the area prior to opening the door. Each second seemed like agony to Dr. Huberdeau, who just wanted to see this table.

“Where is it?” asked Dr. Huberdeau.

Merton interrupted the question that was aimed at the bank manager.

“It’s in the vault, let’s check it out,” said Merton. The bank manager got the hint; he was there to turn a key and not to inspect evidence, or in this case, something out of this world potentially.

As the vault opened, Dr. Huberdeau stood at the table with a look of awe. To the layman, it was a piece of wood. To Dr. Huberdeau, the look on his face would indicate that he had just seen the Holy Grail.

“My God,” he said.

“What? What is it?” asked Detective Howard, now even more curious than he’d been.

“Do you know what this is? Do you have any clue what this is?” said the doctor.

“If I did, the good taxpayers of Naugatuck wouldn’t have just fronted your airline ticket,” a laughing Detective Merton replied.

“Sir, what you are looking at is the table of Nostradamus. Madame Blavatsky,” Dr. Huberdeau said.

“Helen Wilson,” the detective replied.

“Yes, yes. Helen Wilson. It appears to be so, doesn’t it? This Helen Wilson, for her to have been bestowed this table…as legend has it, there are very few in the world who would be given such an honor," Dr. Huberdeau said.

"Any why would someone be given such an honor?" replied Dr. Howard.

Dr. Huberdeau just looked him directly in his eyes.

"She would have to be real."

That was about the only thing Dr. Huberdeau said that he had already known.

The two men would spend hours viewing all of the details of the table, as Dr. Gary Huberdeau viewed with awe the item before him. Merton Howard explained the appearance of the colors in their eyes, and Dr. Huberdeau did all that he could to bring a detective from Naugatuck, Connecticut up to speed with a table that had likely been birthed in Egypt.

CHAPTER FORTY-ONE

AC Nicolo sat in his penthouse apartment with Luigi and several security men as the television re-ran the events of the Macy's Day Parade in what seemed to be a 24-hour-a-day loop. Even the network TV Land, which typically ran old TV shows, was covering the event in between reruns of *The Andy Griffith Show*.

"Shit, there's not a channel on this damn thing that I can find," AC said as the telephone rang. This wasn't AC's cell phone. It was his landline, and only three people had that number. His aging mother, Mauro, and the Police Commissioner of New York City.

"I think you have a problem," the voice on the other end of the phone said. It was Commissioner Rebecca Gaston. "A serious problem. We need to meet, and by meet, I mean right now."

The meeting place with the police commissioner was at Central Park in New York, a spot at the west end that had become typical when there was something to convey to AC from a woman he'd been paying off for years to keep any investigation into this family from reaching first base.

AC, Luigi, and security men Michael Bonanno and Massimiliano Milano made the trip.

"I don't even get the point of security right now, boss," said Luigi. "Doesn't even make sense to me."

"It makes me feel better. Besides, I don't see any crabs walking around today," AC replied.

The park was completely dark as they walked toward the commissioner.

Rebecca wasted no time in her Gucci woman's suit as she approached the mob boss.

"Nice suit," he replied.

"Cool it with the pleasantries. I'm just here to convey a little information. There's a cop, a captain out of Naugatuck, that's pulling a lot of favors for something related to your family. I don't know what it is they've got, but they've got something, and you're the target; you and your entire family. Something about a local psychic one of your henchmen took out," she said.

"That we took out? I had several very fine associates whose deaths, in my opinion, are directly related to that woman," AC replied.

"Then why haven't you taken care of the situation?" Rebecca replied. "Why am I getting calls about this?"

"I don't know if you've been watching the news lately in between your stops to high-fashion shopping malls on your police commissioner's paycheck, but in case you haven't noticed, it's a little hard to target some of the things that have been coming after us. I'm working on it though," he replied.

"Well, his name is Captain Delaney, a Frank Delaney, and he's got his seal of approval on a lot of pieces of paper that are floating around right now, and he apparently is a lot more connected than I am," she replied.

"You're connected with enough; you're connected with me. That's why you're police commissioner, and don't you forget it," AC replied firmly.

The ground beneath them suddenly vibrated and pounded, a large *thud!* knocked all of them to the ground. While there wasn't a sound exactly, the vibration buckled their knees.

"Shit," said Luigi. "Shit, shit."

Looking above, they saw a large figure that looked to be about two stories tall behind them. Rebecca herself was accompanied by two men who couldn't quite be made out in the dark, but who were obviously there to make sure she walked out of the meeting she'd walked into.

Then came the scream. It was a piercing scream that sounded like the wailing of a whale in the ocean in pain, as from the trees came what appeared to be a giant fish tail that looked as if it were being swung like a bat. It completely slammed into Rebecca and her two security men, causing them all to be shot up over the trees, and what appeared to be a small building behind them. At the front of that tail was the head of a goat, and a very angry one at that.

"Jesus," said Luigi.

The men leaped into the limousine that security had already jumped into. Unfortunately, security didn't jump into the front seat, but in their panic had leaped into the passenger seat section.

"What the fuck are you doing back here? Who's driving the damn car?" said AC. "Luigi, climb through that and get us the hell out of there!" AC said, as he referred to the partition. AC's security men would never fit through it, and neither of them intended on trying to get out of the car to get in through a passenger door.

Luigi did as he was told as he saw what stood before him.

"You are the Capricorn," Luigi said. "I'm sorry."

But sorry wasn't enough, as the tail of the beast swung across the front of the limousine and tore it completely off the vehicle. Luigi remained in the front seat as the front portion of the car slammed into a tree, leaving the cabin completely open from its front as the giant creature slowly approached the limousine that now was just a small room with a couple of tires on the back of it.

Sitting ducks, the men all leaped out of the car and ran towards the park, which remained pitch-black.

Michael Bonanno and Massimiliano Milano pulled out their weapons and began firing at the monster. It paid no attention to the bullets as it watched AC running as if he knew how, completely out of breath, and wondering himself if he'd make it out of the park without having another heart attack, never mind whether or not this beast would get to him first.

The beast walked towards AC as its tail fin crashed to the ground and knocked down anything in its way. The force of the tail vibrated the entire park as if it was firing electricity through the ground. As AC approached an exit that he was able to see cars driving down, he headed as fast as he could to get to them.

Michael Bonanno and Massimiliano Milano still fired at the creature, a bullet apparently hitting its tail.

For the first time, a creature had been effected by a bullet, by something human. This wasn't supposed to be, but it happened. The creature turned towards both men, who froze in disbelief of what they were seeing. The creature stood there for a moment, eyeing each man, and sizing up how it intended to handle this. It began its thunderous movement towards both men as they turned around and began to run away, shooting backwards as they ran, while now knowing what they were aiming at. Massimiliano fired as he ran, only to hear an *umph* sound.

He'd just shot Michael in the face. He was dead.

"Shit!" said Massimiliano, as he continued to run and the Capricorn ran towards him. Suddenly, with nowhere to go, the beast with a fish tail cornered the man against a wall he could not possibly climb over. It lifted its hoof, and smashed it down upon Massimiliano with a forced that splattered the man like an egg. There was nothing recognizable about the man, only that the suit was an expensive one.

And it would take quite a dry cleaner to clean up that mess.

Meanwhile, AC had found solace in a taxi cab. His cell phone rang. Michael Zhang Wei was on the other end of the call.

"It just tried to kill me! It killed my guys, and the damn police commissioner and a couple of her men just got sent flying over a damn building! What the hell is going on?" AC said.

"We're working on it right now, AC. We are here. We are getting the help we believe will change this, all of this; but there is just one problem," said Michael.

"What is that problem, Michael? Tell me the problem!" AC said.

"What we are doing here is taking a bit of time. The signs are not supposed to be used in this manner, the Western signs or the Chinese signs. We are asking signs that are meant to do good, to do something else, and it's taking some time," Michael replied.

“Time? I don’t got time. I’m getting killed over here, and no one is doing anything about it!”

“AC, you need to tell me something. I need to know something,” said Michael.

“What? What?” AC screamed.

“Did any of you fire on it, or hit it, or do anything to try to defend yourselves?” Michael asked.

“Yes, one of my guys got a shot off, nailed it in its, I can’t believe I’m saying this…its fish tail. A goat with a fish tail!” yelled AC, as he laughed the words in a frenzy of insanity.

“Well, then, if you were able to impact it, then what we are doing here is working.”

This stopped AC from panicking for just a moment, a calmness suddenly coming over him.

“That’s right! Nothing we ever did stopped them before. One of my guys got a shot off, it hit the thing. How did it hit the thing?”

“It hit the thing, because they are not the only powers in the universe. We have some friends just like them over here.”

AC smiled at the thought.

“Good. Well, it just cost the lives of five people to get off a shot, so hopefully you boys over there come up with something a little more impactful, and very soon.”

AC ended the call. The taxi driver was just looking at him through the rearview mirror.

“What are you looking at? Just drive the car,” he said.

The taxi driver did just that, and in doing so, replaced two of his men and a custom made limousine.

Destroyed by the sign of the Capricorn.

CHAPTER FORTY-TWO

Mauro sat in the small tent with Michael in the small village in China. The man before them was Delun Huang, a man of 94 who continuously murmured to himself, regardless of who was speaking, but who clearly understood whatever anyone was telling him.

Michael felt uneasy about the trip. The connection he was now having as a result of the introduction by Boodemun Budiman was contrary to everything his family had taught him about the family business. Carry a gun, but use it to imply strength, not to show it. In the same way the world had nuclear weapons to intimidate, do so without killing anyone. Business is business, and there are ways to impose fear without ending the life of someone who can help you. It's far better that they be scared and useful, than dead and one less contact.

Delun Huang was not a man Michael's family had known, and here he was, challenged with being involved in a situation that he felt too deeply involved now to extract himself from. Once the word of his family was given, it was seen through. It was dishonorable to not keep one's word, even if it meant sacrificing yourself for the sake of that honor.

Delun Huang had the same abilities that Helen Wilson had, the only difference being that Helen didn't know she had them. His use of his powers were not to better mankind, but to wreak havoc on a world in which he had to grow old, one of those powers being that he could stay alive as long as wanted to, but he would age just as anyone else would. In his 94 years, he was a feared man who lived in a village where no one bothered him out of fear of the things they had been rumored to see from the area surrounding his tent.

Several villagers left the area when they witnessed what they believed to be snakes flying over his tent, some hovering. His powers could manipulate the good and turn them into weapons. If he had to grow old, the world would suffer for it. He was more than delighted to engage in helping the Nicolo family in their time of crisis, and he did not share the same honor that Michael did.

"What we must do in order to defeat those who are defeating you is to manipulate the celestial plain. I have already begun my work, but I'm fighting the forces and what those forces perceive to be their mission to do only good, and this is not easy. I am a mere man; but a man who has seen many things. I know that when the day comes that I no longer wish to remain on this planet, that my powers will be withered away like my body is here," he said. "I must live here, or I will surely die there."

Mauro looked a bit lost in all of it, but knew that there was something very bad occurring in New York. Learning of the deaths of Michael Bonanno and Massimiliano Milano was reality, despite his opinion on the reality everyone was attempting to convince him was occurring. He couldn't care less about the police commissioner and her men, as they were hired hands in his mind. Their bodies were found about 600 yards from where the fin of the Capricorn had launched them into the sky and over a ten-story building.

"Mr. Huang, I have come from New York City to seek your help for my family. I'm not sure I understand what is going on," said Mauro.

"You have betrayed your family, and you are here to be a messenger, not to ask questions. You broke a code, and you are the reason we are sitting here now. You chose to go up against a force that you shouldn't have," Mr. Huang replied.

Mauro just shook his head. Delun responded with a smile.

"What? You do not believe in such things?"

Mauro looked down to the ground he was sitting on, then looked up at Delun.

"I know that people in my family are dead, and I know I'm the reason. Thanks for rubbing that in, by the way. I'm not there now though, and it doesn't seem like the killing has stopped any," said Mauro.

"This is true, and it won't for some time. I do hope you have a big family," Delun replied. "What I am already doing is trying to weaken the signs of the zodiac as you know them through the stars. From what Michael has told me, it has been an effort that has paid off, has it not?"

"Well, I heard someone shot a goat, yes. A big goat," Mauro replied.

Delun just looked at Michael as if to cerebrally say "Where did you get this guy?" Mauro simply wasn't coming off as the brains of the organization at the moment, but more or less like a man in denial.

"We will prevail, because you have me. Be warned, I will not be as forgiving as your brother, should you ever betray me. In fact, your brother does not care if you live or die at the moment," Delun said.

"And how would you know that, old man?" Mauro said, getting pissed off.

"If he was concerned about you, he wouldn't have put you in a tent with me."

Michael just looked down.

"I would like to go to my tent and sleep now," said Michael.

"I know, and you will sleep. Go on, Michael. Go sleep," Delun said. Delun looked back towards Mauro.

"And what about you? What questions would you like to ask of me?" he said, as Michael left the tent.

Mauro seemed as if he had no questions, and a million of them, both at the same time. His anger at the moment was that he was sitting on dirt in a tent in China, unable to do anything productive. His plans had been changed. This entire deal with Jens Maes introducing his family to Michael was to engage in the gem-dealing business, and now he was sitting, literally, in the middle of nowhere with someone who appeared to be an aging nut.

"I think that I'm gonna go get some sleep as well," said Mauro. "I've got a headache."

"Go do that then," said Delun. "Sleep, and we will talk tomorrow about what we will do next."

Mauro got up and walked out of the tent, and as he did, came face to face with a tiger that just stared at the petrified New Yorker. In shock, Mauro jumped backwards into the tent, first landing on the flame that was on the ground in the middle of it before rolling off back onto the dirt.

Delun was gone. Mauro sat there in panic for several minutes before peeking his head outside of the tent. The tiger was now nowhere to be seen.

He breathed a sigh of relief as he sat back in the tent.

"Relieved?" asked Delun.

Completely freaked out about the old man's sudden appearance back in the tent, he shook his head.

"What the fuck was that?" said Mauro.

"That, my friend, was your proof."

Delun just looked at Mauro, and shook his head as he smiled.

"Not everything is based on what you can see, you know. There's always something going on that you can't. You live in a world where, if you can't see or smell it, or taste it, it's not real. I assure you that the tiger you just came face to face with was very real. It is gone now, and that, too, is real," Delun said.

"I'm just…this is all just new to me, Mr. Huang. This is not the life I typically live," he said.

Delun burst into laughter as Mauro looked at him, a bit annoyed.

"What's so funny to you? What is so funny to you that you sit there and laugh at someone like me? I could fucking kill you right now if I wanted; then what good is your power?" Mauro said.

Delun smiled again.

"You are silly. You are a silly man. I am going to insist you now go to sleep, as I have much work to do to save your brother."

Mauro stood up.

"What if I don't want him saved?" Mauro said. "What if it's better if he's not saved?"

Delun shook his head again and smiled.

“You have no honor. I see why you were sent here now by your brother. You are without loyalty to anyone, even to yourself. You do not even know who you are,” Delun replied.

“I’d rather not know who I am and live the way I do, than live like you do in this fucking tent, that’s for sure. You can be all-knowing for all I give a shit, but I’d rather know less under a down comforter,” Mauro said.

Mauro stood up, peeking his head slowly out of the tent before he walked out of it, to make sure the tiger wasn’t still out there.

“Do you really believe this tent would prevent that tiger from getting you?” Delun said. “Do you know how easy it would be for that tiger to get you if he wanted to?”

“I asked you a question,” Mauro said. “What if I don’t want AC around anymore? What if what I want is to steer this family, with your help, in the right direction?”

“I will ponder your words, but the bigger concern to me is whether or not you know what the right direction is,” Delun replied.

“Yeah, this coming from a guy who lives in a tent in the middle of nowhere land,” Mauro replied.

“My friend, I can go anywhere I want, everywhere I want, before you even wake up in the morning,” Delun said.

Mauro just looked at him, unable to figure out a reply that would make any sense.

“Goodnight, Mr. Huang. You have yourself a good night,” said Mauro.

"I will," Delun replied. "Watch out for the tigers. Some of them don't exactly look like the animal."

Mauro left the tent, having no clue what the old man was talking about, but biding his time. He would not allow himself to be AC's bitch. He had risen to the top with the man who was now condemning him to a village in China while wearing Louis Vuitton.

The morning came quickly as Mauro woke up and exited his tent.

"Hey, Michael, I'm up, let's go," he said.

There was no answer.

Mauro stuck his head into the tent, shocked to see that a tiger was standing over Michael's lifeless, half-eaten body. As he ran back towards Delun's tent, he realized that he was no longer in control. It was a feeling he hadn't known before. In his world, he called the shots.

"Worry not about that man," Delun said. "He was weak, and he was about to do the same thing to himself for the sake of his honor. I just helped him do it in a more interesting way."

Mauro walked back into his tent, and realized that it was he who was caged, and it was the animals who were now his captors.

And one day, AC was going to pay for this.

CHAPTER FORTY-THREE

Merton Howard sat at a table in his living room, with only a light emanating from the kitchen, a bottle of Jack Daniels in between them as they discussed the events of the past few months. They had seen a woman save the lives of three children, then put a murderer away in North Andover, Massachusetts, only to have the mob threaten her to assist them in their wicked ways. The coma that had incapacitated AC Nicolo for several days resulted in Mauro taking on what he'd call "Presidential Duties." Unfortunately for Mauro, all of his commands had torn a hole between himself and his brother, and had shown the present world that the mystical exists. Mauro was no longer "Vice President" of his family.

As the FBI had combed through the affairs of the Nicolo family, it was now well known that Mauro, despite having an alibi during the attempted shipyard heist, was now in China for reasons unknown to anyone, and reasons unknown usually meant that something wasn't right.

Merton and Frank just stared at their glasses as the faint sound of Freddy Fender, the Mexican-American Tejano singer, played on Merton's CD player in the background. Fender's "Wasted Days and Wasted Nights" played as they both drank their troubles away.

"I like Freddy Fender," said Captain Frank Delaney. "They don't play his stuff enough anymore."

"He was one of the greats," Merton replied of the Latin-American singer.

The two of them had been overwhelmed by the big city events. They ran a small-town police force, and were unable to comprehend what they seen, or what to do with the information that they had.

"And Neil Sedaka, my wife loves him, too. We went and saw him in Vegas once. He was great. Bobby Vinton, too," said Captain Delaney.

"Real music; what ever happened to it?" replied Merton.

"No idea. A lot of stuff nowadays sounds the same. I don't even turn the radio on anymore," Delaney replied.

The two men sat and stirred their drinks, Merton with a toothpick, Captain Delaney with a butter knife. The ice in his drink clinked against it.

"They say when you get home you should leave your cases at the office, but it never happens," Merton said.

"Do you have any idea how many times I've used that line in my life? Hundreds, and you can't leave it at the office. It's what we chose to do," Captain Delaney replied.

"Yeah," said Merton.

The two men just sat there in deep thought, but enjoying the company. Captain Delaney was never really a fan of Merton Howard's in the past.

"How long has it been since Samantha has been gone?" Captain Delaney asked Merton. Samantha was his wife of 27 years who had passed away after a car accident in Dorchester, Massachusetts while visiting her mother.

“Three years,” Howard replied.

The Freddy Fender song ended as the next track on his CD began, a track called “Before The Next Teardrop Falls.”

Feeling a little more free with the discussion thanks to their good friend Jack Daniels, Merton looked at Captain Delaney.

“Ya know, I’ve always tried to do the right things in my life. I’ve always tried to do some good. I thought that’s what I was doing. I always thought of the big picture in the decisions I’ve made, thinking that if I just held on long enough, some good would come of my efforts,” Merton said.

“They have. I mean, you are a little off the wall to most people, Merton. Your methods are a little weird sometimes. You’ve always been sort of the black sheep at the department; but I don’t think I’m telling you anything new,” Captain Delaney replied.

“True. The past month has shown me that all I can do is try to keep on going. It’s me versus the world right now, I feel,” Merton replied.

“Ah, bullshit. You’re not alone in the world. You just don’t talk to anybody anymore. This is what, the second time I’ve ever been to your house? And the first time was after Samantha left.”

“She died, Frank. She didn’t leave,” Merton said sadly.

“I’m sorry. I don’t know, I just don’t like to use those words, especially after what I’ve seen the last few months. I don’t know a damn thing about a damn thing,” said Captain Delaney. “I just gotta see more. I’ve been trying to take my wife to Kenya for one of those safari trips.”

“Kenya? Is that a safe place to go? Don’t people get killed over there all the time on those things?” Merton replied.

"Listen, people are afraid to go anywhere people think they might die. Egypt, places like that, people should see. But they don't go, they don't see anything. I mean, everyone's gonna go some time, right? It's not like you're gonna prevent it. So I say, see it all until you can't, because you don't know when your ticket's up," replied Delaney.

"True that. So go to Kenya, ride one of those elephants or something with the thing on your head, whatever those things are," said Merton, as the Jack Daniels flowed nicely through him.

"What thing on your head? What the hell are you talking about, a thing on your head?" Delaney laughed.

"I don't know, the hats that Robert Redford wears, those cowboy rustic things like hunters wear," Merton said.

Both men went silent, then broke into laughter.

"Thing on your head, what the hell are you talking about?" Delaney said, as he continued to laugh.

Both men looked down at their drinks.

"So what am I going to do?" questioned Merton.

Delaney took the bottle of Jack Daniels and poured some more into his glass.

"I think I'll be stealing your couch for the night, if that's all right," said Delaney.

"That's fine," replied Merton.

"But about your question, what should you do. I'll tell ya; you're gonna wake up and do what you do every day. You're gonna get up and keep on keeping on. That's your only choice, anyway," Delaney said, as he was swaggering a little himself thanks to the drink.

"That's not what I meant, I meant about this," as he pointed his hand towards his drink.

"Ah, yes. Well, we're gonna hope no one ever realizes what we did, because this could get us both into a lotta hot water. I mean, I don't know. I think people are gonna be looking for it, just don't know who yet," replied Delaney.

Captain Delaney and Merton Howard both looked down.

"It is amazing, isn't it? To think that Nostradamus actually used to write at this very table we're drinking from," said Merton. "And here it is in my living room, wasting away, not telling me anything. I don't feel anything different when I'm sitting here. I mean, I look down, I see all these things in the wood. It's pretty amazing."

"Yes, indeed. People are finding out about it now, though," Delaney said, as he pointed drunkenly at Merton. "You are gonna have to be careful."

"I'm always careful," said Merton. "I think I'm always careful. Maybe I should be more careful."

"Exactly," slurred Frank.

"I think that Gary Huberdeau doctor is going to be able to help us. I told him to bring back his crew of braniacs and I guess they wanna look at it more, but I'm not letting them take it out of this house. I already told them that," said Merton.

"Good, good. They know more about this stuff than we do anyway, these types," Delaney said, referring to Dr. Huberdeau.

"You shoulda seen him; he was like a kid in a candy store when he saw this thing. Didn't take him but a second to realize what it was."

Both men sat there listening to Fender, and tried to comprehend the months they'd just experienced, as well as the table they now sat at that may or may not hold the answers to the events in Naugatuck, Connecticut, North Andover, Massachusetts, and New York City.

"I think people aren't ready for this kind of shit," said Frank Delaney. "I mean, who is? It's like some government project, right? I mean, what does that? How is any of this shit possible?"

Again a pause, as they both looked down at the different engravings on the table.

"I'm telling ya, I saw this table before you brought it to the evidence room. I saw…I mean, it changed. These eyes on a couple of these, they weren't colored," said Merton, clearly slurring his own speech.

"They are like little rocks," said Frank. "Like little rubies or stones in the eyes, not really paint, I don't think," said Frank.

Merton stared down at the engravings, running his fingers through the signs of the zodiac that made the table top.

"I never noticed," Merton said, a bit surprised. "But ya know what? You're right. I didn't, it didn't look like this before."

"Ah, yeah, I know, I know. Frankly, I think I've seen and heard about enough of this topic for at least a few nights, which I'm happy to say I've taken off. What I'd really like to know is what that punk is up to in China. They are up to something over there," Delaney replied.

“Out of our jurisdiction, whatever it is. We’re Naugatuck, and they are the F…B…I. They got it all covered.”

Both men slowly looked up at each other, both having a “feeling” that they were not alone in that room. Merton looked to his right, and Frank looked to his left, both now looking in the same direction, as they were looking at something they couldn’t possibly be looking at.

“Gentlemen,” the voice said. “I think you underestimate yourselves. And if I were you, I’d start preparing for something for which you have never seen before.”

What the female voice didn’t realize was that they both had just seen something that they had never seen the likes of before.

“May I sit down?” said Helen Wilson. “Because we have a lot to talk about.”

INFINITY – Helen's Notes Retrieved by Detective Merton Howard

The following are confidential files from the evidence room of the Naugatuck Police Department, copied by Detective Merton Howard. The information includes notes by Detective Howard following his extensive investigation, as well as notes by Helen herself. While some statements have not been completely verified, it is true insight into the investigation by Helen Marie Wilson into the history that inspired and became her craft, and just how far back her research was. A portion of these records are various assessments made by Detective Howard in what has been an investigation, to this day, that he has been unable to conclude.

That being said, the investigation continues, as will this story.

Helen began researching astrology at a very young age, always questioning its antiquity, and the truth from which it originated. From her studies at many libraries, and books she'd bought from numerous stores, she learned that the most ancient form of astrology was an integrated system of knowledge used by the Neo-Sumerians around 1950-1651 BC. However, paintings on cave walls showed that lunar cycles were being recognized as far back as around 30,000 years ago.

Civilizations developed calculated and sophisticated knowledge of the celestial cycles. Great, massive temples were built in alignment using the heliacal rising of the stars. Supposedly these temples where built before the third millennium BC. Increasing knowledge of constellations became one of the most important aspects of these newly arising civilizations.

Astrological texts, called the Venus tablet of Ammisaduqa, may have been made during the time of King Sargon of Akkad, around 2334-2279 BC. Another ancient form of astrology, known as electional astrology, began about the time 2144-2124 BC. It was given to the Sumerian King Gudea of Lagash by the gods who appeared to him in dreams. The constellations were the divine key to his planned constructions of temples.

Babylonian astrology was possibly the first organized system of astrology, beginning around the time of the second millennium BC. However, Helen believed that the fallen continent of Atlantis was truly the lost brilliant city behind what she believed held some true form of astrology. Helen felt there was something missing, not just in Western astrology, but the history of astrology as a whole had missing parts, and pieces to a puzzle yet to be found. The pieces were slowly being put together. To Helen, however, it was seemingly very difficult to place each piece one by one together, because the whole picture of astrology was most definitely lost somewhere out there in the atmosphere, only showing its stars briefly in her dreams, but not long enough for her to yet understand it's lucid meaning.

Something seemed to be guiding her as she searched through endless bookstores and libraries from small towns to big cities. Even in her own dreams she began to see images of a celestial being shining its symbols into the night, as she slept with what appeared to be angels gazing into her subconscious psyche, shining luminous signs forming lucid dreams. These dreams were waking her with a blinding awe of wonder, and mystery, a feeling love, and of the search for everlasting truth. She knew spirit guides were guiding her into the unknown, uncharted territory which was ever so dangerous, but ever so enigmatic. As the search continued, she began sitting quietly in a library near her home, reading away joyfully into the origins of astrology, always the last one there, as the night slowly covered the stained-glass windows.

Her studies began to uncover that the Neo-Sumerian era, around 1950-1651 BC, showed signs of the use of astrology as a system of knowledge of an integrated system of the stars in the heavens. After many books and research involved in the endless pursuit of astrological knowledge, she began to understand the ancient form of Babylonian astrology. During the second millennium BC, there seemed to be an organized system, and even as far back as the third millennium BC there was knowledge of ancient celestial omens. Scholarly celestial divination arose within the texts of ancient Babylon in 1800 BC, progressing into the Middle Assyrian and Middle Babylonian era of 1200 BC.

Omen-based astrology, known as Enuma Anu Enlil, began by the sixteenth century BC. It contained 70 cuneiform tablets encompassing 7,000 celestial omens, predicting issues concerning politics, and even the weather. At this time, the understanding of astronomy was that of an abecedarian, a beginner. Future mathematical methods had advanced copiously to formulate future planetary alignments with equitable veracity, and vast ephemerides began to develop.

Divination was the core of Babylonian astrology, and 32 tablets with inscribed liver models detailed texts of divination. Blotches and imperfections found on the liver of sacrificed animals were considered as symbolic images sent from the gods to the kings. Gods appeared in celestial images inside the planets and stars.

Omens and magic revolved around rituals that involved lunar eclipses and astrological macrocosmic events corresponding with the native microcosm of earth. Mundane astrology is possibly the oldest form of astrology, according to the history of Babylon. The development of horoscopic astrology as a whole, however, progressed, and by the sixth century BC, had been refined into the craft of natal astrology.

Hellenistic astrology began in Egypt, and as Helen's search for the truth began to unfold, her feeling was that the Sphinx in Egypt was much older than the Pyramids, more ancient than Mesopotamia and Babylon by many thousands of years. It possibly held the truth about astrology inside what could be the Hall of Records, deep in a mysterious tunnel yet to be found inside one of the most magnificent, mysterious wonders of the world.

Helen's intuitive feelings were that these records may have even surpassed those of Atlantis' astrology, in theory of course. But she had this deep inner knowing that the history of astrology was only that of a half-truth hidden from the human race. Nonetheless, she dug deeper into this possible false history of the meaning of these celestial elements, planets and stars, gazing into her heart and mind, ever questioning this history.

As Alexander the Great roamed the world with titanic power and authority, triumphantly conquering the massive lands of mystery and magical beauty, he finally set eyes on the golden Pyramids of Egypt. Realizing that astrology may have played a huge part in this unbelievable site by guiding him, through the stars, the information came to him to conquer the world, as well as Egypt, in 332 BC. The city of Alexandria was established by Alexander the Great, and Egypt was now under the ordinance and ascendancy of Hellenistic Egypt.

The city of Alexandria now became the place where Babylonian astrology was fused with Egyptian decanic astrology to formulate horoscopic astrology. This contained the Babylonian zodiac, a system of planetary glorification, the triplication of the signs and the relevance of the eclipses. Egyptian decanic astrology is comprised of the concept of dividing the zodiac into thirty-six decans of ten degrees each, with an accentuation of the rising decans, as well as the Greek system of planetary Gods, sign rulership, and four elements.

There is some possible Mesopotamian influence on Egyptian astrology, after it was conquered by the Persians in 525 BC. They share two signs; the Balance, known as the Scorpion's claw from the Greeks, and in the Dendera zodiac. The decans, a system of time measurement, was in accordance with the constellations. They were directed by the constellations Sirius. They were used as sidereal star clocks, bantam constellations which numbered a group of thirty-six stars rising on the vista horizon throughout each earth rotation.

The risings of the decans in the twilight were used to divide the night into hours. Concluding the course of the year, each constellation arises just before the present sunrise for ten days. The decans associated with ten degrees of the zodiac became a part of the astrology of the Hellenistic Age. Decans were now, for the first time, correlated with the ten degrees of the zodiac. The Dendera zodiac established in Egypt dates to the first century BC, and may be the first primeval form. Second century BC texts record relations to the positions of the planets in zodiac signs at the time of the rising of certain decans, mainly Sothis.

The astronomer and astrologer Ptolemy, living in Alexandria, Egypt, founded the basis of Western astrological tradition through the work of Tetrabiblos, which became the evolution of horoscopic astrology. Plato later translated the Tetrabiblos from Arabic into Latin, and it became one of the first astrological text to be distributed into medieval Europe through Spain. Astrologers were familiarized with the Hermetic text, and of the current system of the new-found creation of horoscopic astrology, being inserted into the current culture of Egypt. The Hermetic text, and the new system of astrology, evolved during the time of an Egyptian pharaoh named Nechepso.

European astrology began to thrive by the thirteenth century, and it became a part of everyday life, so much so that eventually physicians in Europe were required by law to have knowledge of astrology before performing medical procedures. During medieval Europe, universities were split into seven specific fields represented by planets, and were known as the seven liberal arts. Dante Alighieri applied these arts to the planets. The arts were revolving in an escalating order, and the planets were in a declining order of acceleration. The Moon was assigned to linguistics, also known as grammar. Mercury was assigned to dialectic, Venus to rhetoric, Sun to music, Mars to calculation and arithmetic, Jupiter to geometry, and Saturn to astrology. Many medieval writers used astrology symbolism in art and literary themes. The astrological signs began to evolve in the Western world as Pisces, Aquarius, Capricorn, Sagittarius, Scorpio, Leo, Virgo, Libra, Cancer, Gemini, Taurus, and Aries. Helen's research was now to find out why these names and signs were a part of our modern-day astrology. Helen began to look at all the books folding before her, and as the library in her home town began to close, she went home. She took all the books with her for more review as to why these signs were so important to so many people, and how they became the images in our modern-day horoscope. Helen, at the age of only sixteen, began a journey into something more exciting and wondrous than anyone could have ever imagined.

Helen began to learn about the branches of astrology: Electional, Vedic, Hellenistic, Decumbiture, Horary, Esoteric, Meteorological, Locational, Financial, Psychological, Chinese, Western, and the Mundane.

Zodiac comes from the Greek vocabulary, which by definition means a circle of animals. Libra remains the only sign that is not related to animals or humans symbolically, even though it intermingled with the constellation Scorpius. The zodiac is a wheel within a wheel, interblending with each other, moving clockwise and counter-clockwise. There are only a few descriptions of Egyptian mythological depictions of the signs of the zodiac, possibly because of the invasions in Alexandria in Egypt. However, there are many mythological stories about the zodiac symbols from Babylon to ancient Greece which did help formulate the alchemy and the mythology developing the horoscope's origin.

There are 88 constellations grouped into what are called Families. These Families of constellations are the Zodiac Family, Hercules Family, Orion Family, Perseus Family, Ursa Major Family, Johann Bayer Family, Lacaille Family, and the Heavenly Waters Family.

ARIES: was identified with the god Amon-Ra in ancient Egyptian astronomy. Aries was portrayed as a man with a ram's head and symbolizes copiousness, fertility and creativity. It was called the "Indicator of the Reborn Sun" because of its position in the vernal equinox. Priests would fashion statues of Amon-Ra to temples during the times of the year when Aries was embossed. Aries captured the title of "Lord of the Head" in Egypt, attributing to its mythological momentousness.

The constellation of Aries in Hellenistic astrology is associated with the brilliant golden ram of Greek mythology that rescued Phrixos and Helle on orders from Hermes, guiding them to the land of Colchis.

Helle and Phrixos were the daughter and son of King Athamas. He also had a primary wife, Nephele.

The king's children were threatened by his other wife, Ino, because of her evil, jaundiced eye looking towards them. She set her heart on murdering them. She created a famine in Boeotia to achieve this, then distorted a missive from the Oracle of Delphi that said Phrixos needed to endure a sacrifice for the famine to end.

On top of Mount Laphystium, Athamas was on the verge of sacrificing his son, when suddenly, Aries, commissioned by Nephele, appeared. During flight, Helle dropped off of Aries' back while soaring in the celestial skies and submerged, drowning in the Dardanelles, additionally termed Hellespont in her honor. Subsequently appearing, Zeus was given the sacrificial ram performed by Phrixos, and gave the brilliant and glorious fleece to Aeetes of Colchis. Zeus than remunerated him by giving him an engagement with Chalciope, his beloved daughter.

The skin was suspended in glory in a magically sanctified place by Aeetes, and that's when it became known as the shining Golden Fleece known to be guarded by a giant, powerful dragon. Jason and the Argonauts somehow snatched the Golden Fleece from the dragon in later Greek mythology.

The location of the vernal equinox is in the first point of Aries, and is named for the constellation.

The Sun crossed the celestial equator from south to north in Aries more than two millennia ago, and this is the reasoning behind part of this mythology and astronomy. In 130 BC, Hipparchus formulated it as a point south of Gamma Arietis. The first point of Aries has since moved into Pisces because of the precession of the equinoxes, and will move into Aquarius. From late April through mid-May, the Sun now rises in Aries. The constellation Aries is still affiliated with the beginning of spring, mainly because of its historical background. Aries is portrayed as a ram squatted down, with its head turned towards Taurus.

Hipparchus depicted Alpha Arietis as the ram's muzzle. Aries has historically been associated with the god and planet Mars.

Aries is the first sign of the Greek zodiac positioned in the northern celestial hemisphere between Pisces to the west, and Taurus to the east. In the second century [BC?], the astronomer Ptolemy characterized this constellation, which also followed another forty-eight found in that era. Aries is from Latin meaning ram.

Even in Babylonian times, this constellation was also mirrored by the ram. It shines four bright stars in the northern celestial hemisphere, becoming the Golden Fleece in Ancient Greek mythology.

The brightest star in Aries is the star Hamal, derived from ancient Arabic meaning "head of ram."

Aries has remained a constellation since ancient Babylonian times, and was the final station along the ecliptic. The description of the Babylonian zodiac is given in clay tablets known as the MUL.APIN, which was a comprehensive table of the final station along the ecliptic. The MUL.APIN was a comprehensive table of the rising and setting of stars. Compiled in the 12th or 11th century BC, the MUL.APIN reflects a tradition which marks the Pleiades as the vernal equinox. The earliest identifiable reference to Aries as a distinct constellation comes from the boundary stones that date from 1350 to 1000 BC. On several boundary stones, a zodiacal ram figure is distinct from the other characters present.

TAURUS: was characterized in Egypt on the Dendera zodiac, an Egyptian bas-relief carving on a baldachin that illustrated the cosmic celestial hemisphere. The familiarization of the horns was outlined as skyward or rearward. The constellation Taurus was a sanctified bull that was identified with the regeneration of lifeblood in spring, during ancient Egyptian times. The constellation Taurus would become covered by the Sun in the western sky as spring began during the spring equinox. To the Egyptians it was the Apis bull, born at midnight on the new moon, which is why it is portrayed with a new moon under its sacred horns.

Zeus was identified with and transformed into the royal ivory white bull Taurus in ancient Greek mythology to seize the mythical Phoenician princess Europa. The imperial Taurus was explained as being partially submerged in celestial waves as he carried Europa out to the briny, deep sea. This mythology is why only the front portion of this constellation was depicted in some illustrations of Greek mythology. The myth of the Cretan Bull, also known as Taurus, was also one of the twelve labors of Hercules.

Taurus being associated with the bull is very ancient, dating to the Chalcolithic as well as the Upper Paleolithic eras. In the caves at Lascaux, Taurus is symbolized in a painting that is called the Hall of Bulls, created around 15,000 BC, shadowed by a representation of the Pleiades. The bull's eye is the brightest star, called Aldebaran.

During the vernal spring equinox in the era of the Chalcolithic and early Bronze Age, the omnipotent Taurus signaled the point of the vernal spring equinox during the Age of Taurus, from around 4000 BC to 1700

BC. Taurus then moved into the neighboring constellation Aries. MUL. APIN noted this constellation in Babylonian astronomy as "The Heavenly Bull" because it marked the vernal equinox. It was also the first constellation in the Babylonian zodiac, and they described it as "The Bull in Front."

The goddess Ishtar commissioned The Bull of Heaven, Taurus, to slaughter Gilgamesh for spurning her proposals in some of the earliest work of literature in the Mesopotamian Epic of Gilgamesh. The Sumerian goddess of warfare, fertility, and sexual love. Inanna was intimately affiliated with The Bull of Heaven in ancient Mesopotamian art. The Taurus stands before the goddess Inanna in one of the most archaic depictions of astrology, exemplifying three stars on its back.

GEMINI: is peered with Polydeuces, also known as Pollux and Castor, the offspring of the Argonauts, and Leda, the spouse of the King of Sparta in Greek mythology. Gemini is paired with the myth of Castor and Pollux, the offspring of the Argonauts and Leda. Zeus was the sire of Pollux, who entrapped and seduced Leda. Tyndares was the sire of Castor, King of Sparta, the spouse of Leda. St. Elmo's fire was affiliated with Castor and Pollux in their lookout for abandoned, lost sailors, to protect them during their voyage over the endless oceans. The mortal Castor inured immortality after his death because of Pollux's requisitioning to his sire Zeus to bring him back to life, so Zeus united them together in the heavenly bright stars.

The Great Twin stars Castor and Pollux were known as MUL.MASH. TAB.BA.GAL.GAL in ancient Babylonian astronomy. They were named Meshlamtaea and Lugalirra, The one "Mighty King" who has arisen from the Underworld. Their names are implicated as titles of Nergal, the supreme god of plague and affliction, king of the Underworld. Gemini is between

Taurus to the west, and Cancer to the east. The brightest star in Gemini is Beta Geminorum which is Pollox; second is Castor.

CANCER: The Northern Gate of the Sun was actually said to have been the place for the Akkadian Sun of the South. The sacred emblem of immortality representing Cancer was characterized as the scarabaeus around 2000 BC in ancient Egypt. Cancer has some affiliation with an Egyptian divinity in concord with Sirius, possibly Anubis, The Power of Darkness.

Karka and Karkata are the Sanskrit names for Cancer, sharing a similarity with Karkinos. They formulate the myth of the creation of the constellation in Greek mythology in which Hercules battled the multi-headed Lernaean Hydra. During battle, Hercules became distracted by Karkinos, sent by Hera, and before it became a disadvantage, Hercules walloped the creature by booting him with such force it flew into the celestial sphere. Hera, sworn adversary of Hercules, was appreciative of Karkinos' heroic efforts, and may have placed it in the starry sky after Hercules was bitten by the crab and stomped it to death.

Cancer can also be attributed to both a snapping turtle and a crab, because the constellation was known as MUL.AL.LUL, a name that can indicate the two of them, coming from Babylonian times. On monuments such as boundary stones, images of turtles are often presented and it is assumed that this represents Cancer.

Death and passage to the Underworld is a part of Cancer mythology regarding the Babylonian Constellation. Al Tarf is the most luminous star in the constellation Cancer, the second is

Arkushanangarushashutu, named by the Babylonians.

LEO: The Nemean Lion King of Beasts lived in a cave in a town called Nemea southwest of Corinth. The beast was devouring the humans in their villages, and the inhabitants were unable to destroy the King of Beasts because its hide could not be perforated by any weapons. Hercules was sent to massacre the Lion but could not kill it with arrows or any other weapons, so he trapped the Nemean. Hercules then slaughtered the Lion by grappling with Nemean; he ripped its mouth open and then choked the Beast to death. Hercules then used Nemean's claws to cut off its own pelt, and it became the cloak of Hercules. The head of the Beast became his crown.

The cloak of Nemean the King of Beasts guarded and protected Hercules, all the while making him even more fearsome. Leo was thereafter placed amongst the stars, forming the constellation Leo to honor the King of Beasts. The brightest star, Alpha Leonis, marks Leo's heart, and the six bright stars forming a sickle exemplify the lion's head (in the sky, the six bright stars that form the shape of a sickle represents the lion's head).

Mesopotamians had a constellation comparable to Leo as early as 4000 BC. The star that is poised in the lion's breast is called Regulus, according to the Babylonians, and was known as "King of the Star."

Babylonians named it UR.GU.LA, The Great Lion.

VIRGO: The Goddess of Justice, daughter of Titaness Themis and Zeus was named Dike, having angel's wings, with an ear of grain in her left hand symbolizing the star Spica. This is how the constellation Virgo was depicted in Greek mythology. This constellation also represents Dike, the goddess of justice, shining next to Libra as she holds the scales of justice. The virgin goddess Dike, daughter of Astraeus, father of the stars, and Eos, goddess of the dawn, was also known as Astraea, and is affiliated with this constellation.

Dike was created as a mortal stationed on earth to rule human justice. This was during the Golden Age, an age where humans never became old. It was a time of amaranthine spring, amity, and fortune.

Zeus eventually produced the four seasons, and humans would no longer honor the gods as they had before. This marked the Silver Age. This happened after an ancient prophecy had been fulfilled after Zeus vanquished his sire.

Dike soared over to the mountains, staying away from humanity after giving a spiel to them warning them about disregarding the ideals of their forbears. She said there were worse things that would appear in the near future because of war and strife amongst themselves, marking the Bronze and Iron Ages.

Dike soared to the stars and left humanity behind altogether, forever.

Tyche, the goddess of chance, or of fortune, is tied in with Virgo, and is holding the horn of plenty cornucopia.

The name Spica, which marks the ear of grain held by the goddess, means the ear of grain in Latin. The Blessed Mother Mary was symbolized as Virgo during medieval times. The goddess of wheat and agriculture was Demeter-Ceres. Other myths also involved the characters Dionysus, Erigone as Virgo, and Icarius of Athens.

In the Babylonian MUL.APIN, dating from 1000 to 686 BC, Virgo was recognized as "The Furrow," characterizing the goddess Shala's ear of grain or possibly corn. Spica, being corn or grain, was a culturally based food supply for these people. The constellation Virgo was also known as AB.SIN, somehow exemplifying fertility.

LIBRA: also known as Chelae, the claws, was chosen as being a component of the Scorpius constellation to the ancient Greeks. Chelae was illustrated as the scorpion's claws, and was pictured as being a part of the Scorpius constellation. It is possible that Rome was founded when the moon was positioned in Libra.

Libra was also affiliated with harmonizing the four seasons, and equalizing the length of daylight and nightfall. It was a blessed constellation to the Romans. The sun remained at the autumnal equinox inside Libra until the year 729, when the procession of the equinoxes shifted the equinox into Virgo. The brightest star in Libra is named Zubeneschamali. The second-brightest star is Zubenelgenubi.

Libra, also known as "The Balance of Heaven," was called ZIB. BA.AN.NA in Mesopotamia.

SCORPIO: The mythical hunter Orion was slain by Scorpius, classified as the scorpion. Orion is seen as retreating away from the poisonous scorpion as it sets while Scorpius ascends, lying diametrically opposed from each other in the celestial atmosphere. One myth is that Scorpius was sent to poison Orion to death for trying to ravish the goddess Artemis.

In another mythological tale, Orion was said to have claimed that he could annihilate any savage wild beast, so earth sent the scorpion after him, possibly to protect the agrarian beasts of earth. Scorpius as a constellation is extremely larger, and encompasses two halves, one with the claws, and the other with the stinger. The Sumerians called it GIR-TAB, which means the scorpion.

PISCES: Known as Anunitum, "The Lady of Heaven" at the location of the northern fish.

Greek mythology tells a story of Giants, Gaia, coalesced with Tartarus in the territory of the fearsome Underworld, an almost unimaginable place, where Zeus detained the mighty Titans. In the Underworld there was also Typhon. Typhon was a one-hundred-headed dragon with a sea of flames pouring out from its eyes, the most horrifying, spine-chilling monster the world had ever seen.

Gaia sent Typhon to defeat the gods, especially the Olympians. The first to see him was Pan. He became terrified as he witnessed Typhon approaching the realm of the gods, so he alarmed and signaled the gods. Pan then morphed into a goat-fish and plummeted into the river Euphrates to escape the scorching fires of hell coming forth from the eyes of Typhon. The Olympian gods eventually defeated the Titans, Gaia and the Giants. However, there was still Typhon approaching with fierce power.

Eros, the son of the goddess Aphrodite, as well as Aphrodite, had only one choice but to call upon the water nymphs for service and support, and leaped into the river Euphrates. Eros and Aphrodite where taken to a place of inviolability by two fish who let them ride on their backs, escaping the pure terror of Typhon. The goddess and her son were then transfigured into fish. In Roman mythology, Pisces represented Cupid and Venus that morphed into fish to escape the bloodcurdling-beyond-pure-evil monster, Typhon.

Pisces, also known as “The Great Swallow,” derives from the Babylonian constellation SINUNUTU4.

In the first millennium BC, in texts called the Astronomical Diaries, the constellation was also known as DU.NU.NU, “The Fish Ribbon.”

AQUARIUS: Aquarius was affiliated with the annual flood of the river Nile, where the banks of the river flooded when Aquarius put his jar into the Nile, which marked the beginning of spring. It was told that a stream of more than twenty stars pours out of the jar of Aquarius.

The constellation also was represented as a single vase which poured out a stream to Piscis Austrinus in Greek mythology. Aquarius is sometimes coupled with Deucalion, Prometheus’ son, who constructed a ship with Pyrrha, his beloved wife, to survive an inescapable flood. They eventually washed ashore on Mount Parnassus, after sailing for nine days.

The cup-carrier to the gods, Aquarius, correlated with Ganymede, the son of Trojan King Tros, who was seized by Zeus and taken to Mount Olympus to be the cup-carrier to the gods.

An eagle representing the constellation Aquila, under Zeus’ requisition, snatched Ganymede, who was taken to Mount Olympus. Some believe it was actually Zeus who transformed himself into the eagle. The king of Athens, the one who sacrificed water to the gods, was another character related to Aquarius, called Cercrops, the water-bearer.

GU.LA “The Great One” is the god Ea, which was frequently represented as possessing an overflowing vase and relating to Aquarius, is shown in the Babylonian star catalogs. This celestial star character appears on cylinder seals as well as entitlement stones from the second millennium.

GU.LA incorporated the winter in the antiquated solstice during the prevenient Bronze Age.

The "Way of Ea" was the rex of the southernmost quarter of the Sun's thoroughfare. The Way of Ea was synonymous with a period of seasons relating to the winter solstice. Babylonians were accustomed to smashing floods, arrogated to Aquarius.

CAPRICORN: is the goat Amalthea, which suckled Zeus after Rhea his mother rescued Zeus from being forever annihilated by Cronos his sire. The future goddess and gods, the offspring of Cronos, were all annihilated by him because of a prophecy that revealed the future of one of his offspring dethroning him.

Capricornus was also seen with a broken horn that was altered into cornucopia, the horn of opulence. The god with the goat head, Pan, and the forest deity, Pan, were also described as Capricornus.

In gratitude for Pan being forthcoming about the dangers to the gods, Zeus positioned Pan in the celestial abode of the gods.

Pan assisted the war of the gods against the Titans by spooking them far afield by blowing on his conch shell, warning them of the monstrous Typhon. Pan was the one who pronounced to the gods that they must put on a guise as animals to escape impending doom from Typhon until the endangerment no longer lingered. Typhon was finally blighted by the omnipotent powerhouse of thunderbolts disposed by Zeus.

In the Babylonian star catalogs Capricornus was recorded as MUL SUHUR.MAS, "The Goat Fish."

The constellation was the representation of the god Ea. It announced the winter solstice in the Early Bronze Age, and symbolized the goat-fish during the Middle Bronze Age. Sumerians recognized it as SUHUR-MASH-HA, "The Goat Fish." During the 21st century BC, it was characterized on a cylinder-seal.

SAGITTARIUS: The Centaur, with the embodiment of a horse and the torso of a male human, aims his arrow headed for the heart of the Scorpius constellation, expressed by the supergiant star Antares. Sagittarius was familiarized with Crotus. According to Eratosthenes, it was a mythical creature with a satyr's two-foot tail. It was a minder to nine Muses, the daughters of Zeus. Crotus survived on Mount Helicon and created the art of archery. Crotus was genuinely close to the Muses, so Zeus sent him up into the stars, requested to do so by the Muses.

In other myths, the son of Saturn and Philyra Chiron the Centaur was believed to have transformed himself into a horse to retreat away from his jealous spouse, Rhea. Chiron became associated with Sagittarius, as well as the constellation Centaurus.

Sagittarius was familiarized with Nerigal, or Nergal, a centaur god pulling an arrow against his bow. Nerigal was illustrated as having wings, a horse's body with a scorpion tail and two heads, one human, and one panther. Sagittarius may have also derived from Pabilsag, an elder, paternal kinsman and chief, somehow translating into "Chief Ancestor" during the Sumerian era.

OPHIUCHUS: The "serpent bearer" is a constellation that was affiliated with Asclepius, the honored healer in Greek mythology. Ophiuchus shines in the northern celestial sky near by the celestial equator. Greek astronomer Ptolemy cataloged the Ophiuchus constellation in the second century, and it was one of the first to be cataloged by him. Ophiuchus is also acknowledged as Serpentarius.

It is illustrated as being a man grabbing a snake representing the nearby constellation Serpens, which is branched into two parts by Ophiuchus: the snake's head, Serpens Caput, and the snake's tail, Serpens Cauda. The serpent is often characterized as coiled around his torso. Ophiuchus is one of the constellations that crosses the ecliptic, stepping into the Zodiac Family, coming forth from the Hercules Family of constellations. It also contains the famous Nebula, "The Dark Horse." Ophiuchus is the 11th largest constellation in the celestial skies, occupying an area of 948 square degrees. Aquila, Ara, Centaurus, Corona Australis, Corvus, Crater, Crux, Cygnus, Hercules, Hydra, Lupus, Lyra, Sagitta, Scutum, Sextans, Serpens, Triangulum, Astrale, and Vulpecula also belong to the Hercules Family of constellations.

Asclepius is the son of the god Apollo, and is usually related to Ophiuchus, who was believed to have the gift to bring humans back to life from death in Greek mythology. A snake was seen by Asclepius giving herbs to another snake, these herbs were very powerful in the art of healing. One story tells that of a son, Glaucus whose sire was King Minos of Crete. Glaucus accidently fell into a giant jar of honey and became submerged in it. All of a sudden he drowned, and died inside the jar of honey. Asclepius watched a snake slithering towards him, and Asclepius killed the snake to protect himself. As the story goes, another snake slithered by and deposited an herb on the dead snake's body, and magically the snake came back to life.

After seeing this, Asclepius took the same herb and put in on the body of Glaucus. The son of King Minos was unbelievably resurrected from death inside the giant jar of honey. The wise Chiron, a centaur correlating with the Centaurus constellation, then taught Asclepius the magical art of healing.

The goddess Athena decided to give Asclepius blood from Gorgon Medusa. The left side of Medusa's body carried deadly toxic poisonous blood; however, the blood veins on the right side of her body had the ability to bring people back to life. Asclepius also brought back to life Theseus the son of Hippolytus identified also with the Auriga constellation "The Charioteer." Theseus was propelled from a chariot and passed away.

The god of the Underworld, Hades, heard about Asclepius' gifted abilities to heal others and raise them from the dead. Hades became extremely perturbed and worried that the oozing of dead spirits into his domain would become parched because of Asclepius' magical healing capabilities. Hades yammered and moaned to his brother Zeus about Asclepius. Zeus made a decision to slay the healer with a bolt of lightning, because of the possibility for the race of humans becoming immortal. Asclepius' appearance was drawn in the sky by Zeus to honor him for his blessed gifts and tour de force. Asclepius then transformed into the constellation Ophiuchus, the Serpent Bearer.

The serpent-god Nirah, depicted as a hybrid being with serpents for legs and the head of a human possibly formulated the mythology surrounding the constellation Ophiuchus coming from ancient Babylon.

Of final note was a file obtained by Captain Frank Delaney that sought to investigate whether or not Helen Wilson had a son. The only actual note from that school that Captain Delaney was able to determine was a notation in an Ipswich High School file with the initials "J.C." though there appear to have been three teachers with those initials, all now deceased. Apparently, on November 21, 1963, an inconsolable Helen Wilson had to be taken to the school nurse facility after frantically screaming during what appears to have been an English class that the president, John F. Kennedy, would be assassinated. While this did indeed occur the next day, there appear to be no additional notes added by any school official.

ORPHIUCHUS "The Lost Tribe"???

ABOUT THE AUTHORS

Brian Evans

Brian Evans is a singer, actor, and author. His debut album, produced by Narada Michael Walden, featured his original song "At Fenway," which included a music video featuring William Shatner that made Brian the only solo artist ever to film a music video entirely at Fenway Park in its history. The music video was added to the library of The National Baseball Hall of Fame in August, 2013, and has garnered more than 11 million views on YouTube since its debut. As an actor, Brian has been featured on such notable television shows as *Full House*, and the major motion picture *Book Of Love* (New Line Cinema), and his music is heard on popular TV shows such as *So You Think You Can Dance* and *Drop Dead Diva*. This is Brian's first novel.

Brian Evans resides in Hawaii, and is currently developing "Horrorscope II," as well as several fiction and non-fiction titles.

For more information on Brian Evans visit www.brianevans.com, or follow him on Twitter at twitter.com/croon1, or on Facebook at facebook.com/croonerman

Helen Marie Bousquet

Helen Marie Bousquet was born in Ipswich, Massachusetts in 1950. The mother of Brian Evans, Helen spent most of her life helping her son pursue his career in the entertainment industry. Helen co-produced her the music video "At Fenway," which was written and performed by her son, the song produced by Narada Michael Walden. As a result, Helen Bousquet's "At Fenway," and her name as co-producer of the music video, was added to The National Baseball Hall of Fame. You would not be reading this book if were not for Helen's tireless efforts and years of patience assisting Brian in his work. While Helen left us in 2012, she is the inspiration behind the character Helen Wilson in this book. It was her love for horoscopes and tarot that gave Brian the idea to write this book. Many of the writings in this book come from notebooks and personal writings of Helen Marie Bousquet, and she was primarily instrumental in the creation of this story.

For more information about Helen Bousquet,
visit www.helenbousquet.com

Mark Andrew Biltz

Mark Andrew Biltz was born in Garden City, Kansas, the son of Mark and Vicki Biltz. He is a writer, a poet, and a painter. This is Mark's first novel, and he is currently developing "Horrorscope II" with Brian Evans

ABOUT THE EDITOR

Enrique M. Grullon

Enrique M. Grullon is an author, writer, and musician. He is originally from Haverhill, Massachusetts. He is currently developing "Horrorscope II" with Brian Evans and Mark Andrew Biltz.

For more information about Enrique M. Grullon visit www.enriquegrullon.com, and follow him on Twitter at Twitter.com/rickygx